Boots – Sergeant Boots – watched Private George Watts of the West Kents being chased across the farmyard by a furious young French woman with a pitchfork.

'What's the trouble?' asked Boots. She was a rather nice-looking girl with blazing blue eyes and black hair. But she was dressed in sombre colours – probably a young war-widow like so many others in this savage and decimating war.

'That man came to steal chickens,' she said. 'Now you 'ave come too. It is most disgusting.'

'I haven't come to steal chickens,' said Boots, smiling placatingly.

'That is what you say. 'Ow would you like my father to set 'is dogs on you!'

'Now, ma'm'selle, have I stolen anything, or tried to?'

''Ow do I know what you 'ave come to take. Perhaps even my honour!'

'Well, that's rich,' said Boots.

He and his men were supposed to be having a break from the turmoil of the trenches. They had thought life on the Descartes farm would be peaceful and tranquil. But faced with the fury of Cecile Lacoste, Boots began to wonder just what kind of trouble he was about to face . . .

Also by Mary Jane Staples

DOWN LAMBETH WAY
OUR EMILY
KING OF CAMBERWELL
TWO FOR THREE FARTHINGS
THE LODGER
RISING SUMMER
THE PEARLY QUEEN
SERGEANT JOE
ON MOTHER BROWN'S DOORSTEP
THE TRAP
A FAMILY AFFAIR
MISSING PERSON
PRIDE OF WALWORTH

and published by Corgi Books

ECHOES OF YESTERDAY

Mary Jane Staples

CORGI BOOKS

ECHOES OF YESTERDAY
A CORGI BOOK : 0 552 14375 8

First publication in Great Britain

PRINTING HISTORY
Corgi edition published 1995
Corgi edition reprinted 1995 (twice)

Set in 11pt Linotype Plantin by
County Typesetters, Margate, Kent.

Corgi Books are published by Transworld Publishers Ltd,
61– 63 Uxbridge Road, London W5 5SA,
in Australia by Transworld Publishers (Australia) Pty Ltd,
15– 25 Helles Avenue, Moorebank, NSW 2170,
and in New Zealand by Transworld Publishers (NZ) Ltd,
3 William Pickering Drive, Albany, Auckland.

Printed and bound in Great Britain by
Cox & Wyman Ltd, Reading, Berkshire.

To Jewelene Epps Jones of Covington, Georgia,
a Southern Lady of grace and charm.

PART ONE

THE SOUND
OF THE GUNS

Chapter One

On the morning of the first Sunday in June 1916, a battalion of the Royal West Kents, out of the line, arrived by train at the town of Albert in Northern France. Albert had come under heavy shellfire during the shifting battles of 1914, and was notable for the fact that the damage suffered by its magnificent Notre Dame church had left the statue of the Virgin and Child hanging perilously high. But it had not fallen, and was still miraculously in place. Not that the West Kents had come to look at it. As far as miracles were concerned, the only one they were interested in was that which would bring the war to an end at noon and put them on their way home to Blighty ten minutes later.

The train came to a stop. The doors of its freight waggons slid back and the men of the trenches showed themselves, khaki-clad, tin-hatted and battle-hardened. They were, for the most part, as lean as winter's grey wolves, a mixture of old sweats and tried and tested volunteers. The old sweats, the regulars, had fought at Mons and belonged, therefore, to that legendary army of artillery gunners and infantry sharpshooters known as the Old Contemptibles. The volunteers were young men who had

9

enlisted soon after the outbreak of war in August 1914, and in surviving until now had become very much like old regulars themselves.

NCOs jumped down from the waggons to regulate the detraining of their platoons. Sergeant Robert Adams, known to his family and friends as Boots, a nickname that had been attached to him in his infancy, landed on his feet, straightened up and took the rifle that was handed down to him. His laden pack on his back, he slung the rifle, an army man's best friend, and gave the order for C Platoon of A Company to leave the waggon. Down the men came, two or three at a time.

'What's holding you up, Corporal Parks?' asked Boots of a slowcoach. Just twenty, Boots looked as if he had come of age years ago. But then they all looked older than they were.

'I've got trouble, Sarge,' said Corporal Freddy Parks, who had joined up at the same time as Boots. Both sometimes wondered how it was they were still alive. 'I've mislaid me gaspers.'

'Had 'em nicked, you mean,' said Boots. 'Well, hard luck, Percival. Get down.'

'Some mate you are,' said Freddy, engaged to a girl he'd met while at training camp in Maidstone, and accordingly given to asking heaven to keep him all in one piece. Down he came, still minus his packet of Woodbines. 'And would you mind re-membering I ain't Percival?'

'Button undone, Corporal,' said Boots, and Freddy examined his jacket. 'No, not there,' said Boots, face straight, and poor old Freddy was mug enough to examine his flies. Even a corporal in the West Kents could be stuck on a fizzer for being improperly dressed. Freddy, however, found himself in proper regulation order.

'Oh, you bleeder, Boots,' he said.

Boots's lurking smile surfaced. The West Kents were in a cheerful mood, knowing they were out of the line for a while and heading for billets.

'Don't want you looking undone in the middle of Albert,' he said, and began to go to work on his platoon. There were old sweats among them, men who had been in the regular Army for years, but had such long crime sheets that promotion always passed them by. They made up for that by acquiring an astonishing amount of illegal perks, including such things as chickens, young porkers and French housewives. The latter, of course, were more borrowed than acquired, the borrowing on a short term basis and agreeable to all concerned. Such men regarded Boots in much the same light as baby's water when he was given three stripes, and did their artful best to figuratively stand him on his head and make him feel he wasn't yet out of his nappies. Boots, however, had his own kind of wiliness, and, moreover, he was never lost for words. The old sweats didn't take long to recognize he could teach their grandmothers to suck lemons, and that he had the makings of being one of their own kind, apart from his gorblimey stripes.

The station became alive with assembling companies, and the battalion's officers appeared. Major Harris, a regular who had advanced since

Mons from sergeant to officer commanding A Company, stopped to observe Boots lining up his platoon in his own kind of way, which always embraced exchanging repartee with his men. Other sergeants achieved order by bawling. Major Harris's eyes, as bleak as Cornish granite, held the faint and unusual light of a smile.

'Sergeant Adams.'

'Sir?' Boots advanced and saluted. Major Harris noted the foward tilt of his tin hat. It shaded his eyes, and there was always something to look out for there. Major Harris had known Boots since their days at the training camp in Maidstone, when he himself had had a few months in Blighty after being wounded at Mons. They were old adversaries, but that didn't diminish Boots's respect for his commanding officer, or change Major Harris's opinion of Boots as a man and a soldier. He had it in mind to recommend Boots for a commission before the arrival of autumn, if they both survived the next battle. One was coming, Major Harris knew that.

'Sergeant Adams, what d'you know about farming?'

'About milking cows and so on, sir?' said Boots.

'Something like that.'

'Well, sir,' said Boots, 'since cows have never done me any harm, I can't see myself insulting them with my ignorance. Live and let live, that's how I feel about cows.'

'That includes French cows, I suppose,' said Major Harris, expression impassive. The station was swarming with noisy infantrymen and barking

NCOs, and only the Major and Boots seemed to be conducting themselves quietly. 'Well, if I know you, Sergeant Adams, it's a cert that if there's any milking to be done you'll conscript volunteers. The point is, A Company's billets will be at Descartes Farm, and it's another cert the farmer will be asking favours of what he'll see as available labour. You and your platoon will go along with what the Army expects, co-operation.'

'Not a bad way to pass the time if the weather stays like this, sir,' said Boots. The June day was warm and sunny. 'I think there'll be a few blokes willing to help, as long as the farmer doesn't ask them to shake hands with his cows.'

'Anything else, Sergeant Adams?'

'Nothing, sir, except would you know if there'll be any French dairymaids in the offing?'

'In the what?'

'Offing, sir. Some of the men might fancy carrying their buckets for them.'

Major Harris hardly batted an eyelid.

'Sergeant Adams, get your platoon ready for a two-mile march,' he said.

'Two miles, sir?'

'Two too many for C Platoon?'

'They haven't got a lot of faith in French miles, sir.'

'Hard bloody luck,' said Major Harris, and strode off.

'What's cookin', Sarge?' asked an old sweat as Boots rejoined the platoon.

'Cows,' said Boots.

13

'How the bleedin' Murphy d'you get a cow in the pot?'

'Chop it up,' said Boots. 'Form 'em in fours, Corporal Parks, we've got some marching to do.'

It wasn't long before the battalion began the march, which first took it through the war-damaged town, Major Harris at the head of A Company, and Boots alongside C Platoon. The long column of Tommies, hobnails ringing on the cobbles, aroused only a passing interest in people used to the comings and goings of British troops. In the south-east, German guns rumbled as their batteries laid down a barrage along the sectors held by the extreme right flank of the British Fourth Army and the corresponding left flank of the adjacent French Sixth Army. It sounded as if the Germans suspected the enemy had a Sunday surprise cooking up, and were warning them off.

All sectors of the Somme salient had been relatively quiet of late, but Boots, in common with the rest of the battalion, had a sure feeling another major Allied offensive was being planned. And they all shared the belief of the disillusioned, that the Jerries already knew everything about it. The Jerries always did, while the French and British High Commands always thought otherwise. However, the Allied generals bore the resulting losses bravely, consoling themselves with the knowledge that the misfortunes of war wouldn't affect their retirement pensions. At least, that was how Boots saw it, and so did Major Harris, a born soldier presently existing in utter disgust at the way regulars and volunteers were being used as cannon fodder.

The rumbling sounds of the far-off guns travelled with the marching West Kents, who took little notice. There was rarely complete silence all along the front stretching from the Belgian coast to the border of Switzerland. It was a monstrously long front, ravaged by destruction, and ugly with desolation and trench systems. All the same, being out of the line and heading for rest billets around the farms outside the town, was something for the West Kents to savour.

With his platoon marching at ease, rifles slung, Boots thought of home.

Chapter Two

In the East Street market in Walworth, South London, the Sunday morning shoppers were in search of bargains. Old ladies in granny bonnets, who could still use a vigorous elbow to get to a stall, were in lively evidence. They knew that Sunday mornings were the best times for bargains, war or no war, for what was on offer in the way of fruit and vegetables was often the last of the week's produce. By noon, anything that was left would be going for a song. Then there were the stalls that only appeared on Sunday mornings, stalls that sold knick-knacks, gold watches – some hopes – old books and comics, magical household cleaners, domestic pets, herbs, and miraculous remedies for all kinds of ailments. The latter were readily bought by the kind of people who believed anything a market quack would tell them or anything that was printed on a label. Such medicines were about as effective as sugared water, and as harmless. It was belief that convinced a purchaser a cure was taking place.

Housewives with families to feed came looking for consumables that were in short supply. The Germans and their U-boats had a lot to do with short supplies, and the general opinion of Walworth people was that Kaiser Bill ought to have something chronically painful done to him for the way his U-boats kept sinking British merchant ships. Some of these ships were laden with frozen meat and tinned food, like corned beef. Corned beef was a boon to families who found they could only get enough meat for one really decent meal a week. It wasn't that the Government had issued ration books yet. They simply saw to it that butchers and grocers were rationed, and so the butchers and grocers, of course, had to ration their customers. And the rampaging U-boats made matters worse. The prevailing opinion was that it was bleedin' criminal for so much good food to finish up at the bottom of the sea, where even a shark couldn't open up a tin of corned beef.

Mrs Maisie Adams of Caulfield Place off Browning Street, Walworth, met a neighbour on her way to the market.

'Morning to you, Mr Blake, nice weather we're havin',' she said.

'Weather's all right, Mrs Adams, I ain't saying it ain't. It's this 'ere war that's gettin' my bleedin' goat,' said Mr Blake, driver of a coal cart.

'Beg your pardon, Mr Blake?' Mrs Adams, known to her family as Chinese Lady because she had amber eyes and had once taken in washing to augment her meagre income, showed slight reproof. Chinese Lady was of all things respectable, especially on the Sabbath. 'I think you're forgettin' what day it is.'

'Yer'll 'ave to excuse me French, Mrs Adams,'

said Mr Blake, 'but that there German Kaiser is fair upsettin' me, and Sundays don't make no difference to me feelings. Like I said to me missus, he's a gorblimey perisher.'

'You can be sure 'is sins will find him out, Mr Blake,' said Chinese Lady, a slim woman in her fortieth year. She had a firm bosom, a straight back and an upright walk. All these features characterized her proud air of respectability. Walworth women set great store by respectability, and it showed in their clean doorsteps and the way they carried themselves, never mind that their best Sunday hats might be in pawn along with a husband's Sunday walkers. 'That man's sure to go to purgat'ry,' she said, 'what with his submarines and his zeppelins.'

'I'd 'ang 'im meself, Mrs Adams, if I 'ad the chance,' said Mr Blake.

'Well, I'm a God-fearin' woman,' said Chinese Lady, 'but if his hanging should come to pass, I wouldn't want to miss it, so knock me up on the day it does.'

'Eh?' Mr Blake, plain-speaking though he was, blinked and coughed. He didn't go in for knocking ladies up, and Mrs Blake wouldn't have let him, anyway, not unless he could get past her rolling-pin. 'Beggin' yer pardon, Mrs Adams?'

'Yes, don't forget,' said Chinese Lady, and went briskly on her way to the market. In pre-war times she would rarely have gone there on a Sunday morning. She would have been preparing a roast dinner, for however hard-up she and her family

18

were, she always made sure there was a roast on Sundays. They'd been hard-up ever since her soldier husband died a martial death on the North-West Frontier ten years ago. As the widow of a soldier killed in action, she didn't get much of a pension. Boots, her eldest son, said governments always took a poor view of soldiers careless enough to get blown to pieces by the enemy, so the widows had to suffer for the vexation caused. What, said Chinese Lady, a war widow like me? Oh, they'll be hoping you'll save them money by passing on at an early age, said Boots. Oh, they will, will they? Well, I'll show them, said Chinese Lady, I'll do me level best to live to a hundred. Good idea, said Boots, that might make them give you a rise when you're eighty.

Boots was with his regiment somewhere in France now, and Chinese Lady hoped he wouldn't be as careless as his late dad and get himself in the way of a shell. Tommy and Sammy, her other sons, were too young to join up, thank goodness. Her daughter Lizzy, poor dear, was suffering on account of her husband Ned being in a military hospital in Middlesex. He'd had his left leg amputated following a battle in Flanders. Lizzy was expecting her first child, and Chinese Lady had insisted on having her at home instead of being all by herself in the house she and Ned were buying in an avenue off Denmark Hill, Camberwell. No expectant young wife ought to be on her own in times like these. Lizzy, in fact, had returned to her old home gratefully, and was able to visit Ned twice a week, on Wednesdays and Sundays.

As soon as Lizzy moved in, Chinese Lady went round to the town hall to ask about rations for the baby. Mr Tupper, the clerk in question, said rations for the unborn, missus? Never mind about being unborn at the moment, said Chinese Lady, I know more about these things than you do, Mr Tupper, I happen to have had four unborn babies that were all born later. But all the while they were unborn I needed food for two, didn't I? Well, Mrs Adams, I'll admit you've got a point, said Mr Tupper, but there's nothing in the regulations about rations for children not yet born. Don't talk so disgraceful, said Chinese Lady, the council's got a bit of Christian sense, hasn't it? There's my daughter's soldier husband with a leg off and my only oldest son fighting for the council and the country in France. And there's me a war widow trying to make ends meet. So I don't want to hear about any regulations, only about a bit of Christian sense, which ought to be able to supply a form that'll tell me grocer and butcher I've got an extra mouth to feed.

Mr Tupper said unfortunately he didn't have the authority. Well, get some, said Chinese Lady, I don't mind waiting for five minutes. Mr Tupper had a sensible Christian think about the situation, then said that as her daughter's husband was convalescing at home with her, he at least was entitled to a fair share of what was going. Chinese Lady, about to say that Lizzy's husband was still in hospital, suddenly realized a bit of the desired Christianity was floating about, so she grabbed it and said oh, yes, I forgot about that, Mr Tupper. Let's have his details, said Mr Tupper.

In that way, Chinese Lady and the human Mr Tupper fiddled the issue of a form to take care of the unborn. But forms didn't solve the problem of chronic shortages, although most families did have a bit more money coming in. Factories were going full blast and employing thousands of girls and women at better wages than usual. The people entering the market with Chinese Lady were looking, like the crowds already there, for something on which to spend their money, the first priority being food of a satisfying kind. The two market butchers sometimes opened their shops in a friendly way on a Sunday morning to sell sausages made from Saturday's left-over bits and pieces. They might look and taste as if they contained a fair amount of sawdust, but kids didn't mind. Kids would eat anything that came hot and sizzling out of a frying-pan, and their mums wouldn't have to blindfold them, either.

Queues formed quickly at any shop or stall offering something a bit better than cabbages or turnips. Women, the hunters who foraged for their families, automatically joined a queue as soon as they spotted one, and without immediately knowing what it was for. Queues were magnets, and over-eager huntresses could get a bit pushy. Fretful protests sometimes broke out.

''Ere, d'you mind, missus? That's me legs you're bruisin' with yer basket.'

'Well, move along, can't yer?'

''Strewth, missus, if I move along any more, the lady in front of me will 'ave me arrested, and I ain't been arrested for movin' along in all me life.'

'Oh, dearie me, me 'eart bleeds for yer, but what're you doin' in a queue, anyway? You ain't a woman. Why ain't you in the war instead of a queue?'

'Well, missus, I 'appen to be on the wrong side of fifty, with four grandkids and fallen arches, as well as 'avin' yer shoppin' basket killin' the back of me legs.'

'Serve yer right, you shouldn't be 'ere. What's this queue for, anyway?'

'Rubber soles for boots an' shoes, missus.'

'Oh, yer silly old bugger, why didn't yer say so? Me kids can't eat rubber soles.'

There was a lot of mutual fretfulness about because of the war.

Because pockets and purses contained more money than usual, most stalls were doing good business. Quack medicines were being bought by furtive alcoholics who thought, in their soggy-minded way, that Dr Ambrose Martin's medicinal spirits at fourpence a bottle might be a better buy than fourpennyworth of methylated spirits. Methylated spirits brought forth pink elephants.

Close to King and Queen Street, Mrs Flora Beamish, wife of a serving soldier, was running a glass and chinaware stall, the trading rights of which were in the name of her widower father, whose rheumatics were presently crippling him. On

Sunday mornings, often her busiest times, she was assisted by young Sammy Adams, probably the brightest and sharpest lad in Walworth. Sammy, fourteen, looked sixteen, being decidedly tall for his age and a lot more grown up than any of his contemporaries. With alert and cheeky blue eyes, a pleasant countenance, an infectious grin, and a peaked cap on the back of his head, he looked as if adolescence had only stayed with him for five minutes before hurrying off to land on someone far more innocent. Growing young girls gave him the eye, and some would offer to show him their legs for as little as a ha'penny. That was money chucked away as far as Sammy was concerned. Tell yer what, he'd say, I'll show yer me chest for tuppence. What, all bare? Yes, and me chest buttons as well, he'd say. Shrieks from collapsing girls.

Sammy had a talent for selling and an ambition to be rich. As her Sunday morning assistant, Flora found him a young marvel. By arrangement, she paid him commission on all he sold. Commission was more profitable for Sammy than a fixed sum. He could sell a teapot to someone who already had six.

Chinese Lady was hoping to get a choice lump of suet from one of the market butchers so that she could make some nourishing suet dumplings with today's stew. Roast beef joints were out for the duration, much to her disgust.

She stopped to run a critical eye over her youngest son. It was at least something to note he was wearing his one and only suit, which counted as

23

his Sunday best. Usually, one of his jerseys and a pair of patched trousers adorned him, and both garments took on a scruffy look only ten minutes after he'd put them on. Sammy had long ago worked out that if he looked scruffy, then he also looked in need, which made sympathetic old ladies give him a penny for running an errand. His store of pennies filled five socks, with a sixth beginning to fill up. He had a separate sock for silver coins.

'Good morning, Mrs Beamish,' said Chinese Lady.

''Ello, Mrs Adams, and how's yer good self?' smiled Flora.

'Still on me feet, I'm pleased to say, and relieved that Sammy's lookin' fairly respectable, except I don't know why he's wearin' his cap on the back of his head like some street corner ragamuffin.'

Sammy, finishing a sale, said, 'Watcher, Mum. About me cap. I always put it on proper, but it's perverse, yer know, it moves about till it ends up where it is now.'

'It looks to me like it'll fall off any minute,' said Chinese Lady who, as a widow, was wearing her best black hat out of Sunday respect for her late soldier husband. 'Still, as long as you're makin' yourself useful to Mrs Beamish, I won't say nothing more.'

'Oh, Sammy's useful all right, Mrs Adams,' said Flora, 'and the way 'e wears 'is cap makes 'im look dashin'. The girls like it.'

'Here, leave off,' protested Sammy. He avoided girls and was quite happy for girls to avoid him.

Girls cost a bloke money. You only had to know one of them for five minutes and it could relieve a bloke of at least the price of a toffee-apple. And after only ten minutes there could be horrendous talk about treating them to a seat at the Fleapit, the cinema under the railway arch in the Walworth Road. Tuppence, that cost. Tuppence. Girls had a seriously damaging way of getting into a bloke's pocket without hardly trying. Sammy considered himself fortunate that he wasn't yet old enough to be expected to take up with one. When he was old enough, he'd try to find one who liked his conversation more than his pocket.

'Well, I won't stop longer, Mrs Beamish, you've got a customer,' said Chinese Lady, 'and I want to see if one of the butcher's shops is open.'

'Porky Palmer's was open first thing, Mum,' said Sammy, 'so I nipped in, told 'im our Lizzy was short of nourishment, and 'e sold me a pound of his Sunday bangers. 'Ere we are.' He fished out the wrapped sausages from a box under the stall.

'Well, I must say you're thoughtful sometimes, Sammy,' said Chinese Lady. 'I'll put them in me shoppin' bag.'

'Could yer settle up before you go, Mum? Sixpence for the sausages and a penny for me time and trouble. And me thoughtfulness. That's only sevenpence in all. Well, you're fam'ly.'

'I'm gratified,' said Chinese Lady with a touch of sarcasm. But she paid up and went on her way.

Flora, having served her customer, said, 'I'm goin' now, Sammy, I've got to get an early dinner

25

for meself and me dad. You can manage all right on your own?' She knew he could, that he'd enjoy the responsibility of looking after things until the market closed at one. It was just after eleven now.

'You hop off, Flora, I'll be all right, and I'll bring yer me takings,' said Sammy cheerfully.

'Good on yer, lovey,' smiled Flora, and departed, knowing she could trust him to be loyal to her and to see that nothing was pinched.

Sammy was soon at work attending to a fairly regular flow of customers. Being on his own was a stimulating challenge, and he was always an enthusiast whenever he was involved in anything that earned him money. Since leaving school at Easter, he'd been haunting the market, and knew everything about it that made it tick. All the stallholders knew him, and most made use of his services in one way or another, paying him a few coppers. His first ambition was to run a stall himself, and to use it as a springboard for making his fortune. He was not only sharp, he was shrewd, cheerful and trustworthy. With his blue eyes and facile tongue he could wheedle custom out of shoppers who only stopped to look, and what money he took during Flora's absence would be handed over to her right down to the last farthing. In return, she would pay him his due commission on all he had sold during the morning. Young Sammy Adams had a wholesome respect for money and for the principles of fair shares between employer and employee. He agreed the boss was entitled to the larger share, especially since he saw himself as an employer one day.

He came up trumps by selling six cheap glass tumblers to a bloke who only wanted two.

'Well, I can sell yer two, mister, if that's all you think you want,' he said to begin with.

'Course it's all I want,' said the bloke, a middle-aged man with whiskers slightly tea-stained. 'One for me and one for the missus. We just broke the two we 'ad.'

'That's me point,' said Sammy. 'I mean, I owe it to yer to mention breakages, which is common in ev'ry fam'ly, yer know. Me own fam'ly suffers 'orrendous, but it can't be 'elped, and you can get over yer grief quicker if you've got spares to hand and don't 'ave to rush out and buy 'em. Look, I can't do it for ev'ry customer, but I'll offer you a set of six of these genuine 'alf-pint tumblers for tenpence, as long as you keep quiet about it.'

'I ain't buyin' six, I don't need six,' said tea-whiskers.

'What, not when the set for tenpence instead of a bob is givin' you discount that's only a bit short of twenty-five per cent?' said Sammy, registering astonishment.

'Twenty-five per cent?'

'Shush, not out loud,' said Sammy.

'Twenty five per cent, you say?'

'Near enough,' said Sammy, 'but I'm beggin' yer to keep it dark.' He placed six tumblers in a cardboard box at the speed of light, then handed the box to the bloke before he could do any more thinking about it. 'There's a war on, yer know, mister, and I ain't legally supposed to do these kind of favours.

27

It's the shortages, yer see, they're something chronic. Still, we're all in it together, so I'll keep to me word and just charge yer what I promised, tenpence.'

Tea-whiskers paid up and went happily home with his purchase. When he arrived, his missus informed him what a dozy old coot he was, and demented as well. He informed her in turn that he'd got valuable discount. You silly old carrot, she said, Flora Beamish always knocks tuppence off for a set of six.

Sammy had most of the wares set out very attractively on the stall, the china including little ornaments dear to the hearts of cockney housewives who always had room for one more on a mantelpiece or in a corner cabinet. He served every customer as if he'd been waiting all his life for the privilege. A little after twelve, three schoolgirls approached. Thirteen-year-olds, thought Sammy, or maybe fourteen. This is where I exercise me fatal charm without it costing me anything.

The three girls viewed the display from a distance, much as if they were hedging their bets.

'Walk up, me darlings,' said Sammy, 'I don't charge for lookin', not even at me priceless cut glass.' There was little of that on the stall, if any.

'What was that 'e said, Ivy?' asked one girl.

'Darlings, 'e called us, Ethel,' said the second girl.

'Saucy devil,' said Ethel, 'we don't want to buy anything from 'im.'

'But Rachel does,' said Ivy.

28

'Well, don't let 'im know,' said Ethel, 'he's got gypsy eyes.'

The third girl, standing behind the others, said nothing. Rachel Moses was just fourteen. Her boater sat like a bright yellow crown on her glossy raven black hair. Her eyes were a dark liquid brown, and she was already a beauty. Sammy placed her at once as a blossoming flower of the Israelites. He had a soft spot for the Jewish fraternity of Walworth. They were good at business, and their young men were doing their bit for the country out in France and Flanders.

'D'you want to look, Rachel?' asked Ivy.

'Who's Rachel?' asked Sammy.

'She is,' said Ethel, turning and nodding at the young beauty.

'Mornin', Rachel,' said Sammy breezily, 'pleased to meet yer.'

Rachel looked up at him, slim and tall behind the stall. Sammy was standing on the reverse side of a kipper box. His wheedling smile made an appearance, and one blue eye winked. Rachel blushed.

'Rachel, what yer doin' that for?' asked Ivy.

'What's she doin', then?' asked Ethel, edging forward to run her eye over a display of colourful little china ornaments.

'She's blushin',' said Ivy.

'What for?'

'She's not sayin',' said Ivy. 'Come on, Rachel, you want to 'ave a bit of a look, don't you?'

'No charge,' said Sammy, 'specially not for Rachel.'

A sudden little smile made its bright mark on Rachel's face, and she came forward to the front of the stall. A woman arrived to buy just one china egg cup. Sammy sold her two for the price of a pair. Then he watched Rachel inspecting a little set of three miniature china bears, Father, Mother and Baby Bear. He had to admit, cautiously, of course, that she was a Sunday morning treat in a very pretty light brown frock with a rich brown silk sash. She glanced up at him. Cheeky blue eyes held the liquid brown. Rachel blushed again.

'Well now, Rachel, it's like this,' said Sammy in conspiratorial fashion.

'Beg yer pardon?' gulped Rachel.

'You 'appen to be lookin' at a secret bargain,' said Sammy. 'Watch my hand.' He passed his right hand over the display and suddenly the three bears were joined by Goldilocks.

'Crikey,' breathed Rachel, 'how did yer do that?' Rachel was a Jewish cockney.

'He 'ad it in 'is hand all the time,' said Ethel scornfully, 'and what's secret about little orna-ments, anyway?'

'It's because this set's the kind of bargain I keep for special customers,' said Sammy.

'Some 'opes,' said Ethel, obviously the awkward one.

Up came a housewife with whom Sammy was acquainted.

'Keep lookin', Rachel,' he said, 'while I serve this other young lady.'

'Complimented, I'm sure, Sammy,' said the

30

housewife, who was in her thirties. 'Which is a nice change from bein' follered down the Walworth Road at night by one of them 'orrible German zeppelins. It'll get me one night and blow me skirts over me 'ead, and I won't know where to look.'

'If I'm there, nor will I,' said Sammy.

The schoolgirls shrieked.

'Well, I can't stand 'ere all day talkin' about me skirts and suchlike,' said the housewife. 'I'll just take two cups and two saucers out of that job lot, Sammy.'

Sammy served her, took her money, said he'd follow her down the Walworth Road himself if he was a bit older, and off she went giggling like a girl. He turned his attention back to the three girls.

''Ow much is Goldilocks and the three bears?' asked Ivy.

'Well,' said Sammy, 'seein' they're Court china—'

'Never 'eard of it,' said Ethel.

'Don't worry,' said Sammy, 'I forgive yer.'

''Ow much?' demanded Ethel.

'Well, I could ask five bob,' said Sammy, 'but I didn't mention a bargain for nothing, yer know, specially as it's Sunday and you've all got yer best frocks on. Let's say four bob – no, if it's for Rachel, I'll make it three and a tanner.'

''E's barmy,' said Ethel, ''e must be at three and a tanner, it's nearly more than me soldier brother gets for a week in the trenches.'

'Oh,' said Rachel, 'I think I could afford—'

'No, you couldn't,' said Ethel. 'Ivy, Rachel's not

payin' all that much for a birthday present for an old aunt in Shoreditch, is she?'

'Course she ain't,' said Ivy, 'I don't call three an' six a secret bargain.'

'That's it, break me arm,' said Sammy. 'Still, what's an arm when there's a war on? All right, seein' Rachel reminds me of me fav'rite cousin, I'll let her 'ave the set for three bob – no, blow it, I tell a lie. 'Alf a crown.'

'Rachel ain't payin' that, either, are yer, Rachel?' said awkward Ethel.

Rachel glanced at Sammy again. Sammy smiled. Rachel's dark lashes fluttered and she did some thinking.

'Well,' she said, 'I—'

'There, told yer she wouldn't,' said Ethel to Sammy. 'Offer 'im a tanner, Rachel.'

'I'll pass out if she does,' said Sammy.

'Come on, Rachel, let's go somewhere else,' said Ivy. 'You don't want to spend more than a tanner on an old aunt.'

'Yes, come on,' said Ethel, and the bossy pair took Rachel away, although not before she had given Sammy one more glance and a fleeting smile. Sammy would never have allowed the loss of a customer if he hadn't had certain feelings. And there was still time before the market closed down. He dealt with two new customers, and then Ma Earnshaw, whose quality fruit and veg stall was on his immediate right, spoke to him.

''Eard from Boots recent, Sammy?'

'Last week,' said Sammy.

'All right, is 'e?' asked Ma Earnshaw, plump and motherly.

'Bearin' up, yer know, Ma.'

'Grown up a real man, Boots 'as,' said Ma. 'Bet them French ladies like 'im.' She chuckled.

'Would yer mind not tellin' me mum that?' said Sammy. 'Me mum don't think too 'ighly of French ladies.'

A shadow fell across the front of the stall and a young velvety voice reached Sammy's ears above the buzz of the market.

'I've come back.'

Sammy turned. There she was. His certain feeling had been right.

''Ello, Rachel.' His welcoming smile was all of friendly, with not a touch of commercial cupidity to it. Well, he knew she was hooked on Goldilocks and the three bears. 'I thought I might 'ave the pleasure again. Give 'em the slip, did yer?'

'Oh, they went 'ome,' said Rachel, 'and I don't really mind payin' two and six.'

Crikey, thought Sammy, a girl her age able to spend all that much on a present for an old aunt was unusual in Walworth.

'Well, Rachel, I want yer to know the set ain't ordin'ry or common,' said Sammy. 'It's quality, cross me heart.' He gave her another smile because her brown eyes looked so trusting. Her dark lashes did another little fluttery dance. 'That's honest, Rachel, believe me. Funny thing, I 'ad this idea you might come back, so I said to meself, Sammy Adams, I said, don't sell that set to no-one else, give

33

Rachel a chance to show up again. If you do sell it, I said to meself, and she does show up, you'll never forgive yerself. I can't 'elp saying I like yer, Rachel, and sometimes a feller's got to let 'is kind 'eart rule 'is business principles.'

'Crikey,' breathed Rachel, fascinated, 'don't you talk all over the place? My life, not 'alf. How old are you?'

'Sixteen,' said Sammy, able in his looks and gift of the gab to stretch the truth reasonably. 'It's me first age of responsibility, yer know.' He began to wrap the set, using spare tissue paper around each piece. 'I think you're fourteen yerself.'

'Oh, but I'm nearly fifteen,' said Rachel, who wasn't.

'Well, I don't tell a lie, Rachel,' said Sammy, 'it's nice to 'ave met yer.'

'Oh, thanks,' said Rachel, and let a little sigh escape. Sammy Adams was just about the most natural and friendly boy she'd ever known. It was sometimes hard being a Jewish girl among so many Gentiles. Some, like Ivy and Ethel, didn't worry a bit. Others seemed to suspect she was capable of putting the evil eye on their grandmothers. Some boys stood up for her. Others called her names. Young street kids were easier, they simply either liked you or didn't, never mind what your religion was. Rachel instinctively felt that Sammy Adams had a liking for one and all, except those no-one could like, even if he was sharp enough to be in charge of this stall. Rachel wasn't simple. She knew about markets and how they were run. It was just that shyly nice feelings for Sammy had been born because of how cheerful and friendly he was, with a smile as natural for her as it would have been for the prettiest Gentile girl. It was his natural friendliness that made her decide to detach herself from Ivy and Ethel and return to the stall.

An elderly couple came up, looking for a cheap glazed basin.

'Serve them first,' said Rachel, 'I'm not in no 'urry.'

Sammy sold them a better quality basin, seeing the elderly lady's Sunday hat was of a superior kind. Then he finished packing Rachel's purchase into a small cardboard box.

'There, 'ow's that?' he smiled, and Rachel felt almost guilty at liking him so much already, seeing he wasn't of her own kind. 'If your Aunt Delilah don't like the set—'

'It's not Aunt Delilah, you silly, it's Aunt Hannah,' said Rachel.

'Well, good old Aunt Hannah,' said Sammy. 'If she turns 'er nose up at the set, me name's not Sammy Adams. Can't say fairer, can I, Rachel?'

That was something else she liked about him, his friendly use of her name.

'Oh, the set's not for 'er,' she said, 'it's for me, to decorate me dressin'-table. I just bought some 'ankies for Aunt Hannah. Well, I thought I'd like Goldilocks and the three bears for meself. D'you think they'll look nice on me dressin'-table?'

'Pretty, like you,' said Sammy, and Rachel went

just a little pink. Here, watch what you're saying, he told himself.

'I think you're nice,' said Rachel.

Help, thought Sammy, if I'm not careful something expensive could happen to me, and it won't be just the expense of a tuppenny seat at the Fleapit. A girl in a frock like that will expect a sixpenny seat somewhere posh.

'Well, I'm nice to me fav'rite customers,' he said, 'but I've got a hard heart mostly, yer know. It's what business does to a bloke.'

'It's not done it to you,' said Rachel, laughing. 'You 'aven't got a hard heart. You're just saying that.'

'Well, 'ere comes the hard-'earted bit,' said Sammy. 'Two and six, if yer don't mind.'

'Oh, that's not hard-'earted,' said Rachel, 'that's easy.' She opened her purse. Sammy blinked. The purse was rich with copper and silver coins. She picked out half a crown and gave it to him.

'Rachel, it's yer lucky day,' said Sammy, and handed her three pennies.

'What's this for?' asked Rachel.

'Discount,' said Sammy. Two and threepence was the correct price, of course, and two and a penny if seriously pushed.

'But you've got to make a profit,' said Rachel.

'Pardon?' said Sammy.

'Well, you 'ave to in business,' said Rachel.

'Blow me, Rachel, you said that out loud. Blessed if you ain't a girl after me own 'eart.'

'Oh, d'you think so?' said Rachel.

For the first time since going into long trousers two years ago, Sammy had an horrendous feeling he was going to fall overboard.

'Profit keeps a business goin', yer know,' he said, 'and I'll remember you for yer kind remark.'

'Oh, thanks,' said Rachel. 'I – well, I s'pose I'd better be on me way 'ome.'

'Good luck, Rachel, nice to 'ave met yer, honest,' said Sammy, feeling another few minutes with her might sink him. His pocket actually hurt at what that might cost. A customer arrived. Good timing, thought Sammy. 'So long, Rachel.'

'Oh, d'you work in the market every day?' she asked.

'Well, I'm in the market ev'ry day,' said Sammy.

'That's nice. Goodbye, then.' Rachel looked wistful as she left:

Chapter Three

It was still morning when the Germans began shelling the road between Amiens and Albert. The trouble was that they held the high ground southeast of Thiepval, and their observation posts always had the road to Albert in view. So from time to time they shelled it. They opened up this morning out of habit rather than with any real reason, it seemed, for there were no columns of marching troops to strafe, and very little traffic, military or otherwise.

An Army lorry did appear, however, a few miles from Albert, belting along towards the town. And a hundred yards behind it was a new Wolesley ambulance, keeping its distance to minimize the target factor. The shells were straddling the road, exploding on either side in a welter of flame, smoke and flying earth, the tired ground softening the impact and reducing the violence of the blasts. The lorry thundered on, and the ambulance, due to be delivered to the combined Red Cross and St John headquarters in Albert, followed. It would be suicidal to stop. Polly Simms, at the wheel, grimaced.

'Keep going, Polly,' said Alice Hurst, her co-driver.

'If that lorry cops it, they'll need us,' said Corporal Johnny Jones of the Medical Corps, seated on the other side of Alice.

'Light me a fag,' said Polly as another salvo variously exploded a little way ahead of the lorry, which visibly shuddered but went on. Polly was edgy. So was Alice. They'd been driving ambulances on the Western Front since September 1914, and no matter how hardened they became month by month, there were always times when nerves were ragged and prayers were said silently.

With all eyes on the pitted road and gashed earth, Johnny lit three cigarettes, one for each of them. Alice stuck one between Polly's lips. She drew on it and exhaled smoke through her nostrils. Over came the whistling shells. One hit the edge of the road midway between the travelling vehicles. The roar of the explosion coincided with the crump of other shells ploughing into earth. Dirty smoke and showers of disintegrating soil painted their obscene pictures in the light of the June day. The blast of explosion rushed, and its heat struck at the great box-like ambulance. Polly, Alice and Johnny felt that heat fan around their faces.

'Nasty,' said Johnny.

Crump, crump, crump. Further shells pitched into the war-torn earth to the right of the road a hundred and fifty yards ahead. The lorry kept going, running into and through the violently disturbed air and the ragged drifts of smoke. The ambulance, still keeping its distance, rocked and swayed in its wake. Polly, after several drags on her

39

fag, chucked it away, at which point the shelling stopped as suddenly as it had begun. Just north of Albert, a British battery opened up to remonstrate with the Germans for disturbing the peace of this summer Sunday. Or so Johnny said in so many words. Polly thought, what peace? When were the guns ever silent? Would she ever get their echoes out of her head?

'Road clear, lovey,' said Alice. She was a young cockney woman of twenty-three, hailing from Albany Road, off Camberwell Road, south London. Polly was nearly twenty and upper class, the daughter of General Sir Henry Simms, a corps commander. The two young women were firm friends for all the difference in their backgrounds.

A clerk in a factory office before the war, Alice took a first aid course with the Camberwell branch of the St John Ambulance Brigade in 1913. She was also taught to drive. The moment war broke out in 1914, she applied to join an ambulance unit that was being made ready for service in France. She was accepted. A typically lively and resilient cockney, with fair hair, hazel eyes and very passable looks, she sent her mum up the wall in her determination to do her bit as an ambulance driver. That wasn't what a girl was for, protested her mum. Why couldn't she be a nurse? Alice said she couldn't, not now she'd been accepted into the ambulance unit and was going to France any moment. Her dad said well, good on you, Alice gel, you won't be out there long, the war will be over by Christmas.

Alice was out there by early September, when she

40

met Polly. They were thrown at once into their missions of mercy, along with male colleagues, by the great battle of the Marne, when the Old Contemptibles of the British Expeditionary Force and the soldiers of France finally stopped the awesome German advance and forced a retreat. But the casualties were tremendous, and Polly and Alice endured their first traumatic days of driving ambulances laden with wounded men to the field casualty stations, and from there to the casualty clearing depots.

Polly was an upper class caution, a madcap. She had no time for the kind of rules, regulations and red tape which, in her opinion, got in the way of commonsense, and she had lied about her age when enrolling. Eighteen then, she got away with a declaration that she was twenty-one. With a thick crown of dark brown hair, wide grey eyes and piquant features, Polly could look a picture of endearing and vivacious charm, with no outward sign of her strong will. She was irresistibly likeable, a young woman who recognized she was advantaged by birth. Privilege, however, had never spoiled her, and she took people as she found them, irrespective of their background. She was quick to befriend Alice, a lone cockney among the primarily middle class women drivers, and helped her whenever it was expedient to cock a snook at authority. Authority was unpopular to the men and women of France and Flanders. It had too much in common with the attitudes of dogmatic generals.

Polly was a well-educated and sophisticated

young woman. Alice, with an elementary education, was undeniably gauche when she first arrived in France, but she soon learned what the facts of life were on the Western Front. She and Polly knew it was a desperate struggle for survival as far as the Tommies were concerned, and as for the women ambulance drivers, theirs was an existence fraught with anger and bitterness at what was expected of the men of the trenches. Polly and Alice had seen service in Flanders and France, from Ypres down to Amiens. Like almost all the other ambulance women, they had a very special relationship with the Tommies. But by 1916, every woman knew what the maxim was. Make love with them, if you want, but don't fall in love, for they're all dead men.

Polly and Alice, with Corporal Johnny Jones as escort, had collected the new ambulance in Dieppe three days ago. They were given twenty-four hours leave there to relax and unwind before beginning the journey to Albert. The two young women took turns at the wheel during the two days of driving. Polly was still at the wheel when they finally arrived in Albert, when she brought the ambulance to a stop outside the headquarters of the combined services, the Red Cross and St John. She stretched her limbs, then climbed down, a supple young woman notable to the Tommies for her brittle sense of humour, her attractive figure and her legs. Most women drivers wore breeches. Not so Polly and Alice. They wore khaki jackets and tough serviceable knee-length skirts, peaked caps, lace-up boots and woollen khaki stockings. They both had good legs and didn't mind giving the appreciative Tommies a look. What Polly and Alice would have relished at times was the feel and look of silk stockings.

Alice followed Polly down, and Johnny alighted on the other side. Due for an immediate Blighty leave, he said, 'Ta for the ride, me loves. Could've been quieter. Don't get tight and break your legs while I'm away. Wait till I come back, eh? I don't want to miss the privilege of tyin' splints to your good-lookers.'

'Hoppit,' said Alice.

'Love to Blighty,' said Polly.

'So long,' said Johnny, a wiry old married man of thirty. Off he went to his billet to pick up some kit and his travel warrant. Quite a few personnel had been getting Blighty leave lately, due to a lull in the affairs of war in the Somme sectors.

Polly and Alice delayed reporting their arrival for a few minutes, Polly digging out a packet of Players Navy Cut from the pocket of her rumpled jacket.

'Another fag, Alice old sport?' she said.

'Won't say no.' Alice took one, Polly struck a match, and they lit up and relaxed. They needed to, for they felt as battle-scarred as the town itself, held by a division of General Rawlinson's Fourth Army. As much as the men themselves, Polly and Alice thought the interval of quiet was suspicious, like the lull before a storm. Something big was being cooked up. Polly had no illusions, and was entirely

43

sceptical about what would come of it, apart from more horrendous casualties. Only the Tommies themselves knew the Germans and their tenacity through and through. The planners, who never came face to face with the enemy, as the Tommies did, relied on maps, numeracy and logistics.

She and Alice smoked their fags reflectively, faint little rims around their eyes. In nearly two years of service, they had driven a succession of ambulances over roads pitted and gouged by gunfire, and frequently in the worst kind of weather. They knew exactly what it was like to come under fire, and most of all they knew what exploding shells and machine-guns could do to the men of the trenches. Wounds could be ghastly. Polly's father, General Sir Henry Simms, had lately been reprimanded for stating his opinions on the deadly lot of the Tommies too frankly to the British Commander-in-Chief, Sir Douglas Haig.

Polly saw the Tommies as a strange breed of men, with little or no respect for the powers-that-be, and they reacted with earthy cynicism to all mention of gallantry and heroism. When they got hold of newspapers that recorded battle incidents in such terms, their comments were obscene and ribald.

'But at least you can look each other in the face,' said Polly once to some such men just out of the line, 'and that's something, isn't it, you old gasbags?'

'Aye, it's summat, lass,' said a Northern man, 'but nowt to do with what you're thinking on. More to do with do I owe Nobby a fag, or does he owe me, by heck. Any road, lass, when Jerry starts his bloody shooting, we start bloody ducking, and there's an end on it.'

But for all their irreverence, they obeyed orders. They went over the top to be shot to pieces, and when the survivors reappeared, they were gaunt of face and blasphemous of voice. They fought and they died, the new recruits, the early volunteers and the Old Contemptibles, and Polly thought that those who died somehow lived on in those who survived. They were imperishable comrades, the dead and the living. It was this, the never faltering nature of their comradeship that made Polly absolve them of all their sins and omissions as men. It was a comradeship that took in Polly, Alice and other women of their kind.

Polly had long had a feeling that somewhere among these thousands of cynical, earthy and sooty-eyed men, tough young officers, hard-bitten NCOs, gunners and privates, there had to be one on whom she was destined to make a very personal claim. It was an odd feeling, a ridiculous one at times, yet it kept surfacing. They were all Tommies to her, whatever their rank, those who were men of the trenches or the gun batteries. But somewhere, she felt, there was one who had to be special, special to her, and to her alone. She was not so fey as to go looking for him, but sometimes she did glance with interest at faces new to her. Again there was a ridiculous element, that of feeling sure she would know a certain man was the one as soon as she looked into his eyes.

She came out of her reverie as Alice touched her arm.

'We're in the way, ducky.'

They were, they were standing with their backs to the ambulance in the middle of the street, and marching at ease towards them was a battalion of the Royal West Kents, packs on their backs and their rifles slung, tin hats at all angles. At their head, on horseback, was their battalion colonel. Their supply vehicles were in the rear. They were marching in the easy, tireless way of veteran infantry. Was there any difference between them and any other infantry battalions? Not to the eye, thought Alice. All British infantrymen looked the same in their worn khaki, their steel helmets and their gait.

She and Polly took themselves out of the way, and the battalion began to pass them. There they were, a long column of khaki, officers at the head of each company, sergeants alongside their platoons.

'Watcher, me popsies,' said a man out of the corner of his mouth.

'Watcher, old 'orseface,' said Alice.

'See yer, maybe?'

'Can't wait, can I?' said Alice, and the man was gone, with his grin. Another made himself heard.

'Out of britches, are you, girls? Well, good on yer legs.'

'You're welcome,' said Polly.

'Who's talkin' out of turn?' barked a sharp-eared corporal.

'Old bleedin' Nick,' said the culprit, and he was

gone too, with his platoon. On came others, marching by, giving the ambulance women an eyes left. A sergeant brushed Polly's arm as she let her gaze travel over the length of the column. Had she looked at him, she might have thought, here's a man a little different from the others, here's a man I'd like to know. As it was, she did not look. Alice did, however, and the sergeant returned her glance. He saw a young woman kitted out in khaki, a cigarette between her fingers, and an immediate little smile on her face. Alice saw the lean face of a man of the trenches, a man matured more by the war than his years. How many years? Twenty-one? Twenty-five? Thirty even? Who could tell with some of them? But such a fine face, and such fine grey eyes, with amusement lurking about in his expression as if the stupidity of men was something to laugh at, not cry over.

All this in the brief seconds of passing. Alice experienced a quickening.

'Good luck, Sarge,' she said.

Over his shoulder, Boots, who had been twice wounded, smiled and said, 'I'm a customer of yours.' Then on he went, alongside his platoon, leaving Alice curious about him.

She stood there with Polly, watching the West Kents come and go. They watched until the battalion and its transport disappeared.

'They're West Kents, Alice,' said Polly. 'They were at Mons, you know.'

'Polly lovey,' said Alice, 'you know too much, and it's all storin' up inside you. You'll get to be like

47

a filin' cabinet, like we had in our fact'ry office.'

'There's going to be another offensive,' said Polly, 'and they're going to be part of it, the West Kents. It's in my bones, ducky, not my filing cabinet.'

'Could be rheumatics,' said Alice. 'Oh, blimey, rheumatics at our age, Polly.'

'Our age?' said Polly. 'What age is that? I've forgotten mine.'

'I don't want to know about mine,' said Alice, 'I keep feelin' I'm fifty at least. Polly, one of those sergeants was a lovely man.'

'Lovely?' said Polly caustically.

'Oh, you know,' said Alice.

'Bless you, old sport,' said Polly, 'there's none of them lovely. They're all grey wolves, they're all men in a way no others have ever been. They're all due for death and the devil, and they all know it, and they spend what time they can spare spitting in his eye. It doesn't make any of 'em lovely, old dear, but do you care, and do I? Not on your life. When they've gone, when our High Command boneheads have managed to see them all off, what'll be left? Shadows and ghosts, Alice, and you and me.'

'That's it, cheer me up,' said Alice. 'You're a laugh a minute, you are.'

'No charge, ducky,' said Polly.

Lady Banks, Area Commandant, came out of headquarters at that moment.

'There you are, you two,' she said. She was a handsome woman of forty-five, smartly uniformed in blue. Polly noted, abstractedly, that her stockings

48

were silk. 'You've arrived on schedule. Excellent. Any problems?'

'Ten minutes of shellfire from Thiepval,' said Polly, her features just a little drawn.

'I wondered about that,' said Lady Banks. 'We heard it, of course. Was it unpleasant?'

'A bit lively, ma'am,' said Alice.

'Well, I'm very glad you got through safe and sound,' smiled Lady Banks. She took a look at the ambulance, its newness somewhat spoiled by a layer of dust pock-marked with specks of dried mud. She ignored that. 'Not a scratch,' she said. 'Splendid.'

'Oh, it'll grow into a good old biddy, another good old bone-shaker,' said Polly, slightly tart. Like other drivers, she could swear her heart out about what the bone-shakers could do to a cargo of badly wounded men.

'Still, I suppose they're all a bit better than a dustman's cart,' said Alice.

Lady Banks gazed sympathetically at the two young women who had been in the thick of things since 1914. They both looked a little drawn. That kind of look was all too common among ambulance drivers.

'I think you can both do with some leave,' she said. 'Well, you're on next month's roster.'

Blighty leave for Polly meant a giddy round of theatres, restaurants and parties, and a quiet time at home for Alice. Yet for both it soon became unreal because it had so little to do with the carnage of the Western Front. They couldn't help their feelings, their whole beings belonged to their missions of mercy.

'That's nice,' said Alice, "'ome leave.'

'I'll face up to it,' said Polly with her brittle smile. Departing for their billets a few minutes later, she murmured, 'Listen, dearie, how many pairs d'you think she's got?'

'Pairs of what and who?' asked Alice.

'Silk stockings. Lady Banks. I fancy pouring myself into some slinky glad rags and silk stockings one evening.'

'You Polly, you just can't get silk stockings except in Paris,' said Alice.

'I know that,' said Polly, 'I'm thinking of you sneaking into Lady Banks's quarters and pinching some of her regulation issue. Say two pairs, one for you and one for me. New, of course. I'll keep watch.'

'Well, blow that,' said Alice, 'me doin' the nickin' and you safe outside smokin' a fag?'

'All right, Alice old love, I'll nick, and you blow the whistle if you have to. One evening, when she's out. Game?'

'Crikey, what a palaver,' said Alice, as they entered their billet. 'Still.'

'Still what?' said Polly.

'Silk stockings,' said Alice, and thought of herself in an *estaminet* in slinky glad rags, and that West Kents sergeant inviting her to sit on his lap. 'Yes, I'm game.'

'Good on yer, sport,' said Polly in the lingo of the hour.

Chapter Four

'What?' said sixteen-year-old Tommy Adams over the Sunday dinner of stew made of scrag ends of mutton, vegetables and plump suet dumplings.

'Yes, did we 'ear you right, Sammy?' asked his sister Lizzy, nearly eighteen and quite lovely with her rich chestnut hair and her large brown eyes. She was eleven weeks pregnant, and enduring the sad fact that her husband Ned was in a military hospital recovering from the amputation of his left leg. 'Did we 'ear you say you actu'lly met a girl?'

'He must've meant accident'lly,' said Tommy. 'Walked into 'er, I suppose, when 'e was on 'is way 'ome and countin' 'is money.'

'If yer don't mind,' said Sammy, 'I never count me money out in the street. It ain't safe to. What was that you was askin', Lizzy?'

'She was askin' if it's true you've met a girl,' said Chinese Lady.

'I dunno what came over me, mentionin' it,' said Sammy. 'Me brains must be gettin' some kind of complaint. I might've known you'd all give me looks. Anyway, it ain't a crime, yer know, to meet a girl.'

'It's a sensation for you to,' said Tommy, a young

stalwart with an engineering job. 'Don't you usually run a fast mile when you see one comin'?'

'Only to protect me savings,' said Sammy, 'they're me future. Anyway, I couldn't leave the stall, and, besides, she was a customer.'

'Was she nice, Sammy?' asked Chinese Lady, who believed in growing boys and girls being sociable together, as long as there were no larks of the forbidden kind.

'Well, she bought a set of nice china figures,' said Sammy. 'Look, all I said was that I'd met a girl. That's all. I met a girl, that's all I said.'

'Yes, you came out with it sort of sudden, as if she was on your mind,' said Lizzy. 'Crikey, and you only fourteen, Sammy, and a woman-hater up till now.'

'A what? I never 'eard the like,' breathed Chinese Lady. 'My own youngest son a woman-hater? It's like a viper in my – well, never mind that, I just don't know where I went wrong with you, Sammy. It'll have to be put right, even if it means boxin' your ears twice a day. D'you hear me?'

'Mum, course I'm not a woman-'ater,' said Sammy, 'it's not natural. It's just that I ain't old enough to 'ave one of me own yet. Nor could I afford it.'

'Sammy Adams, are you speakin' of holy matrimony?' asked Chinese Lady.

'Not yet I ain't,' said Sammy, 'I ain't made me fortune yet.'

'Well, you'd better understand, me lad, that I didn't bring any of me sons up to be woman-haters,' said Chinese Lady. 'Mind you,' she went on, as she ladled out seconds of the nourishing stew, 'I wouldn't want Boots gettin' too fond of them fast Frenchwomen. I 'ear there's a lot of them about in France. Sammy, did you mention if this girl you met is nice?'

'Pardon?' said Sammy, chasing his extra dumpling around on his plate. His fork caught up with it, and pinned it. 'What girl?' he asked.

'The girl you met,' said Tommy, grinning.

'I can't remember exactly,' said Sammy.

'Oh, is it all over, Sammy, before it's 'ardly begun?' asked Lizzy.

'I couldn't afford to let anything like that begin,' said Sammy, 'I've got me savings to protect, like I already told you. One day,' he said darkly, 'you'll all thank me for what me savings'll do for the fam'ly.'

Lizzy laughed, then thought about her visit to the hospital this afternoon. The war had crashed into her life like a thunderbolt when the news came that Ned had lost a leg. They'd been married only a month when he was recalled to his unit and to a battle that resulted in the amputation. How thankful she was about his gradual recovery. It was a comfort, living with Mum and the boys for the time being, but she could hardly wait to have Ned home in the house in Sunrise Avenue, off Denmark Hill. It actually had a bathroom and a garden. She and Chinese Lady went there regularly to let in the fresh air, to do one or two household jobs, and generally to keep the place nice for when Ned came home.

'Now, who wants rice puddin' for afters?' asked Chinese Lady, at which point the front door opened to a pull on the latchcord, and a girl's voice called.

'Coo-ee, Mrs Adams, can I come in?'

'Yes, come through, Em'ly,' called Chinese Lady.

Emily Castle from next door darted energetically through the passage to the cosy kitchen. A thin young lady the same age as Lizzy, she had a peaky nose and a pointed chin. But she also had magnificent dark auburn hair and huge swimming green eyes. An only child, she had attached herself to the Adams family as if such attachment was the best thing in her life. Her beery but kind old dad had recently died of cancer, and her good-natured but blowsy mother was hoping to move and to live with a sister in Camberwell. Emily was fighting that tooth and nail.

''Ello, ev'ryone,' she said in her eager and lively way. 'Oh, yer still 'avin' yer dinner.'

'Rice pudding afters, Em,' said Tommy.

Emily, nicely dressed in an apple green Sunday frock, said, 'Oh, you do bake a lovely rice puddin', Mrs Adams.'

'Well, sit down and 'ave some,' invited Sammy. They all knew Mrs Castle wasn't much of a cook, and that wartime rationing hadn't helped her to improve.

'Yes, get yourself a plate from the dresser, Em'ly love,' said Chinese Lady, 'and sit down with us.'

'Bless yer, Mrs Adams, I don't mind if I do,' said Emily. She fetched a plate and sat down at the table, looking happy at being one with them, and even happier when Chinese Lady served her a large helping. She tucked in with the relish of a young lady whose own Sunday dinner hadn't done a great deal for her healthy appetite. 'Oh, ain't it lovely?' she said. 'Lizzy, I actu'lly only popped in to see if you'd like me to go with you to the 'ospital this afternoon, just for company, like. I won't come in, of course, I'll wait while you 'ave yer visitin' time with Ned.'

'Love you to come with me, Em'ly,' said Lizzy, 'and you can say hello to Ned, I'm sure he'd like to see you for a bit. Then on our way back, we can go to the house and see 'ow the garden's lookin'.'

'Oh, I'd be pleasured to see yer house again,' said Emily.

'We'll take something with us so we can 'ave a late tea there,' said Lizzy. 'And do some gardenin', shall we?'

'Crikey, I never done gardenin' in all me life,' said Emily. 'Don't you 'ave to learn a bit about it first?'

'You can help me just to dig weeds up,' said Lizzy, 'you don't need any learnin' about weeds.'

'Tell yer what, Lizzy,' said Sammy through a mouthful of rice pudding, 'I'll do some gardenin' for yer next Sunday, I'll sacrifice me whole afternoon.'

'Well, that boy's got some good in him, after all,' said Chinese Lady.

'Yes, that's really nice of you, Sammy,' said Lizzy.

'Wait for the catch,' said Tommy.

'There ain't no catch,' said Sammy. 'I'd only charge a tanner for the whole afternoon. Lizzy's me one and only sister, and I wouldn't charge 'er more, not if you broke me arm.'

'Sammy, I don't know 'ow you can be so graspin',' said Emily.

'Well, you ought to know,' said Tommy, 'you've been livin' next door to 'im nearly all 'is life.'

'Oh, all right,' said Sammy in a burst of generosity, 'fourpence-'a'penny, then. That's twenty-five per cent discount. Could I say fairer?'

'I'll give you fairer,' said Chinese Lady, 'I'll get Boots to give you a tannin' when he's next home on leave.'

'Oh, 'ave you heard from Boots recent, Mrs Adams?' asked Emily in an impulsive little fit of eager enquiry. The family looked at her. She coloured up. Not that it would have made any difference if she hadn't. They all knew how she felt about Boots. She'd followed him about like his own shadow from her schooldays, craving his attention to the point of being a terror.

'I'm expectin' a letter any moment now,' said Chinese Lady, 'and if I don't get one by Tuesday, I'll want to know the reason why. The war's bad enough, but 'avin' it goin' on in France is even worse. Like I said before you came in, Em'ly, there's a lot too many of them fast Frenchwomen about, and if any of them get their hands on Boots, we'll all have to pray for him.'

'Oh, lor',' breathed Emily, and in a silent panic

said a hasty but heartfelt prayer for Chinese Lady's only oldest son.

Private George Watts of the West Kents came running from the large yard that lay between a French farmhouse and its dairy. In his cap, braces, shirt, trousers, puttees and boots, he was moving at speed. He needed to, for on his heels was a furious young Frenchwoman, wielding a very unfriendly pitchfork. Boots, arriving with an innocuous jug in his hand, sidestepped as Watts accelerated and rushed by him. The young woman shouted.

'What's the trouble?' asked Boots. She stopped, her sun-browned face expressive of temper, her blue eyes fierce. Carmen in a fury, thought Boots. No, not Carmen. Carmen's Spanish. I'll settle for Fifi in a paddy.

'Ah, you,' she said in fierce, spitting English, 'you 'ave come to steal our chickens too? It is disgusting. 'Ow would you like for me to stick you with this fork, eh?' She gave him a prod. Boots retreated a step. She lunged, the prongs looking wicked. He back-pedalled, tripped and fell, his peaked cap falling off. She leapt and stood over him, booted feet astride his hips, the hem of her long skirt brushing his trousers. She dug the fork into his jacket. Mother O'Reilly, thought Boots, what's she after, blood? ''Ow would you like some 'oles in you, you English thief?'

'I wouldn't, it'll let out my dinner,' said Boots. It was four in the afternoon, and his midday meal, eaten a bit late because of the time taken for the company to settle into their billet, was still being digested. 'Who's that behind you, by the way?'

Falling for it, the young woman turned her head. Boots knocked the fork aside, drew his hips and legs free, and came quickly to his feet. She hissed a fierce imprecation, drew a breath and looked him over as he picked up his cap and put it on. She saw a tall British soldier with three stripes on each sleeve of his jacket and the air of a man who could take care of himself. She knew that his company, billeted in her father's largest barn, hadn't long been out of the line, but already the hot sun was healing his trench greyness. His face wasn't in the least unpleasant, although it should have been – the thief – and his deep grey eyes, slightly rimmed from his time in the trenches, weren't at all furtive or shifty. But they were a little wary. So they should be. She was quite ready to use the pitchfork. She thought him in his mid-twenties, an Englishman inured to the war. She frowned, much as if she would have preferred him to have a hangdog look.

'That man came to steal chickens,' she said. 'Now you 'ave come too. You are a sergeant. It is most disgusting.'

'Well, it would be if—'

'Do not speak to me.'

'I haven't come to steal chickens,' said Boots, and smiled placatingly.

'That is what you say. 'Ow would you like my father to set 'is dogs on you?'

'Now, ma'm'selle, have I stolen anything or tried to?'

58

''Ow do I know what you 'ave come to take? Perhaps even my honour.'

'Well, that's rich,' said Boots, and laughed. Most Frenchwomen, as far as he could make out, were more concerned with what the Boche were doing to their beloved France than with their honour. But this one looked as offended as a virgin who'd caught a saucy market pickpocket with his hand in her blouse. He spoke in French then, for his time in France had helped him perfect what he had learned at school. 'Ma'm'selle, believe me, I haven't come to relieve you of anything that's precious to you, your honour or your livestock.'

She frowned again, as if she disliked the fact that he could speak her language. Using it herself, she said, 'I am not a single woman, I am a widow. My husband, a brave soldier of France, fell to the Boche a year ago.'

'I'm sorry, then,' said Boots, 'very sorry.' He accepted, like most of the men, that he was at the mercy of the luck and the percentages of war, but no man could get used to the slaughter and the tragedies, and this young woman's tragedy was a very personal one. He judged her to be about twenty-one, and noted that her blouse was a sombre grey, her skirt an unrelieved black, her braided hair a shining Latin black. The high neck of her blouse was fastened by a filigree brooch, and her farm boots marked by patches of dried mud. 'Accept my sympathy,' he said.

'You are a sergeant,' she said again, 'and should keep your men away from here. They have the big barn. Here it is private.' The large stone dairy was at her back, the farmhouse a little way on, part of the farmyard visible. Chickens began to appear, strutting and pecking. She turned to look at them. 'There, they have come back after flying for their lives from you.'

'Not from me,' said Boots, realizing old sweat Private Watts of A Platoon, a redoubtable kidnapper of French poultry, was responsible for putting her hens to flight. 'I'll speak to the man you were chasing.'

'What did you come here for, if not to steal?' she asked.

'To tell the farmer – your father?'

'Yes.'

'To tell him that my company commander says he can make men available if you're short of labour. It's the usual thing when a company is allowed the use of a barn as a rest billet.'

'Ah, you think so?' she said scornfully. 'The usual thing is to lose chickens or eggs or suckling pigs.'

Boots tried another placating smile. She made a face at him. Eighteen months ago, he might have found it difficult to deal with her, for at that time he hadn't been at the Front all that long, and he'd felt disconcertingly raw among the hard-bitten regulars. Since then, however, the attitudes of a young man had been lost forever, and one could have said of him that if he survived, little would ever disturb him again, for what would ever come close to this carnage? He was mature in a way that stood him in good stead with the old sweats and with what was expected of him. But it was an unspoken regret of his, the certainty that he had lost any feeling of being young, although he wasn't yet legally of age. Even that, however, was acceptable when set against the percentages. If he survived another six months, it would be despite the odds. He lived, as all the others did, in the shadow of the grim reaper. A fretful and mettlesome young Frenchwoman was a very small problem.

'It's the war, madame, we're all losers,' he said. 'But there it is, in return for the use of your barn and its water supply, Major Harris presents his compliments and says if you need some labour, you only have to ask.'

'That is what you came for?' She seemed dissatisfied at being deprived of a reason for using the pitchfork.

'That, and to ask if you've a little dairy milk to spare,' said Boots.

'Ah,' she said triumphantly, 'now I know, yes, you came to steal milk, and perhaps cheese as well.'

'Young lady,' said Boots, reverting to English, 'if you keep this up, I'll smack your bottom.'

She let go a little yell of outrage.

'Ah,' she cried, also in English, 'you are a pig as well as a—'

'Don't say it,' said Boots, thinking it a pity that on a day of golden summer, with the guns only an intermittent rumble, this young widow was choosing to play the quarrelsome madam. 'I'm sure we'd get along much better if you cooled down. What is it you don't like about me?'

'It is because you look so pleased with yourself.'

'But I'm not pleased with myself,' said Boots. They were back to French again. 'I'm not pleased with where I am, or with what it means. I'd much rather be at home and reading that there's been an armistice. But I'd be very pleased with you, young lady, if you could spare a little fresh milk.'

'If I give you some, you will come again and ask for your own cow. I know the Tommies, always asking or taking. Go away.'

Boots, with a resigned smile, said, 'Sorry to have troubled you, madame.' He touched the peak of his cap and left.

'Come back!' she called. Boots stopped and turned. 'Come back!' He returned to her, and she looked him up and down. Her farm-tanned face took on a challenging look. 'You are very provoking,' she said.

'I don't think so,' he said.

'Who is the milk for?'

'Myself and my corporal,' said Boots. 'He's about to boil a kettle in the hope we can make some real English tea. With dairy milk.'

'Tea with milk is disgusting,' she said. 'But give me the jug.' He handed it to her. 'Wait here,' she said, and disappeared into the dairy, casting the pitchfork aside on her way. Boots waited. The chickens clucked and ventured in his direction, cocking enquiring and wary eyes at him. The hot afternoon sunshine flooded the farmhouse and the fields. The rumble of guns stopped, and the day became as quiet as any he could remember since arriving at the Front a thousand years ago. His company was at rest in tranquil surroundings, the other companies similarly situated at other farms. How long the lull would last was anybody's guess. Major Harris knew, perhaps, but if he did his bleak eyes were guarding the information.

The young widow reappeared, carrying the jug.

'That looks promising,' he said.

'You are smiling? The war does not worry you, after all?'

'Is that a good question, do you think?' countered Boots.

'Perhaps not. Here is some milk.' She gave him the jug. It was nearly full.

'Well, I'm much obliged,' said Boots. 'Thank you, young lady. *Au 'voir*.'

'Wait. What is your name?'

'Adams, Robert Adams.'

'You are Sergeant Adams?'

'Sergeant Adams of A Company,' said Boots.

'Very well, Sergeant Adams, you may go now.'

'Thanks,' said Boots, and smiled as he left. Widow she might be, but she was very much the madam in her dismissal.

She watched him leave, a British Tommy of the sergeant fraternity, who had not come to steal her chickens, after all. It was a terrible war, it had widowed her when she was only twenty, but for once there was a little smile on her face.

* * *

Boots returned to the huge barn, some way from the farmhouse. It was full of lounging and relaxing soldiers. Some were playing cards. Some had found sacks, or purloined them, and were filling them with straw to make palliases of them, although in the main the Tommies could sleep on anything barring a bed of nails. Several men were already out to the world, and would probably sleep the clock round. Boots's own sleeping quarters were in a much smaller barn, along with the rest of the sergeants. A little way from the main one, a disused pig shed was being used as a cookhouse, and some forty yards beyond that was a farm cottage housing the officers.

Corporal Freddy Parks had a fire going outside the south end of the big barn, and a tin kettle was on the go. When Boots arrived with the milk, Freddy spilled tea leaves from a packet into the bubbling, boiling water. Up came Sergeant Boxall of A Platoon, a rugged fighting man, but abrasive.

'No fires,' he growled.

'Do us a favour,' said Freddy.

'What favour?'

'Shove off,' said Freddy.

'Sod that,' said Sergeant Boxall. 'I'm here now, so I'll stay for tea.'

'You ain't been invited,' said Freddy.

'I'll still have some,' said Boxall, a regular.

'Please yourself,' said Boots. 'By the way, Watts has been after the poultry.'

'Get any, did he?'

'None. Just as well,' said Boots.

'Just as well?' said Boxall, who had an aggressive bone structure. 'Who's bleedin' side you on?'

'Watts's,' said Boots. 'He needs saving from the farmer's daughter and her pitchfork.'

'Some young farm tart's a problem?' said Boxall.

'I don't think she's a tart,' said Boots, 'much more like a six-foot iron maiden. She'll feed Watts to her chickens. Ask him.'

'I like you, mate,' said Boxall, 'but you're a ponce.'

Boots laughed.

'I thought that was you, Boxy,' he said.

'So did I,' said Freddy.

'We all make mistakes,' said Boxall. 'Where'd you get that milk from?'

'I stopped a wandering cow, and Corporal Parks milked it,' said Boots.

'Thought so,' said Boxall, 'he's another ponce. But more like you've been up to the farmhouse and tickled the six-foot daughter. You sure she's that size?'

'Ask Watts,' said Boots.

'Bloody 'ell,' said Boxall, 'a six-foot French bird ain't natural.'

'Same size as her pitchfork prongs,' said Boots.

'Six-foot pitchfork prongs?' said Boxall, a born sergeant but with a thick head.

'Ask Watts,' said Boots again.

'Jesus,' said Boxall, 'she sounds like blue bloody murder.'

'Well, slightly dangerous,' said Boots, with Freddy grinning all over his chops.

'Sometimes, yer know, Adams, I feel sort of sorry for you,' said Boxall. 'You're not only a ponce, but you talk like one, did yer know that?'

'Course he knows it,' said Freddy. 'We both know it, but if he can live with it, so can I. Well, I got to, I'm only his corporal. All right, tea's brewed.'

'Don't pour yet,' said Sergeant Boxall, grinning as he went to fetch his mug.

There was a fair amount of this kind of camaraderie on the go. The West Kents, out of the trenches and at rest, were in a good mood, and had few grumbles apart from the usual ones about head-lice, bleeding officers, lousy grub, and perishing Jerries.

Someone was singing, 'Oh, when this bleedin' war is over, oh, how 'appy we shall be . . .' to the tune of 'Jesus wants me for a sunbeam.'

Chapter Five

Alice and Polly, lodging with a middle-aged French couple, left their billet that evening to visit an *estaminet*. That was their preferred choice of entertainment during a lull in their sector at the moment. At other times, when the warfare was persistent, they often came off duty too physically exhausted and too mentally drained to do more than simply fall into their beds. The continuing lull in the whole of the Somme sector was as welcome to them as to the men of the British Fourth Army.

Reaching the *estaminet*, one run by proprietor Jacques Duval, an avuncular Anglophile, they entered and looked around. Blue smoke filled the place, the smoke from pipes and inveterate fags. The haze shifted about, its patterns created by the movements of bodies or the intermittent gusts of laughter from men seated at tables laden with bottles of French beer or wine. There were an unusual number of regiments presently stationed or resting in and around Albert, and men who could get passes made for the *estaminets* in the evenings.

So many men in the area represented another sign to Polly that a new offensive was coming. Were the Germans taking note? You bet they were, she thought, and most of the men in this *estaminet* would take the bet. So for them it was drink, smoke and be descriptive about their sergeant-majors, for they knew they were going to cop it.

She and Alice showed themselves in the blue smoke. Men of the West Kents, newly arrived in the area, were present, the few who had wangled immediate passes. So were men of the Warwicks, Royal Scots, Irish Fusiliers, the Essex and other regiments. They hailed in boisterous fashion the arrival of the women ambulance drivers. Pipes waved, and men took fags from their mouths to invite them to Paris this year, next year, sometime, never. The comradeship that existed between the Tommies and such women was imperishable. They were all in it together, and that was a fact.

'This way, girls, we saw yer first. Room 'ere for yer *derrières*.'

'Stuff the Essex leavings, Alice, join the War-wicks.'

'Dinna mess aboot wi' Sassenach fairies, lassies, the Royal Scots'll gi' ye a fine welcome.'

Polly made herself heard.

'You hairy lot, you all need a barber. Never seen such riff-raff, and all as tight as a one-eyed parrot in a beer barrel. No, don't get up, old dears, you'll only fall over, and there's a squad of redcaps outside waiting to cart you away.'

They roared with laughter. Behind the bar, Jacques grinned. He knew Polly and Alice, and many other women drivers. Of them all, Madem-oiselle Polly Simms was the joker in the pack.

68

She and Alice looked around again. Along with the bottles and glasses on the tables were packets of fags and pouches of tobacco. The weed was the solace of almost every Tommy. There they were, these specimens of a strange wartime breed of men. Polly accepted that they were as imperfect, basically, as all men: blasphemous, complaining, scrounging and womanizing. They thought nothing of attempting to seduce every French housewife who came within reach, and within reach could be as much as half a mile to their trained eyes. All the same, they were men of extraordinary resilience and character, for whom the Germans, a tough breed themselves, had unqualified respect. Perhaps French housewives responded to such men, for none had ever been known to cry rape as far as Polly was aware. She had once rescued a Tommy fleeing from a farmhouse in just his shirt-tails, a white-bearded and red-faced grandfather roaring after him with a shot-gun. The Tommy jumped aboard her ambulance as she slowed down for him, and afterwards she went back to the place to persuade the woman in question to let her have his uniform and boots. The young woman willingly handed them over and said with a smile, 'Tell Gus, Monday afternoon when my grandfather will be at the market.'

Polly herself had not been immune. Owning a particular regard for the men of Mons and the Marne, and increasingly bitter about their gradual decimation, she came to share the opinion of other ambulance women, that virginity could hardly be considered sacred in a war like this one. She was nineteen when she delivered hers to an Old Contemptible, a man of thirty-four, who had fought as a young soldier in the Boer War. She had her eyes shut tight throughout. But she need not have worried, for he was experienced in other arts besides those of war, and she was able to be a pleasure to him because of his understanding of her body. There were others like that. Not many, just a few, a few who came close to her armoured heart. One did grow that kind of armour, to escape the risk of falling in love with a man who was not really the right one and whose time, in any case, was limited.

They're all dead men. That knowledge, that certainty, repeatedly came to mind.

Alice stood apart from making love with those who were about to die. But cockney girls, of course, as Polly realized, were far less inclined to go all the way than she and her kind were, even in a world turning hideously upside down.

They moved forward between tables. No hands reached to grab at them, although Helene, the proprietor's buxom daughter, always had a terrible time when she was squeezing her way through with a tray of orders. The Tommies, however earthy they were, had a respect for all the women who drove their ambulances close to the shot and shell of the trench warfare.

Five Northumberland Fusiliers made inviting room at their table. Alice and Polly stopped.

'You blokes fairly decent?' smiled Alice.

'Nobbut else, lass.'

'Chance it, Polly?' said Alice.

'Well, ducky, you've got more to lose than I have,' murmured Polly, and Alice laughed. They sat down with the Northumberland men. An open packet of fags was proffered, and they took one each. The light of a struck match hovered, putting a little glow around Polly's piquant nose and delicately carmined lips as she leaned. She lit up, and the match moved to serve Alice. She dipped the end of the cigarette into the flame, and the tobacco glowed as she drew. Polly called to Jacques and ordered a bottle of wine and two glasses for herself and Alice. In the main, everyone bought their own drinks. The Tommies rarely had much money to spare. The Government didn't feel that going over the top was deserving of high wages. After all, with so many soldiers doing it – and in their thousands, what was more – it was very commonplace by now. Nor did the Paymaster-General think much of soldiers' wives who wrote asking if their husbands couldn't have a bit of a rise.

Alice and Polly struck up a lively conversation with the Northumbrians. At an old piano in a corner of the *estaminet*, one of their sergeants was running his hands lightly over the keys, playing some kind of tinkling sonata barely heard above the general noise.

'Liven it up, Sarge,' called an Essex man, 'give it a go.'

The sergeant, cap tipped back, took no notice, apart from a brief smile. He continued his light trilling. The *estaminet* buzzed with anecdotal conversation that was punctuated with bursts of laughter. It was all very familiar to Alice and Polly, who had shared many such evenings in the *estaminets* of France and Flanders with men of the British Army. Progressively, there were fewer old sweats, fewer Old Contemptibles. But in an *estaminet*, the survivors could still laugh, and still make their sardonic jokes about the unfortunate.

'Poor old Jock, Alice. Found his boots, yer know, just his bleedin' boots. Still running, they were. Pointin' to Glasgow. Hope they can run on water, or they'll never get there.'

Through the smoke, Alice caught sight of the sergeant at the piano, a pipe between his teeth, his eyes watching the keyboard, his hands travelling lightly over it, the tune difficult to hear above the noise.

'Who's the sergeant?' she asked.

'Old Horse,' said the man beside her.

'How'd he get that name?'

'Well, lass, he were Young Horse once.'

'Ask a silly question, get a silly answer,' said Alice. She got up, asked to be excused for a moment, and made her way to the man at the piano, taking her glass of wine with her. She looked down at him. He lifted his head, little trails of smoke issuing from his pipe. She met his eyes. They were blue overlaid by the inescapable grey of the trenches. With his cap tipped back, his black hair showed a widow's peak. His face was weathered, his expression enquiring.

'Hello,' she said, 'I 'aven't seen you before.'

'Nor I you, lass,' he said, taking his pipe from his mouth and laying it alongside his glass of beer on the scarred top of the piano. Alice placed him as a man in his late thirties, and a hardened regular.

'Why are you called Old Horse?' she asked.

His hands returning to the keyboard, he said, 'Ask me another.'

'Were you at Mons?'

'Aye.'

'And the Marne?'

'Aye.' He was playing the same light sonata.

'That was where I first found what the war was all about,' said Alice.

'Time for you to call it a day, then, and to go home.'

'Well, I can't, can I?' said Alice. 'I'm in it till it's over.'

'You're too young,' he said. 'Go home, lass.'

'But you can't go 'ome yourself till it's over,' said Alice.

'Not even then,' he said, his Northumbrian accent perceptible without being broad.

'You're a regular?'

'Aye. Started as a drummer boy. What're you doing here in France, lass, at your age?'

'Pickin' up the bits and pieces,' said Alice. His hands were deft, the music lilting. 'Who taught you to play the piano?'

'Nobody. There were an old upright like this once. Somewhere. I thumped on it, like noisy boys do, and one day thumping pensioned itself off and playing began. Of a kind, after a fashion.'

'Well, I suppose you're a natural.'

'So-so, lass.'

Alice felt drawn to him. There were men from time to time who touched one's emotions more than others. There had been a few men like that for Polly, men with whom she'd made love before they were thrown into one more battle and perhaps to finally die in the mud. Other women had also had their giving moments, and Alice thought how emotional it must be, pleasuring a man who was a little more special than others in the knowledge that sooner or later he would be dead. But she could not do it herself, even if most of the women drivers considered virginity on the Western Front laughable. Alice wondered if any of the women had pleasured this man, for she thought most of them would see him as very special. He looked like so many veterans did, as if he would last for ever, but in this kind of war he was as vulnerable as they all were. They knew it, and one saw it in their eyes.

'How long will your unit be here?' she asked.

'A few days, maybe,' he said, playing a different melody, but still of a light character. 'A few weeks, maybe. Depends on when the trumpets call.'

'Some blinkin' trumpets,' said Alice, and he looked up at her, a little smile on his face.

'Aye, they're different in this war,' he said, 'and so are young women like you, though you're still nobbut a girl when all's said and done.'

'That's all you know,' said Alice.

'Shouldn't be out here, lass.'

'You're an old Victorian,' said Alice.

'Aye, I'm that,' he said, and stopped playing to finish what was left of his beer. Replacing the glass, he said, 'I were born and brought up in the old Queen's time, and sorry I was to see the end of her and her iron petticoats, never mind her widow's sulks.' He stood up. 'Well, time to go, but a pleasure, meeting you.'

'You can't go yet, I want to talk to you,' said Alice.

'Another time, lass, another time. I'm duty sergeant tonight.' He put his pipe back between his teeth, and off he went, through the haze of smoke to the door. Then he was gone. Alice rejoined Polly and the Northumbrians.

'Like Old Horse, did you, lass?' asked one man.

'Wild about him,' said Alice.

'Made of iron filings, that one,' said another man. 'Saw him standing in the rain once, at Wipers. Watched him turning rusty.'

'And then?' said Alice.

'Ah, well, he were all right when the sun came out.'

A Warwickshire private sat down at the piano. A local Frenchman with an accordion took up a position beside him, and music of the right kind began. The next moment the Tommies were singing 'Mademoiselle From Armentières.' Polly and Alice joined in, and so did other long-serving women drivers now present. Women new to France or Flanders might have found the Tommies' own version somewhat blush-making. Polly and Alice, and other old hands, took it in their stride.

As the evening turned into a rousing round of music hall songs and wartime ditties, Alice and Polly shared fags with the Northumbrians and sang along with them. Polly, getting heady, bought several bottles of beer and wine as a treat for everyone at the table. Polly was never short of funds.

'Tha doesn't have to do that, lass.'

'That's where you're wrong, old love. Of course I have to, now and again.'

'It's not regular.'

'I know that, but we all like to break the rules, don't we?'

'Mud in your eye, lass.'

'Mud? Bloody hell,' said Polly, thinking of Tommies who had drowned in it, 'anything but that, old sport.'

'Language, ducky,' said Alice.

The singsong went on, the haze thickened to a fug, and eventually men began to leave. There was a time limit on their passes. And when Alice and Polly were finally on their way back to their billet, it had to be said in the parlance of the times that they were pretty squiffy.

'Tell me something,' murmured Polly, as they waveringly crossed a cobbled street, 'is it night-time?'

'Beg pardon?' said Alice.

'Is it night-time?'

'Not 'alf,' said Alice.

'No wonder it's dark,' said Polly. It was. The sky was inky, the Somme sector blanketed by the night. The guns were silent. 'Alice, where are you?'

'Wish I knew,' said Alice, and giggled.

'Is this the time to see if Lady Banks is dining out?' asked Polly.

'What for?' asked Alice.

'Silk stockings,' said Polly. 'Look, hold me up, will you, sport?'

'Can't,' said Alice, 'me legs won't let me.'

'But you can get into Lady Banks's quarters if she's not there, can't you, dearie, while I keep watch?'

'Some 'opes,' said Alice.

'Alice, what's wrong with you?'

'I've 'ad one over the eight,' said Alice.

'That's funny, so have I,' said Polly.

But they made it to their billet, where their condition at least helped them to get quickly to sleep, and to put a rosy glow into their dreams. Tomorrow might bring an urgent summons from a sector that had suddenly erupted into fire and slaughter, and a sound night's sleep was a good preparation for heart-breaking action.

Chapter Six

'Crikey, the time,' said Emily, finishing a late evening pot of tea with Lizzy, 'we'd best go.'

They were at Lizzy's home, having travelled there from the hospital after visiting Ned, who was making a slow but satisfactory recovery. Not only had he had his left leg amputated, he'd also had shrapnel dug out of his ribcage. He was happy to see Emily, who spent ten minutes talking to him with Lizzy before leaving them to themselves for the rest of the visit. Afterwards, on the way back to South London, Emily mentioned in an awkward way that it was going to be rotten for Ned only having one leg when he was finally home. Lizzy said not to be daft, he'd have an artificial one. She said she wasn't going to let the army fit him up with some old wooden thing, that it had got to be a proper new artificial leg. She said that when Ned was home, they were going to walk out on Sunday afternoons, just like any normal married couple.

Having enjoyed a late tea in Lizzy's marital home, they then attacked the weeds in the overgrown garden. Emily was always in her element whenever there was anything to do, and although she'd never worked in a garden before, she attacked the weeds with enthusiasm, using a little fork from the old shed. Enthusiasm counting for more than knowledge, it wasn't surprising that Lizzy had to tell her she'd dug up some plants as well.

'Still, never mind, Em, your heart's in the right place, even if you are a bit cross-eyed.'

'Lizzy, course I'm not, I've never been cross-eyed in me life. I 'ad mumps once, and the flu, but that's all.'

'Well, I'm happy for you, Em'ly,' smiled Lizzy.

'Oh, thanks,' said Emily.

Now, as she and Lizzy began to make sure the kitchen was left looking nice and tidy, Lizzy said, 'Yes, we'd best go in a couple of minutes, Em, it's already dark.'

'We'll catch a tram by King's College Hospital,' said Emily.

The German zeppelin, which had left its base at twilight, slipped out of cloud cover and hovered north of London, a city enveloped by night. Painted black to render it a difficult target for searchlights, the invader was invisible against the clouds that had rolled in half an hour ago. As it hung, it slowly turned until its nose was pointing due south, and then began to glide. Hundreds of feet below, the maroons were going off, warning the people of London of the presence of a German night raider. On went searchlights to scour the dark sky.

There were a few people on the streets, and at the first sound of the maroons, some began to run. Others continued walking, not wanting to let any ruddy German sausage balloon get the better of them. Of course, there were one or two doubters as to the wisdom of this.

'Alf, p'raps we ought to get a bit of a move on, seein' what 'appened to me sister when she was caught out in the last raid.'

'Well, I tell yer, Maggie, if you wet yer drawers like she did, I ain't goin' to 'old me 'ead up as yer 'usband.'

A few people here and there stopped to look up at the night sky, to watch the bright moving discs of searchlights. The zeppelin, still unseen, glided on.

Chinese Lady was sewing while she awaited the return of Lizzy and Emily. Tommy was reading a Sherlock Holmes story. Sammy was sitting at the kitchen table, a notebook in front of him, a pencil between his fingers, calculating Post Office Savings Bank interest at two and a half per cent. It was a question of whether or not he should part with his sockfuls of coins and trust them to the Post Office. Would they take the same care of his money as he did himself? What sort of safe did they have, and did anyone stand guard over it at night?

Chinese Lady looked up then.

'There's maroons goin' off,' she said.

'I got objections to zeppelins comin' over of a Sunday night,' said Tommy.

'Me too,' said Sammy, hoping a bomb wouldn't drop on his savings.

'Lizzy's not home yet,' said Chinese Lady. At this precise moment, Lizzy and Emily were waiting

for a tram by King's College Hospital. They'd
already been waiting twenty minutes. The war had
reduced tram services, especially on Sunday nights,
and omnibuses were even scarcer.

'Oh, Lizzy'll be 'ere any minute now, Mum,' said
Tommy.

'It's a problem, yer know,' said Sammy, ruffling
his hair with his pencil.

'It will be if Lizzy and Em'ly can't get a tram,'
said Chinese Lady. 'They stop running in an air
raid.'

'They'll get 'ome all right,' said Sammy. 'What's
worrying me is would the Post Office lose me
savings if I 'anded them over?'

'You implorable boy,' said Chinese Lady, 'worrying more about money than about your own sister.
And I don't know we shouldn't get under the table
in case a bomb drops.'

'You get under, Mum,' said Tommy. 'Make
yerself comfy, and I'll pass you yer sewing.'

Mr Finch, their lodger, came down from his
room and knocked on the kitchen door.

'Come in,' said Chinese Lady.

Mr Finch, a handsome man in his forties, was a
river pilot, and hadn't long returned from his
Sunday stint. He worked all kinds of awkward
hours, but that didn't stop Chinese Lady regarding
him as a very respectable gentleman lodger. He was
on the friendliest terms with the family. Entering
the kitchen, he smiled reassuringly.

'You and the boys are all right, Mrs Adams? You
wouldn't like me to take you to some kind of

shelter, such as the basement in the workingmen's club on the corner of Browning Street?'

'Kind of yer, Mr Finch,' said Tommy, 'but we went there durin' one of the air raids. They play billiards in the basement, yer know, and we sat there with other people, watchin'. But Mum said if the roof and the basement ceilin' and the billiards table as well, all fell on top of us, we'd be better off 'ere at 'ome.'

'Yes, and we can keep our mince pies on things 'ere at home,' said Sammy. 'Valuable things.'

'Understood, Sammy,' smiled Mr Finch. 'But where's Lizzy?' He had a very soft spot for Chinese Lady's one and only daughter.

'She went to see Ned in hospital this afternoon, with Em'ly,' said Chinese Lady, listening for the dreaded sound of bombs falling. 'They were goin' to Lizzy's house from there, to have some tea and do a bit of gardening. I must say they've left it disgraceful late to come home.'

'If they can't get a tram,' said Mr Finch, 'they're probably walking. I think I'll take a walk myself, and look for them along the Walworth Road.'

'I daresay I might come with you,' said Tommy, trying to sound casual.

'I think I'll come too,' said Sammy.

'Suppose you stay, Sammy, and look after your mother?' suggested Mr Finch.

'Oh, all right,' said Sammy, 'I'll do that, I'll look after Mum and 'er best ornaments. And other suchlike things.'

Chinese Lady, hiding her worst worries, said,

'Well, I would be grateful if someone went and met Lizzy and Em'ly. I'm sure that if any bombs drop you'll see that Tommy and the girls don't stand about waitin' for them, Mr Finch, that they take cover like they should.'

'Leave it to me, Mrs Adams,' said Mr Finch, and out he went with Tommy.

Searchlights by the dozen had blazed into being, their elongated fingers of dazzling white creating criss-cross patterns in the sky. They probed for the gliding airship, for its huge sausage-like shape. It passed directly above Dalston, heading for the river and the factories of East and South London. The searchlights darted and fidgeted, crossing, uncrossing and crossing again.

The first bomb dropped close to Liverpool Street railway station, the explosion a roar of sound combined with a blinding flash. Two adjoining office frontages fragmented, and a warehouse on the corner of Middlesex Street collapsed. Windows of adjacent buildings burst and shattered. In Liverpool Street itself, a man and a woman were blown off their feet, the blast tearing their clothing to shreds.

The zeppelin continued its planned flight. It passed over the river, a little east of London Bridge, and travelled above Bermondsey, Walworth and Camberwell, dropping its bombs at intervals. The searchlights sprayed their frantic white beams, while ack-ack gunners peppered the sky with shellfire. Miraculously, a searchlight caught the raider as it began a turn to the east over Herne Hill. The gunlayers homed in on it. Shells whistled upwards. At once the zeppelin jettisoned ballast and soared for the clouds. Zeppelins could reach incredible heights, and fast, making it impossible for RFC fighter planes to catch them.

The beams of light stabbed at the clouds, and the clouds flung their impenetrable blanket over the escaping airship. Ambulances were rushing through the streets north and south of the river, and the clang of fire engines could be heard.

Mr Finch and Tommy seemed to be the only people abroad in the Walworth Road. Shops were closed and shuttered, and there were neither trams nor omnibuses running. Street lamps were out, but searchlights were still probing the clouds. Mr Finch was hoping for Lizzy and Emily to appear. So was Tommy. They'd heard a bomb drop in the distance, not far from Camberwell Green.

'Blimey,' Tommy had said, 'I don't like the sound of that.'

'Yes, a little too close for comfort, Tommy,' said Mr Finch, 'but at least it means you and I are safe now. The zeppelin's travelling ahead of us.'

'But 'ow safe are Lizzy and Em'ly?' asked Tommy. 'If they decided to stay in Lizzy's house, the next bomb might cop Denmark Hill. I reckon that last one dropped near Albany Road.'

'Chin up, old chap,' said Mr Finch.

They reached Camberwell Road, keeping their ears and eyes open, and in a little while they approached Albany Road. At that moment a fire engine, coming from Camberwell Green at speed, braked hard and turned into Albany Road. It picked up speed again, clanging as it went.

'There y'ar,' said Tommy, when he was able to make himself heard, 'didn't I say Albany Road? I bet—'

'Tommy, is that you?' Tommy jumped at the sound of Lizzy's voice issuing from the dark shelter of a deep doorway. 'Tommy?'

'Lizzy?' said Mr Finch. A thinking man, he had brought an electric torch with him. He switched it on. A muffled yell greeted the little beam of light.

'Oh, me gawd, don't do that!' Emily, sharing the shelter of the doorway with Lizzy, sounded as if panic had set in. 'Put it out!'

'Crikey, what's up?' asked Tommy in alarm. The torch having been switched off, he peered at the figures in the doorway of a shop. One shadowy figure hastily hid behind the other. 'Lizzy, is that you and Em'ly? What's 'appened?'

'Oh, we're all right,' said Lizzy, 'we're not hurt or anything, but – oh, lor', you'll never believe it, Emi'ly's lost the skirt of 'er frock, and 'er petticoat. And hat.'

'Crikey Moses,' breathed Tommy, 'is that right, Em'ly? Where are yer?'

'You Tommy, I'm in 'ere,' gasped Emily, 'don't you come any nearer.'

'But you're safe and sound, Emily?' said Mr Finch.

'Lizzy is,' said the distracted Emily, 'but I ain't. Oh, them zeppelins and their rotten bombs, it just ain't right or decent, blowin' a girl's clothes off 'er,

85

and 'er best Sunday 'at as well.'

'Emily, that's very unfortunate,' said Mr Finch. An ambulance raced up and turned into Albany Road. 'But are you sure you're not hurt?'

'Well, I'm not wounded, Mr Finch, but me modesty's taken an awful 'iding.'

'Oh, blimey,' said Tommy, 'you don't mean you're down to yer knickers, do yer, Em'ly?'

Emily uttered a yell of outrage.

'You Tommy, don't you 'ave no respect when I'm close on eighteen? Oh, me gawd, Lizzy, don't move, he'll lose 'is eyesight.'

'What happened exactly?' asked Mr Finch, regarding the shadowy figures. The zeppelin was far away now, searchlights still conducting an ineffectual chase, and as far as these young ladies were concerned, the only damage was what the German airship had done to Emily's modesty.

'What happened?' said Lizzy, still shaken by the incident. 'You might well ask, Mr Finch.' She explained. She and Emily hadn't been able to catch a tram, or any omnibus, so they began walking. They'd heard the maroons going off, and seen the searchlights, and then they'd heard what they were sure was the sound of a bomb a long way off. They hurried, and just as they reached the corner of Albany Road, they thought they actually heard the noise of the zeppelin itself, a sort of low engine drone high up in the sky. They thought about finding shelter somewhere as they crossed the entrance to Albany Road. Lizzy ran. A bomb dropped way down Albany Road just as she reached the safety of the corner building. Emily, a little way behind her, was a second too late to get the building between her and the rushing wind of the blast. It didn't hurt her, but it blew her hat clean off and ripped away the skirt of her frock and her Sunday petticoat. They just disappeared, just like that.

'I felt like I was in a sort of hot stormy wind just for a split second,' said Emily, keeping herself behind Lizzy. 'It was a wonder it didn't knock me over, but it was more as if it blew me forward, because next thing I was beside Lizzy, and she was pullin' me into this doorway. Oh, I nearly passed out when I found what it 'ad done to me clothes.'

'Never mind,' said Mr Finch gently, 'we'll get you home, Emily.'

'And it could've been worse,' said Tommy consolingly, 'it could've blown yer summer vest and whatsits off as well, Em.'

There was another little yell from Emily.

'Mr Finch, hit 'im,' she begged.

'Spare her blushes, Tommy,' said Mr Finch.

'I ain't goin' home like this,' said Emily.

'Take my jacket and wrap it round your waist,' said Mr Finch, 'and then I'll carry you home. I think it'll be too awkward for you to walk.' He took his jacket off and handed it to Lizzy, who passed it to Emily behind her. Emily wrapped it around her middle and legs. Lizzy stepped aside, Mr Finch stepped in and lifted Emily up into his arms.

'Oh, bless yer, Mr Finch, you're such a kind gent,' said Emily.

'Jacket's comin' off, Em,' said Tommy, and

Emily shrieked. But it was a false alarm, and Lizzy gave her grinning brother a piece of her mind. Then she made him carry her shopping bag, and she also made him walk ahead with her, Mr Finch following, Emily in his arms, hands clutching the jacket as if it were a lifebelt. Mr Finch knew there was nothing they could do about the bomb that had dropped in Albany Road that the police, the fire service and the neighbours couldn't do better.

Chinese Lady, extremely relieved when they all showed up, said it was thanks to the Lord that Emily and Lizzy had been spared, and that although it had been a discomfortable time for Emily, she could probably write to someone in the government about her ruined clothes, and perhaps the Prime Minister would send her a government postal order. Emily, hiding herself in the scullery for the moment, said it was the German government that ought to pay, really. Chinese Lady said no-one was on speaking terms with the Germans while the war was on. Emily said she was sure of one thing, that she'd never forgive that German zeppelin. Tommy nearly copped for having his ears boxed by Chinese Lady then, for he said it was the first time he'd seen Emily in her Sunday knickers.

Lizzy did the necessary for Emily by finding her a skirt she could wear before going home to her mother, and Sammy more or less closed the proceedings by informing everyone he could now go happily to bed with his savings.

Mr Finch, calm and reassuring throughout, laughed and said goodnight.

Chapter Seven

'Find Sergeant Adams,' said Major Harris to his runner on Monday morning. 'Tell him to come and see me immediately.'

'Right, sir.' Away the runner went. He found Sergeant Adams in his shirt and trousers, braces dangling, giving himself a leisurely shave in the open air.

'Ruddy fanackapans, Sarge, ain't you up yet? You better be, the Major wants you immejiate.'

'I'm up, I've had breakfast, and now I'm shaving,' said Boots.

'Well, would yer mind gettin' yer French skates on, so's you can report double-quick to the officers' quarters? Better do yer braces up.'

'Enjoying the war, are you, Private Potter?' said Boots, dipping his hands into a bucket of water and washing a residue of lather from his face.

'Bleedin' hell, love it, don't I? Hope it keeps goin', don't I? Can't wait to jump the barbed wire, can I? Hope I get me perishin' legs shot off, don't I?'

'Best of luck,' said Boots.

'Bleedin' comic, you are, Sarge. You'll get medals for it one day. The Major's waitin', by the way, and he's got his tick-tock out. Hope you're hearin' me.'

'I'm hearing you,' said Boots, and was on his way five minutes later. The large cottage made over to A Company's officers had been spruced up by general duties men, and a room on the ground floor provided Major Harris with an office. In the hall, Boots came up against Company Sergeant-Major Rowlands.

'Morning, Sergeant Adams, you're after what?'

'Seeing Major Harris.'

'Got a request to put to him about someone's sick mother?'

'Not today, Sergeant-Major, just an order to present myself.'

'Ever thought where general army orders come from?' asked the Sergeant-Major, who had seen the Boer War and a lot more besides.

'Yes, from under cavalry moustaches in the War Office,' said Boots.

'Right first time, Sergeant Adams. Make a regular of you yet. Carry on.'

Boots knocked on the Major's door.

'Come in.'

Boots went in. Major Harris was sitting at his desk, cap off. He took a look at the pocket watch on his desk, and glanced up at Boots, his bleak eyes expressionless.

'Had a struggle to get here, did you, Sergeant Adams?'

'Can't say I did, no, sir.'

'I'll pass on what kept you, then. Today's orders.

Take eight men to the farm. I've had a request for labour. Get them to take their dinner rations with them. Shirt-sleeve order is permitted. Got that?'

'Yes, sir. Do I leave them there?'

'No, you'll stay. The request included a Sergeant Adams. That's you. How'd the farmer get your name?'

'From his daughter, I'd say.'

'I see.' Major Harris studied his youngest sergeant. Youngest he might be, but never the simplest. 'Farmer's daughter. Did you take her into town last night?'

'No, sir. Accidentally ran into her yesterday afternoon.'

'Accidentally sounds like a put-up job to me, as it did when you managed in 1914 to accidentally run into my own daughter.' The bleak eyes were caustic. 'Let's see, what came of that?'

'Nothing, sir.'

'Yes, you escaped in time, you fortunate sod. Well, that's all. Get your eight volunteers organized.'

Boots, a smile lurking, returned to the barn. It was full of lounging soldiers.

'On your feet, C Platoon,' he said.

'Give it a rest, Sarge.'

'On your feet. Orders from the Major. Eight volunteers required for work on the farm.'

'Now you're talkin'. Chicken farm, Sarge?'

'You won't like their chickens, there's a shot-gun and a pitch-fork in charge of them. Let's have you. You, Greenwood, and you, Williams. You,

91

Plummer.' Boots put names to eight volunteers, and was accordingly advised by an old sweat, in so many words, that his family credentials were suspect. 'Don't get my goat,' said Boots, 'I'm giving you five minutes before I march you up to the farm.'

'Bloody 'ell, what a case,' said Private Plummer to Private Williams, 'I bet his Ma found him on her doorstep, marked unwanted.'

Young Madame Cecile Lacoste emerged from the farm dairy clad in a remarkably attractive white smock and a wide-brimmed straw hat.

'Good morning,' said Boots in English.

'Ah, you 'ave come with your men. Good. Jules!' she called, and an elderly farm labourer appeared from behind the dairy, a large collection of hoes resting on his shoulder. She instructed him to take the Tommies to the fields and show them how to use the hoes.

'Come,' said Jules, and the team of West Kents, muttering all kinds of asides, followed him as he led the way. Boots ambled along behind them.

'No, no, not you, Sergeant Adams,' called the young madame.

'Right, I'm leaving you in charge, Private Jones,' said Boots to the senior man.

'All right for some,' growled Jones. 'You get the French hen, we get bleedin' French sunstroke.'

'Do you good,' said Boots. He stopped and watched his men filing along in the wake of the labourer. They began to whistle 'Men of Harlech' in derisory fashion. Boots smiled. He knew they were glad to be out of the line. It was a filthy existence on top of everything else.

'Sergeant Adams!' The young madame was peremptory. Boots turned, walked to the dairy and presented himself to her. He touched his cap. She eyed him suspiciously. 'I do not trust you,' she said in English.

'Why?'

''Ow do I know? Perhaps it's the way you look at me. Perhaps you say to yourself, "Ah, 'ere is a poor 'elpless widow."'

Boots laughed.

'Far from it,' he said. 'Well, you have the labour you asked for. I can go now?'

'No.' She spoke in French. 'You are to help in the dairy. I have permission from your officer. The churn is full and needs turning. Come.' She led the way into the cool, stone-flagged dairy, where a large wooden churn, brass-bound, awaited his muscle power. 'There it is. You may talk while you work. But in English. I wish to speak it better. You will help me, then perhaps I won't have to shout at you. Commence.'

Boots began to turn the churn by its handle. Full of curdled milk, it began to revolve. It was heavy, but rotated smoothly. He whistled softly. The young madame uttered an imprecation.

'You're not happy?' he said.

'I said to talk as well as work, I did not say to whistle. And I said to talk in English. You may call me Cecile. That's my name, Cecile Lacoste.'

93

'I've never met a Cecile,' said Boots. 'How'd'you do, Madame Cecile.'

'No, no, not madame.' Cecile was watching him. He was in his shirt, trousers and cap, his sleeves rolled up, his arms sinewy.

Boots, turning the churn with passable rhythm, said, 'Will this do?'

'No, I will show you,' she said.

Boots stood aside, she took hold of the handle and turned the churn strongly and quickly.

'I'm a stranger in a dairy,' said Boots.

'Pooh, that is no excuse. Do it again, more stronger.'

Boots had another go, and the churn revolved faster.

'How's that?' he asked.

'Yes, better,' said Cecile. 'You 'ave a family in your English 'ome?'

'Yes, I've a family,' said Boots.

'A wife?'

'No, a mother, a sister and two brothers.'

'You are not married, Sergeant Adams?'

'Fortunately, no,' said Boots, keeping the churn revolving strongly.

'Fortunately?'

'Very,' said Boots, 'under the circumstances.'

'Ah.' Cecile regarded him understandingly. 'Yes, it's a terrible war. Terrible for everyone. Please to keep working, I 'ave other things to see to.' She disappeared, and Boots kept turning. Well, it was something to do, something a lot better than having trench rats running over his feet. He had letters to write, but they would have to wait. Major Harris had given the young French widow permission to make use of him, and, however he had put it, Boots would bet he'd done so without hardly moving his lips.

He opened up the churn after half an hour. What was in there looked like thick congealing cream. He supposed he was winning. He resumed turning, and let his mind encompass thoughts of home and family. Those kind of thoughts helped to push suspicions of a coming offensive into the background.

Sammy was a bit late getting home for his midday meal. Chinese Lady asked him where he'd been.

'In the market, Mum, as usual,' he said.

'You'll turn into a market cabbage one day,' said Lizzy, who'd been writing to Boots. She was fond of all her brothers, but was closest to Boots and was praying he wouldn't be another war casualty. 'Mind, you won't be as green as most cabbages.'

'Kind of yer to say so, Lizzy,' said Sammy, sitting down to a light wartime meal of fried potatoes and brawn, the brawn made of meat from ox-feet and pigs' heads, cut up, boiled and pickled. It was very cheap and off ration. 'But what kept me, Mum, was tryin' to get some cracked eggs for Lizzy. Well, seein' she 'ad a bit of a shock last night, I thought I'd better do what I could. I remember Em'ly's mum saying once that eggs can be good for an expectant woman that's 'ad a shock. Lizzy, you all right today?'

'Yes, course I am, Sammy love,' said Lizzy, 'I don't panic easy.'

'Wait a minute,' said Chinese Lady. 'You Sammy, boys with big ears shouldn't listen to talk about women that's expectant. It's not proper. And what d'you mean, you tried to get some cracked eggs? You can't get eggs, whole or cracked, except when our grocer rations some out.'

'Well, some people can't get more than a few a month from their grocers, Mum,' said Sammy, tucking in, 'but informed people can get some from elsewhere.'

'Informed people?' said Lizzy. 'Where'd you get that from?'

'Well, I've always been admirin' of Boots and 'is educated talk,' said Sammy, 'and it don't 'urt a bloke to copy some of it, specially a bloke that wants to go into business later on. Anyway, bein' informed 'elped me get the eggs.'

'Bless you, then, Sammy,' said Lizzy. 'Mum, who's the clever boy in this fam'ly?'

'Me,' said Sammy, who had an instinctive feeling that a bloke couldn't earn his fortune by being modest. 'Well, I 'eard from a market mate of mine that old Joe Slash—'

'Joe who?' asked Chinese Lady.

'Well, that's what they mostly call Joe Slattery,' said Sammy. 'He's got weaknesses, yer know, and 'as to make a quick run to the public convenience ev'ry—'

'We don't want any common talk, if you don't mind,' said Chinese Lady.

'No, Mum, of course not,' said Sammy, 'but it's why they call 'im old Joe Slash, yer see. Anyway, I 'eard he'd be at 'is stall midday with a crate of cracked eggs, which he 'ad to sell quick in case the market bobby wanted to know where 'e got 'em from. So bein' informed about it, I joined the queue as soon as I could and managed to get six for Lizzy and 'er shock. It took a bit of time, which was why I've only just got 'ome. Lizzy, they're in that shoe box, and I 'ope they do yer good. One or two's leakin' a bit, but not much.'

'Sammy, you love,' said Lizzy, 'that's really nice of you.'

'Oh, that's all right, sis,' said Sammy, 'I'm only askin' yer the same as I paid old Joe. Mind, 'e charged tuppence each on account of eggs bein' scarce, which makes a bob. Course, if yer want to add on tuppence for me trouble, I suppose that 'ud be fair.'

'Sammy, you crafty 'a'porth,' said Lizzy, but she laughed.

'That boy and his graspin' ways'll disgrace us all one day,' said Chinese Lady. 'Still, I suppose he showed a bit of Christian goodness in thinkin' of you, Lizzy.'

'And only chargin' tuppence for his trouble and a bob for the eggs,' said Lizzy.

'It's me kind 'eart,' said Sammy.

Boots was sitting on an old bench outside the dairy. So was Cecile. On the bench between them was a plateful of French bread and cheese, together with a bottle of wine. They were dining on the simple but satisfying repast, which Boots thought was equivalent to manna from heaven compared to trench cuisine.

'You are not very good at dairy work,' she said, 'but also not too bad.'

'I'd say not bad at all, I churned out a whole barrel of butter,' said Boots.

'That is a lie, you do not get a full barrel, or even 'alf,' said Cecile, 'and all morning to do it. You must improve.'

'Improve?' said Boots.

'But of course. I 'ave permission from your officer for every day.'

'Hold on,' said Boots, 'I'm to report to you every day?'

'Yes, every morning,' said Cecile, brim of her straw hat shading her eyes.

'Look,' said Boots, 'I could probably find you a bloke—'

'A bloke? What is a bloke?'

'I'm a bloke,' said Boots.

'A sergeant is a bloke?'

'We're all blokes. Anyway, I can probably find you one who knows a lot more about farms and dairies than I do. He'd be far more useful than I am.'

'I do not wish some other bloke,' said Cecile haughtily, 'I 'ave permission from your officer for you.'

'I could get you permission to use someone more suitable,' said Boots.

'Ah, you do not like coming 'ere?' Cecile waved her hands about, and a piece of bread flew.

Chickens pounced on it. 'Why not? What is wrong with 'ealthy work?'

'Hold on,' said Boots, 'have I said I don't like coming here, even if you did try to poke me full of holes yesterday?'

'But 'ow was I to know you were not a thief?' said Cecile. 'You looked like one.'

'What sort of a look is that?' asked Boots.

'Should I know 'ow to answer all your questions?' said Cecile. She bit into bread and followed that with cheese, then a mouthful of wine. 'Ah, no wonder your officer said I must watch your tongue.'

'Did he say that when you brought your father's note?' asked Boots.

'Of course. 'E said not to let it get too near my ear. You are laughing? Why are you laughing?'

'Because I know my commanding officer, and because you're very amusing,' said Boots.

'Ah, do I 'ave a funny face?'

'Do you?' said Boots. 'I don't think so. You're amusing to talk to, that's all.'

'But what 'ave I said that is amusing? All the time I am serious. Who could not be when the war is so terrible, and our brave soldiers are dying every day?'

'Don't you think I know that?' said Boots.

'You are to come 'ere each morning, your officer said so. You are not to find some other bloke. Are you sure bloke is right when I 'ave never 'eard of it? Oh, name of a pig, you are laughing again.'

'It's hearing you say bloke, Cecile.'

'But you say it too, and I do not laugh at you. Is it my English? It is not very good?'

'It's excellent,' said Boots, 'and far better than my French was when I landed.'

'But I do not speak English as you do.'

'That's because you're French,' said Boots. 'In the same way, I don't speak French as you do.'

'But I wish to speak English like you do,' said Cecile, watching him chewing bread.

'Why?'

'I like 'ow you speak it. I do not like your eyes, of course.'

'What's wrong with my eyes?'

''Ow do I know? Except that they look at me and my honour trembles.'

Boots laughed his head off. The young madame's conversation and her French imagination were having a recuperative effect on his nerves. When out of the line, one could recover much quicker from the physical wear and tear of trench warfare than from what it did to the mind and the nerves. There were always thoughts of being hit and drowning in the mud, or dying slowly on the barbed wire. Private Jones and the seven other men had whistled on their way to the fields, but Boots knew that every one of them had yesterday's ghosts and tomorrow's dead on their minds. Madame Cecile Lacoste, a young French war widow, was good at helping to repair a man's ragged nerves, even if she didn't realize how she was doing so.

'Not your honour again, you goose,' he said.

'Goose? Goose? Who is a goose?' Cecile's blue eyes flashed. ''Ow would you like a blow on your silly 'ead, eh? My honour is funny to you?'

'Not a bit,' said Boots, 'I treasure it as much as you do.'

'Treasure it? That is what you say? You are a crazy bloke, Sergeant Adams.'

'Well, I've enjoyed the bread and cheese, and your wine, Cecile—'

'Stay where you are,' said Cecile.

'Have I moved?' said Boots.

'You are not to move until I say so.' Cecile spoke in French to make sure she expressed herself clearly. 'Then you must turn the churn again. A government man will come to collect the butter next week, and there must be enough or he will ask questions. Do you like this weather? It's better than English weather, isn't it?'

'No comment,' said Boots. If there was one thing the British Army had learned in Northern France it was that the weather could be even fouler than in Britain. The French, of course, refused to admit it.

'Ah, now you are going to insult our weather when you are sitting in our sunshine?' said Cecile.

'No comment,' said Boots again.

A stocky middle-aged man appeared. He wore black serge trousers, heavy boots, a dark blue shirt and a black beret. There was a rifle under his arm. He strode up and addressed Cecile.

'This is the sergeant?' he said.

'This is Sergeant Adams, *mon pere*,' said Cecile.

'You have said things about him.'

'Don't repeat them,' said Cecile, 'he speaks French very well.'

'Is he married?'

'No.'

'Remember you are in black. However, as he isn't married, you may use his help.' Monsieur Descartes turned to Boots. 'I am grateful, Sergeant Adams, for the men you brought with you. We are behind with everything. All our best young men are fighting for France against the Boches. My daughter Cecile will tell you each day how you may help her. I am François Descartes, owner of this farm.'

'A pleasure to meet you, m'sieur,' said Boots.

The farmer smiled briefly.

'Well, it is good, the English and the French together at last,' he said. 'Now excuse me, if you please, I am very busy.' Off he went to the fields, stocky, sturdy and as strong as a horse. A dog followed him, frisking at his heels.

'Why is he carrying a rifle?' asked Boots.

'Why? Why? To shoot you, of course, and also the other Tommies if my honour is not respected.'

Boots laughed yet again. It wasn't very often that a Frenchwoman carried on about her honour. Perhaps a widow's honour was that much more sacrosanct, although he doubted if certain of the West Kents would say so.

Cecile, frowning, and still speaking French, said, 'Why do you laugh so much?'

'Is it out of place?' asked Boots.

'Yes, it is,' she said. 'You should be crying. Everyone should be crying. And the whole world should be weeping.'

'Yes, I daresay,' said Boots.

'Come, you are not to sit there all day,' said Cecile. 'The churn must be filled again, and you must turn it again. I have to do other work.'

Boots spent the afternoon in the dairy. Cecile spent it elsewhere, except for the occasions when she looked in on him and made him talk in English with her. The occasions were many, and sometimes she even smiled.

Not until five o'clock did she tell him he could go. Boots's expression suggested he wasn't sure if he should smack her bottom or grin and bear her provocations. It wasn't usual for a sergeant to be given the run-around by a farmer's daughter.

'Why are you looking at me like that?' she asked.

'Like what?' said Boots.

'It's true, yes, that I do not like your eyes. But you must be 'ere in the morning, and with your men.'

Boots shrugged.

'*Au 'voir*, Cecile,' he said.

She watched him go on his way, the little smile back on her face.

Boots walked the long lane to the barns. At the end of the lane he saw Major Harris, cane in his hand. The Major waited until Boots reached him.

'Sergeant Adams?'

'Sir?' Boots stopped and saluted.

'Have you been at the farm all day?' asked Major Harris, height matching that of his youngest sergeant. Boots was just a little short of six feet.

'It feels like all week, sir.'

'Too much for you, farm work?'

'It's the farmer's daughter,' said Boots.

'She's too much for you, Sergeant Adams?'

'Not so far, sir. It's her churn.'

'Damned if you don't smell of butter,' said Major Harris.

'Yes, damned if I don't, sir,' said Boots. 'And she tells me I'm under orders to report to her every day.'

'So you are. It's a question of Anglo-French co-operation. But don't shout about your luck.'

'Well, I wonder, sir,' said Boots, 'is a young French widow good luck or bad luck?'

Major Harris's granite-grey eyes glinted.

'Work it out for yourself, Sergeant Adams,' he said, 'while you've got time. By the way, Kitchener's gone.'

'Lord Kitchener?'

'Went down with the *Hampshire* some days ago on his way to Russia.' Major Harris looked bleaker than ever. Boots suspected he would have preferred Haig to have been sunk. 'Either torpedoed or mined. That's all, Sergeant Adams.'

'That's enough, sir.'

'Dismiss,' said the Major.

Chapter Eight

The following day Cecile made herself quite pleasant to Boots, and Boots made the churn race round, while Jules, the labourer, put the eight so-called volunteers to work in the fields again. The sound of the guns in Flanders did not reach them. No-one would have commented if they had.

'Ah, you are working better, yes,' said Cecile on one occasion.

'Hoppit,' said Boots.

''Oppit? What is 'oppit?'

'Never mind.'

'But I want to know.'

'It means close the door when you leave,' said Boots.

'Ah, that is funny, isn't it?' said Cecile, and laughed, and left without closing the door. She came back a minute later. 'Do you 'ave an English girl?'

'Here, you mean, in the small barn?' said Boots.

'Ah, you crazy bloke, no, no, 'ow could you 'ave an English girl 'ere?'

'Good question,' said Boots, churning on.

'I mean, do you 'ave an English girl at 'ome waiting for you?'

'Just my family, that's all,' said Boots. 'Why'd you ask?'

'Because you are so funny,' said Cecile.

'Hoppit,' said Boots again.

'English is a crazy language,' she said.

'Think so?'

'Yes,' she said, 'but you speak it very nice, which I like.'

'Don't mention it,' said Boots, and Cecile smiled and departed.

'Alice, what's up with you?' asked Polly. She and Alice, in overalls, were doing some maintenance work on their ambulances in the large yard behind headquarters. Other drivers were doing similar work, with the help of mechanics. There was no call for missions of mercy at the moment, not in the sector controlled by the British Fourth Army. Relatively, the trenches were lightly occupied, for large numbers of battle-hardened men were out of the line, resting and recovering. And instinctively waiting. In and around Albert the atmosphere of quiet was growing daily more ominous.

'What's up with me? Nothing,' said Alice, 'except when this bloomin' war is over, oh, how 'appy I shall be, Mother.'

'You're glooming a bit,' said Polly, and tossed a spanner down.

'Me? Now look 'ere, Polly, I've never gloomed about anything in all me natural life. I'm happy-go-lucky, I am, except about blown-up Tommies.'

'All right, old sport, don't get shirty.'

'I'm not shirty,' said Alice, 'I'm just saying. And I was thinkin', anyway, about the Northumberland sergeant I talked to the other night.'

'Found him a bit special, did you, ducky?' said Polly. 'Would you like to send some of our generals over the top in place of men like him?'

'Not 'alf I wouldn't,' said Alice, and looked up as two RFC spotter planes, high in the sky, passed over Albert towards the German lines. 'That's where I'd like to be, Polly, up there in the sky, shakin' hands with me Maker.'

'Well, dearie, I think you'd find our Maker dark with thunder at what mankind's up to down here, and more likely to chuck sulphur and brimstone at you than shake your hand,' said Polly. 'Oh, sod it, ducky, I'm getting oily. I don't mind getting muddy, filthy and looking like something the cat brought in, but I hate getting oily. And soap's no good. Alice, pinch a can of petrol.'

'That'll make you smelly,' said Alice.

'I'm always smelly. We all are. That's why we don't notice each other. Dear Jesus, I just hope if I ever meet the one man who could be my soulmate, my smell won't put him off.'

'Crikey,' said Alice, 'are you lookin' for a soulmate, Polly?'

'Just a passing thought,' said Polly, and grimaced at the smell of oil. 'I think I'll have one over the eight again tonight, old love.'

Sammy, having spent most of the day doing odd jobs for some of the stallholders, thought about going home. But no, not yet. Chinese Lady might get on to him about finding regular work in some factory. The last thing Sammy was in love with was the idea of factory work. It would pin his feet to the factory floor, and stop him in his tracks. Fortunately, he was able in his market activities to pick up quite a tidy little bit of what had been invented by a thinking cove in somewhere like Ancient Greece. The Greeks called it spondulicks, according to an old bloke who collected fag ends. Of course, it came to be called money later on, as not many people spoke Greek.

'Oh, hello.' A shy but warm voice travelled into his ear. He turned. At his elbow was the girl from Sunday, wearing a school frock and a round school hat of blue felt. A smile made her brown eyes look melting. Crikey, thought Sammy, me alarm bell's ringing. The money nestling in his pocket lost its sense of security and sort of shivered. He wasn't sure that it didn't even rattle.

'Well, I'm blessed,' he said, 'it's you, Rachel.'

'Oh, I just thought I'd come down the market before I went 'ome,' said Rachel, not at all put off by the fact that he was in jersey, cap and well-worn trousers instead of his Sunday suit. Well, his clothes didn't matter. What did were his blue eyes and his immediate smile of friendliness. Nor did it matter that she was only fourteen and not yet old enough for a nice Jewish boy to take an approved interest in her. Rachel Moses had a crush, and simply didn't mind that it was on a Gentile boy. 'Fancy bumpin' into you,' she said, as if it had been an accident.

'Oh, but I remember now, you did say you were 'ere every day.'

'It's where me future lies as a start, yer see,' said Sammy. 'I mean to 'ave me own stall as soon as I can.'

'Oh, I think you'd be ever so good, running a stall,' said Rachel, and Sammy brought her free of the thinning crowds and stood with her on the corner of King and Queen Street. She took a little breath and said, 'What's your name?'

'Sammy Adams.'

'And you're sixteen? My life, ain't you nice and tall?'

Hello, hello, thought Sammy, what's going on?

'You're not so bad yerself, Rachel,' he said.

'Oh, thanks. I'm Rachel Moses.' Rachel knew that would tell him she was Jewish, if he hadn't already guessed.

'Well, ain't that a privilege?' said Sammy. 'Moses is the best-known name in the Bible, Rachel. Well, along with Jesus and Abraham. Who's yer dad?'

'My Daddy's Mr Isaac Moses,' said Rachel.

'Not the Mr Moses that runs pawnshops and lives in Lower Marsh?'

'Yes, that's my Daddy,' said Rachel quite proudly.

'Well, blow me, I know 'im,' said Sammy. Many Walworth people did, because of his pawnbroker's business. He was known as Ikey Mo, but not in an unfriendly fashion. He knew the people of South London through and through, and his pawnshops would lend on items almost worthless. If such items weren't redeemed, the business absorbed the loss but gained goodwill. *You Bessie, take it to one of Ikey Mo's shops, you'll get a penny more on it there, even if it is all wore out.* That was a common injunction from hard-up mums to young daughters. 'Yes,' said Sammy, 'I've met 'im a couple times, when I was in 'is Walworth Road shop, redeemin' some valuable items of me mum's, and he 'appened to be there. We had a chat, yer know, each time. Well, yer dad's the kind of bloke that's 'elpful to someone that's got ideas of 'is own about business. Imagine you're 'is daughter. Does he know you're a good-looker?'

'Oh, d'you think I am?' said Rachel.

'Well, yes, I do,' said Sammy. Here, half a mo, he thought, what'm I saying? More formally, he said, 'You can tell yer dad Sammy Adams sends 'is regards and is pleasured to 'ave met 'is daughter.'

'Sammy, I – oh, can I call you Sammy?'

'Well, I don't answer to Charlie, yer know.'

'Sammy, d'you mind—' Rachel went just a little hesitant. 'D'you mind that I like you?'

'Funny you should say that, Rachel, I was just goin' to say you're fav'rite with me.'

'Oh, crikey,' breathed Rachel in bliss, 'I think you're the nicest boy I've ever met.'

Gallopin' elephants, thought Sammy, now what've I done? I've as good as invited her to put her hand into me pocket. His pocketed coinage shivered again.

Slightly hoarse, he said, 'Mind you, don't forget I'm a bit hard-'earted.'

'Oh, you've got to be sort of practical when

you're runnin' a stall,' said Rachel, 'you've got to make a profit.'

That did it. Sammy had a mad moment.

'Here,' he said, 'would yer like to come roller-skatin' with me at the Brixton rink on Saturday afternoon?' Roller-skating was his one and only pastime. He had a passion for it, and closed his eyes to the pain of what the price of admission did to his savings each week.

'Oh, crikey,' breathed Rachel again. She didn't look ahead, she didn't have to. She knew she could only have a Gentile boy as a friend up to the time when an acceptable young Jewish man would begin consideration of her. If she could have Sammy Adams as her best friend just for a few years, she'd really like that. Her eyes danced in the light of the afternoon sunshine. 'Oh, my life, Sammy, would yer really take me? I've never been roller-skatin'.'

'Don't be downhearted, you ain't too old to start,' said Sammy. I've gone right off me rocker, he thought, I'm saying things I don't believe I'm hearing. 'I'll call for yer in Lower Marsh say about two on Saturday afternoon.'

'I'll be ready, I'll buy some boots and roller skates in the week,' said Rachel, all velvety bliss. 'Thanks ever so much for askin' me. Your—' Again the little hesitancy. 'Your fam'ly won't mind?'

'Why should they?' asked Sammy. Point is, he thought, will me pocket mind?

'Well, I'm—'

'Oh, you're a Moses.' Sammy smiled. 'Well, I'm

an Adams. My fam'ly's not goin' to worry about that. Nor am I.' It's just me hard-earned dibs, he thought, that's where all the worry is.

'Oh, you're so nice I could kiss you,' said Rachel in a warm girlish rush.

Blimey, thought Sammy, now she's gone off her own rocker.

'That's all right,' he said, 'I'll pick you up next Saturday as per me promise.' Giving a thought or two to expenses incurrable, he added, 'Mind you, Rachel, I ain't exactly related to Rockefeller, I'm a lot more hard-up than he is.'

'Oh, I'll pay for both of us,' said Rachel, 'I'd like to.'

Crikey, what a good idea, thought Sammy. No, wait a minute, Chinese Lady would never let him get away with having a girl pay for both of them. Even if he didn't tell her, she'd get to know. Somehow, Chinese Lady always got to know everything.

'Well, it's nice of yer, Rachel,' he said, 'but I tell yer what, I'll pay my share and you pay yours. It's only right I should be gen'rous.'

'Yes, all right,' said Rachel. 'Oh, I'd better get a tram 'ome now. See you Saturday, then?'

'Me pleasure,' said Sammy, and Rachel departed on light and happy feet for a tram home.

Her father, Mr Isaac Moses, owned a large flat above shops in Lower Marsh, off Westminster Bridge Road, from where he conducted his business. A widower, he had a daily woman who came in to do the housework and to cook whatever meals he wanted. For all that he was known as Ikey Mo, he was a surprisingly handsome and distinguished-looking man in his mid-forties. The light of his life was his only child, Rachel. His wife had not lived long enough to have others.

He listened with a smile to Rachel's glowing description of a lovely boy called Sammy Adams.

'I know that young man,' he said.

'Daddy, yes, he said 'e'd met you a couple of times in your Walworth Road pawnshop.'

'Yes, that's why I know him,' said Isaac, 'twice seen and listened to, never forgotten. He was in business by the time he was ten.'

'Of course 'e wasn't, how could 'e have been?'

'He was born for business,' said Isaac. 'Rachel, you want him for a friend?'

'I should want 'im instead to leave the milk outside the door?' said Rachel.

'A friend, then, no more,' said Isaac, who was not strictly orthodox. Had he been, he would have discouraged his daughter.

'My life, Daddy, what more could there be at my age?'

'Other ages arrive,' smiled Isaac. 'There'll be your age next year, when you'll attend college.'

'Oh, that,' said Rachel.

'Yes, that,' said Isaac, 'to make more of a lady of you and less of a cockney. Now, should I mind that Sammy Adams is a Gentile boy?'

'Well, I don't mind, do I? D'you know what he said? That it was a privilege for us to be called Moses because that was the best-known name in the Bible, along with Jesus and Abraham.'

Isaac laughed and said, 'That boy is exceptionally gifted in his outlook.'

'Daddy, let me go roller-skatin' with 'im.'

'Of course I shall let you, Rachel. If a man can enjoy a good book on the Sabbath, then a girl should be allowed to put roller skates on her feet. Do we not in England open our market stalls on our Sabbath because most of our customers are Gentiles?'

'Oh, good on yer, Daddy,' said Rachel, born within the sound of Bow Bells.

'Yes, you 'ave worked much better today,' said Cecile, fanning herself with her straw hat. 'You may go now and come back in the morning.'

'More churning?' said Boots, rolling his shirt sleeves down. His cap was off, his head bare, his face, lean from the privations of trench existence, a healthy colour now and free of greyness. Cecile, very French, wondered what his body was like, and a slight flush deepened her tan.

'No, tomorrow you can mix meal for the pigs,' she said.

'Not on your sweet life,' said Boots, 'I'll need a bath if I go anywhere near pigs, and all we've got is a cold water tap.'

'Oh, I will bring out some warm water and soap, and you can wash down in that,' said Cecile.

'Sorry,' said Boots, 'but I'm having nothing to do with your porkers.'

'Porkers?'

'Pigs.'

'I shall report you to your officer.'

'Stop playing about,' said Boots, putting his cap on.

'You are supposed to do as I say, Sergeant Adams.'

'Behave yourself,' said Boots, 'or you will get your bottom smacked.'

'You think that is funny?' said Cecile.

'Good for a bit of a laugh when you think of everything that's not,' said Boots, and left. Cecile called after him.

'You are a peasant, you 'ear?'

'Keep smiling,' called Boots.

'Oh, tail of a donkey, I hate you!' she called in French.

Boots stopped and turned.

'Shall I send someone in my place tomorrow?' he asked.

Cecile rushed at him and shook a finger in his face.

'No, you must come, your officer said so, and I say so!'

'I'll think about it,' said Boots, and went on again.

She watched him go. She was not really angry, of course, or she would not have been silently laughing. She was French and she liked provoking him.

Somewhere in the south-east, where the French held the line, guns were rumbling, while above the trench systems of the British sector, German Albatros fighter planes and British Sopwiths were attempting to shoot each other out of the sky.

It was always going on somewhere, the war.

Young Madame Cecile Lacoste stopped smiling and sighed.

Chapter Nine

'Sammy, what did you say?' asked Chinese Lady over a supper of sausages and mash, referred to these days as zeppelins in a cloud.

'Yes, did we 'ear you say you're takin' Ikey Mo's daughter roller-skatin' next Saturday?' asked Lizzy.

'I did remark to that effect,' said Sammy.

'He's 'ad a dangerous rush of blood,' said Tommy.

'Sammy, you sure that what you said was right?' asked Chinese Lady.

'Well, I've got to be honest,' said Sammy, 'I think I must've fell on me 'ead somewhere. I don't know what else could've made me invite 'er. I ain't really well-off enough to take girls out, yer know.'

'You Sammy, you didn't do no fallin' on your head,' said Chinese Lady. 'Tommy's never fell on 'is head in all his life, nor has Boots, nor Lizzy. I didn't bring any of you up to be as careless as that.'

'Well, somethin's given 'im a funny complaint,' said Lizzy. 'Invitin' a girl out at his age, takin' her to a Saturday afternoon at the Brixton rink and puttin' his hand in his pocket, you sure you 'aven't come over ill, Sammy?'

'No, I ain't sure,' said Sammy.

'Poor old Sammy,' said Tommy, ''e'll come back 'ome from the rink seriously ill over what it's cost 'im.'

'It must be the war,' said Lizzy.

'The war's done something to all of us,' said Chinese Lady, frowning. 'Well, I was against it in the first place, but no-one took a blind bit of notice of me, specially Boots. He went and joined up the moment me back was turned. Still, it's hard to believe it's made Sammy invite this girl Rachel Moses to the skatin' rink.'

'Unfortunately, it's done now,' said Sammy.

'Oh, dear, what a shame,' said Lizzy.

'But fortunately,' said Sammy, 'Rachel's 'elpin' me out, I'm only payin' for meself. She's payin' her own share.'

'What?' said Chinese Lady, sitting up straight except for her firm and tidy bosom. 'Now, you look 'ere, Sammy, I don't expect any of my sons to let young ladies pay for theirselves.'

'But I've got the tram fares on me mind, Mum,' said Sammy.

'Never mind that,' said Chinese Lady, 'you're not to let her pay for anything, d'you 'ear?'

'But if a bloke can't afford it—'

'Not much,' said Tommy, 'you've got old socks bulgin' with bread and honey.'

'But they're me savings,' said Sammy. 'I can't touch them, they're me capital, me future lifeblood. Don't forget Rachel might want tea and a bun. No-one can say that won't be 'urtful.'

'I don't want any talk like that,' said Chinese

Lady, who had a firm belief in the right order of things, including whose privilege it was to do the treating in a sociable relationship. Sammy was a bit young for being sociable with a girl, but Chinese Lady wasn't going to discourage him. It would help him to get things right. Besides, Mr Moses was a very well thought of Jewish gentleman in the pawnshop business, and if his daughter was anything like him, she might just civilize Sammy a bit.

'Listen, my lad,' she said, 'if Mr Moses' daughter feels like a nice cup of tea and a bun, you make sure you treat her.'

'Well, I'd like to, Mum, but fourpence is fourpence, yer know,' said Sammy.

'I don't want any answerin' back,' said Chinese Lady.

'It's still goin' to be 'urtful,' said Sammy.

'Well, if it kills you, Sammy,' said Lizzy, 'your savings won't go to waste. We'll divide them up and spend them usefully.'

'Best if Mum 'ad the lot,' said Tommy.

'Here, mind what you're sayin',' protested Sammy.

'Yes, you could 'ave them, Mum,' said Lizzy. 'You could buy a shilling wreath for his funeral, say, and then use the rest to treat yourself to a nice winter coat from Hurlocks or Gamages.'

'Lizzy, you shouldn't talk like that,' said Chinese Lady, 'not about funerals, love. It's not nice.'

'And it ain't funny, neither,' said Sammy. 'I ain't daft enough to pass on and leave me savings be'ind. I'll face up to Rachel bein' a bit expensive on me pocket. It's only for this once.'

'I think 'e's goin' to live,' said Tommy.

'Yes, but for how long, when you think of all the pain 'e'll be suffering?' said Lizzy. 'You can't live very long with that sort of pain.'

'Still, there's Chinese Lady,' said Tommy. 'She's a woman, yer know, Lizzy, and women are good at lookin' after someone's pain and bandagin' it. She's bandaged a lot of mine in me time.'

'Yes, all those cuts and grazes of yours, Tommy,' said Chinese Lady.

'I don't know Mum can bandage Sammy's kind of pain,' said Lizzy.

'Is someone laughin'?' asked Sammy. 'Because I ain't. Besides, I've always been 'eroic about me occasional suffering, and I'll be 'eroic all through Saturday afternoon and all day Sunday too, you'll see.'

'Oh, that's good,' said Lizzy, 'he's goin' to live till Sunday evening at least.'

The packed *estaminet* was uproarious with noise, and even a sharp-eared stevedore couldn't have heard a cargo of pig-iron drop as Polly stood on her chair and then stepped on to a table. She was lit up, in a manner of speaking. With the contents of a bottle of Jacques' best claret.

'Give it a go, Polly!'

'How about Salome, Polly? I'll hold yer seven veils.'

'Never mind any veils, Polly, just Salome'll do.'

Men of the Australian 1st Division, the Buffs, the West Kents, the Royal Scots and the Warwicks

were among the many soldiers present. Several
women ambulance drivers were also in evidence.
Polly up on high above them, was wreathed by
the blue smoke, a slightly dotty smile on her face.

'Quiet, you ratbags,' she said.

'Come on, Polly, give us "Barnacle Bill the
Sailor".'

'Who let Nelson in?'

'Chuck 'im out, someone.'

'Quiet,' said Polly again.

'Yes, let's 'ave some hush,' said Alice.

A certain amount of quiet reigned.

'Pin your ears back,' said Polly, 'and listen out
for "Angels of Mercy".'

'We're 'earing yer, Polly.'

Polly did her piece.

> Take her up to Hellfire Ridge, girls,
> Give the old bone-shaker a go,
> Let her jump all the craters and bumps, girls,
> Let her gaskets gurgle and blow.
> Take her up to Hellfire Ridge, girls,
> And pick up the pieces of Jim,
> And when you've put him together,
> So what if he's short of a limb?
> Take her up to the road south of Wipers,
> Fill her up with our glorious dead,
> Load her up to her jolly old roof, girls,
> With feet and arms and a leg.
> Take her back to the fields of Mons, girls,
> Where Jerry first peed on our lads,
> And when you're searching those fields, girls,

See if they left any fags.
Cheer up, you Tommies and fleabags,
Listen out for our merciful toots,
We'll always arrive in time, boys,
To pick up what's left of your boots.

Roars of applause.

'Encore, Polly!'

'Not tonight, Napoleon,' said Polly, and jumped. Arms caught her, swung her and set her on her feet. At which point, Alice got up and worked her way through to the old piano. The Northumberland sergeant, lately arrived, was there again. Pipe in his mouth, cap tipped back, fingers light on the keyboard, he looked up at her.

'Yes, it's me again,' said Alice, and his blue eyes, filmed by the trench grey, smiled. He placed his pipe on the piano, next to his beer.

'Aye, it's you, lass,' he said, and resumed playing the kind of music he seemed to favour.

'What's your name?' asked Alice.

'What's in a name?'

'I'm Alice.'

'Aye, I know.'

'How'd you know?'

'Everyone knows. Heard that you once stood on a table in Poperinghe and asked for votes for women.'

'Not me, that was my friend Polly,' said Alice. Polly had been a bit high on some vintage Burgundy. The Tommies pulled her leg unmercifully, and a Middlesex corporal came up with a scribbled limerick.

There was a young lady called Polly,
Who thought votes for women were jolly,
When a bloke disbelieved her,
She said, 'Oh, you bleeder,'
And flattened his conk with her brolly.

It had made Polly yell with laughter, and since then she'd never mentioned votes for women. It was a subject out of place among men fighting to stay alive. In any case, most of them didn't seem bothered one way or the other, as long as women didn't compete for the jobs they hoped were waiting for them back in Blighty. If they got back.

'That young lady's fond of standing on tables?' said the Northumbrian.

'You've just 'eard her recitin', have you?' said Alice.

'Aye.'

'And did you hear all the noise?'

'I heard. You're in the jungle now, lass.'

'With the men?' said Alice. 'Well, you don't think I'd rather be in Hyde Park with the nurse-maids, do you?'

'You're still no man, lass,' he said. 'You're a young lady. You can't run with hounds, nor with wolves, nor live in a jungle as men do. Aye, men are wolves, lass, and women are civilized.'

'Don't you believe it,' said Alice, 'I've 'ad times when I could have torn our gen'rals to pieces.'

'Wrong for a woman,' said the sergeant, facial bones etched by his starved flesh.

'Not for our kind of women it's not,' said Alice.

'And it's not a jungle out 'ere, it's hell on earth.'

'Same thing, lass, dogs are eating dogs.'

'Listen, who are you?'

'Name's Ben Hawes.'

'Hawes?' said Alice. 'Oh, now I see, young Hawes, old Hawes. Old Horse.'

'That's how they call me,' said Sergeant Ben Hawes. He stopped playing to drink his beer and to talk. He belonged, he said, to the Northumberland Fusiliers. Thirty-four, he joined up in 1898 as a drummer boy, when he was seventeen, fought in the Boer War and saw service in India. In 1914, he was at Mons, Le Cateau and the Marne. Now he was here, and out of the line for a while.

'Well, you've got my blessin',' said Alice. 'Are you married?'

'No time for that, lass, nor am I right for it as a regular. Not fair on a woman, don't you see, to ask her without thinking on it. What's in a marriage for a regular soldier's wife when it's nobbut a few nights together and then nought for a year or two years? That's not marriage, that's loneliness, and loneliness doesn't fit a woman.'

He was laconic but very direct, and Alice felt emotions stirring. He had no future, nothing, unless a miracle spared him.

'But didn't you ever want to marry?' she asked.

'Aye, there was a pretty lass once, from Hexham.'

'But you didn't marry her?'

'I thought on it, and didn't,' said Sergeant Hawes.

'Well, what did you do, love her and leave her?' asked Alice.

'Fetch up, young lady, that's nought to do with love, that's nobbut selfishness.'

'But if you were in love with her?'

'She were a sweet lass, so I didn't marry her and make a lonely wife of her. Nor did I bed her, if that's what you mean. It's wrong to spoil a young woman.'

Alice could hardly believe her ears. In all the hell of France and Flanders, there was a man who thought like this? A man who was living on borrowed time? Not many were like him.

'Is that a joke, Ben?' she asked.

'It's no joke when a sweet lass finds herself spoiled for another man. Aye, leave her with child and she'll not remember it as an act of love.'

'Have you met a woman since Mons?' asked Alice.

'Met?' said Sergeant Hawes, and gave her a quizzical look.

'Oh, you know.'

'Are you offering, lass?' he asked, and Alice turned a violent pink.

'No, I've never – I don't be'ave like that.'

'Then you're a sweet lass, Alice, and should stay so.'

'What-oh, Alice, who's your friend?' A hearty-voiced woman ambulance driver appeared out of the drifting fug and the boisterous blue. She was holding a pipe, her other hand in the pocket of her breeches. She looked buxom and cheerful.

'This is Sergeant Hawes,' said Alice.

'Hello, you bugger,' said the woman. 'Hilda Cummings,' she said by way of introducing herself.

'You're full-grown,' said Sergeant Hawes.

'Glad you noticed,' said Driver Cummings. 'What beats me is how I manage to hang on to all of it on ambulance unit grub.' She drew up a chair and sat down next to him at the piano. 'Manage a duet, Sarge, can you?'

'Aye,' he said with a brief smile.

'That's the stuff. Right, then, let's bash out "Blaydon Races". The lads'll let rip on that one. Off we go, Sarge.' She stuck her pipe in her mouth and put her hands on the keys. Sergeant Hawes took control of his own half of the keyboard, and away they went as a duet.

The Tommies did let rip as soon as the music began, four hands moving over the piano, and that was the end of Alice's time alone with the Northumbrian for the evening. She had an unfriendly wish to kick the chair away from under Hilda Cummings.

Later, when she and Polly were on the way back to their billet, they passed a standing Army lorry that was filling up with West Kents.

'Goin' our way, you gels?'

'Not tonight, old sport,' said Polly. They went on. Two more soldiers approached in the semi-darkness. One was Boots, the other Freddy Parks. They'd spent the evening in an *estaminet* near the town centre.

''Night, girls, sleep tight,' said Freddy.

'Same to you, and 'ow's yer father?' said Alice.

They passed each other, the two men of the West Kents and the two ambulance drivers, and as they did so Boots's left arm very lightly brushed Polly's. She hardly noticed. She was close to being one over the eight again.

Chapter Ten

The following day, Boots still refused to have anything to do with the pigs. Cecile threatened again to
report him to his officer. Boots said no officer, not
even the battalion colonel, would crime a sergeant
for refusing to shake hands with porkers.

'Why do you call them porkers, you crazy man?'
asked Cecile.

'All right, pigs,' said Boots. '*Cochons*. But they're
not favourites with me.'

'But I told you yesterday, you are supposed to do
as I say.'

'I pass,' said Boots.

''Ow would you like my father to speak to you?'

'Send him along,' said Boots.

'Perhaps,' said Cecile in French, 'perhaps I
should fetch my mother, who is even more formid-
able than my father.'

'Why not fetch them both?' said Boots.

'Or perhaps I will ask your officer for someone
else, after all.'

'I'll go and ask him for you, Cecile.'

'No, no,' she said. 'No, go and collect the eggs in
the chicken house. You will see the basket. Ah, I
despise you for refusing to feed the pigs.'

'Sorry about that,' said Boots, 'it's just that I don't want one more smell to live with.'

She looked sober then. She knew, as did most French and Belgian people who lived relatively close to the Front, that the men of the trenches existed in a miasma of horrible odours, including that given off by the dead.

'Please to collect the eggs,' she said, 'Jules will see to the pigs.'

'Give him my regards,' said Boots, and off she went in search of the elderly labourer.

She reappeared an hour later. Boots was sitting on the bench outside the dairy, smoking a fag. The basket of eggs was on the ground at his feet.

'You are not doing anything?' she said, taking her straw hat off and letting the sun dance on the shining health of her braided hair.

'Yes, I'm having a smoke,' said Boots.

'That is not doing something.'

'I'm not complaining,' said Boots.

''Ow would you like—' Cecile smiled. 'Some coffee?'

'Thanks very much.'

'Ah, you are not too bad,' said Cecile, and disappeared again, taking the basket of eggs with her.

They drank hot strong coffee a little later. It tasted slightly of acorns, but coffee beans, of course, were in short supply. Cecile sat next to him on the bench, giving him frequent glances. His eyes were a deep grey, and she noted the little hollows and fine lines that the war had drawn on his face. She felt sad for him. She had felt sad for herself at the loss of her husband Maurice, but the worst of that was over now. Perhaps the war would end soon, and then Sergeant Adams could go home to England and his family.

Boots thought about the weather. It was hot and dry, and had been for some time. That there was a new offensive was a fixture in everyone's mind now. The percentage factor was less in his favour with each battle. It would be even less if the weather turned wet, when men would slip and slither over torn ground that quickly turned muddy. He gave up on those kinds of reflections and thought of Ruskin Park on a summer Sunday.

Cecile asked him what he was thinking about.

'Home,' he said.

'But you are looking at me as if you are thinking of kissing me.'

'Am I?'

'Yes, of course. That is what all British Tommies are thinking of doing.'

'They're all thinking of kissing you?' said Boots.

'No, no, not me, you crazy bloke, but every woman they see.'

'Well, I suppose it's better than thinking about kissing the back of a bus, Cecile. Not much fun in that.'

Madame Descartes appeared then, a middle-aged woman dressed in a high-necked grey blouse and black skirt, her long hair tied in a knot on the top of her head.

''Ere is my mother to see what you are thinking about,' whispered Cecile.

Madame Descartes had actually come to take a good look at the man with whom Cecile was spending so much time. She introduced herself and thanked him for all his help. Boots, on his feet, said it was a pleasure, except that he drew the line at getting mixed up with the farm's piggery.

'Cecile has asked you to see to the pigs?' said Madame Descartes. 'Cecile, is that the way to treat an English sergeant?'

'I'm treating him very well,' said Cecile, 'giving him simple work, and look, coffee as well. What is wrong with that? Jules has seen to the pigs.'

'So he should,' said Madame Descartes, and turned again to Boots, inspecting him with interest. Naturally, one should inspect a man when one's daughter talked about him so much. She liked what she saw. She smiled. 'My daughter, Sergeant Adams, isn't always to be taken seriously.'

'So I've discovered,' said Boots.

'Good,' said Madame Descartes. 'Be firm with her and do only what suits you. Cecile is not to take advantage of your kindness.'

'Oh, I assure you, Mama,' said Cecile, 'no-one could easily take advantage of a man like him.'

'Good,' said Madame Descartes again. 'If he can get the better of you, Cecile, then he has much to commend him.'

Cecile made a face. But she was extremely pleasant to Boots for the rest of the morning, and at midday took him to have a light lunch with herself and her parents amid the sound of British bombers high in the sky. Boots knew the French ate lightly at midday, and in the large farmhouse kitchen he sat down to a meal of bread, cheese and spring onions, with white wine. Madame Descartes regarded him with visible interest because of her widowed daughter's own interest, and with a mother's regret for any sorrow this could cause Cecile. Her daughter was headstrong, of course, and had suddenly become tired of being a respectable widow. Monsieur Descartes thought the guest typically the soldier of the times, agreeable on the surface but guarded in all his references to the war. They were all like that, they all seemed to dislike letting civilians know exactly what trench warfare did to them. The farmer thought they could only discuss it with each other.

Boots provided a few details about his family and his background; then Cecile's father asked him what he thought of farm work. Boots said it was preferable to the kind of work he'd brought on himself by joining the army. No-one commented on that. Instead, Madame Descartes said he looked as if he would make a very good farmer. Cecile rolled her eyes. Her father said a farmer was a slave to his calling, and that no-one born with any real sense would choose to be one if God would allow him to be anything else. Madame Descartes said politicians had no sense at all, otherwise they would not choose to go to war. Cecile said they at least had enough cunning not to do the fighting themselves.

That aside, the meal was congenial and the rest of the day passed quite pleasantly for Boots. So did following days. Cecile gave him agreeable jobs and

132

refrained from arguments. She was sometimes teasing, sometimes scolding and sometimes provocative. She took him around the farm to help her with work here and there, and whenever the men of his platoon caught sight of the two of them, they ribbed him in loud and bawdy fashion from a distance. Boots took absolutely no notice. Cecile took him to task for allowing impertinence from mere privates.

'It's not important to me,' he said.

'It would be to French sergeants,' said Cecile.

'It'll be different,' said Boots, 'when we march out of here.'

Cecile bit her lip.

Alice and Polly, along with colleagues, waited for the curtain to go up, the curtain on one more horrendous drama. Nerves twitched, nerves that relaxed each evening in the rumbustious atmosphere of Jacques' *estaminet*. On Friday evening, Alice met Sergeant Ben Hawes again, and this time sat with him at a table and kept him to herself. She had wrong feelings about him. All emotional feelings towards one particular man were wrong, for they were feelings that had no future. Nevertheless, Alice couldn't help herself. She had met hundreds of Tommies, some for a brief few minutes and some for much longer, and while all aroused that special sense of comradeship in her, she had never seen any of them as Mr Right. There were no Mr Rights among the fighting men. Sergeant Ben Hawes, however, was having a dangerous effect on her, and she felt herself teetering on the brink.

Recklessly, she saw off a whole bottle of wine in a very short time. It gave her a welcome amount of Dutch courage, which put her on a par with the Northumbrian as far as arguments about women's presence close to the Front were concerned. Sergeant Hawes began to smile at her quips and sallies.

'You'd all miss us if we went 'ome,' she said.

'True, lass.'

'So why'd you keep sayin' I should go?'

'Only said so once tonight,' said Ben.

'Oh.' Alice puzzled over that. 'You sure?'

'I'm sure.'

'All right, but don't look so cocky about it.'

Driver Hilda Cummings emerged again from the fug.

'Hello, hello, Alice,' she said, beaming, 'is that my sergeant you're hogging?'

''Oppit,' said Alice.

'I'll pull up a chair,' said Hilda.

'I'll kick its legs off,' said Alice.

'Now, lass, there's always room for one more in a pub,' said Ben.

'Not for Happy Hilda and her pipe there's not,' said Alice.

'Hello, got the bit between your teeth, Alice?' said Hilda cheerfully.

''Oppit,' said Alice.

'I will at ten-thirty or thereabouts,' said Hilda. 'I've just dropped our Commandant off at Divisional HQ. She's dining there, lucky old biddy.

I'm detailed to pick her up at eleven. Anyone want to buy me a drink?'

'Oi, 'Ilda!' A cockney soldier called. 'Over 'ere, darling. Bottle of beer for yer, if yer want.'

'Coming, old-timer,' said Hilda, who was well-known for breaking the unwritten rule about buying her own drinks. Over she went to a table occupied by men of the Essex Regiment.

Crikey, thought Alice, Lady Banks out for the evening. She turned, looking for Polly. Polly, in company with some Australians and Middlesex men, was laughing her head off, the soldiers roaring.

'Listen, Ben, would you like to 'elp me look for some silk stockings?' asked Alice in a whisper.

'Speak up, lass.'

'Well, come closer, you daft thing,' said Alice, and Ben shifted his chair and himself until he was touching elbows with her. Under the table her right knee made contact with his left one. It was only knees, but it did something to her. 'Ben, you up to something?' she said lightly.

'Not with you, lass.'

'Look, I'm not sixteen,' said Alice.

'I know, Alice, I know. But you're still not for spoiling.'

'I don't know how you can say things like that in a war like this,' said Alice, then asked him if he'd go with her to the Red Cross and St John headquarters and keep watch for her.

'Keep watch?' said Ben.

'Yes, while I do me best to borrow some of Lady

135

Banks's silk stockings,' whispered Alice.

'Say that again, lass.'

'Well, all right, pinch some. For me and me best friend, Polly Simms.' Alice smiled as winningly as any young lady would who was well into her second bottle of wine. 'Come on, Ben, be a sport, you'd like to see me in silk stockings, wouldn't you?'

Ben laughed. Alice felt happy with herself for making him laugh.

'Not in the light, lass.'

'Don't be daft,' said Alice, 'what's the point of silk stockings in the dark?'

'Didn't mean that, lass. Only meant I'll not keep watch till it's dark. Nor will I then.'

'Oh, come on, don't be a sergeant all your life,' said Alice, 'be one of us.'

'All right, Alice,' he said.

'Oh, you'll come with me, then?' said Alice.

'There's a saying. Generals own the works, for the rest there's perks.'

'Too blessed right,' said Alice.

Later, at dusk, she let Polly know what she was going to get up to with Ben. Polly said bloody top-hole, that she'd go with them.

'No, you won't,' said Alice, 'you'll be in the way.'

'Hello,' said Polly, 'three's a crowd?'

'Yes, one too many,' said Alice.

'Listen, Alice old sport, don't get serious.'

'All right, Grandma, I won't,' said Alice, but not at all confident that she wasn't already emotionally committed.

Ben did his stuff outside the building, keeping

watch, his pipe between his teeth and a little smile on his face. The place was devoid of staff except for two night-duty personnel. Alice had no difficulty in avoiding them as she went up to the quarters of the Commandant. She wasn't long in finding what she was looking for with the aid of struck matches. Crikey, a rectangular cardboard box in one of the dressing-table drawers held at least a dozen neat white manufacturer's envelopes, each containing a pair of silk stockings. She pinched two.

Outside, her laconic Northumbrian was waiting for her.

'I've got 'em, Ben.' They were tucked inside her shoulder bag.

'Right, lass, now be on your way.'

'You're goin' to walk me to my billet, aren't you?'

'No time, lass. Off you go.'

'Will I see you tomorrow?'

'Can't say,' said Ben.

'When, then?'

'We'll see.'

'Look, can't you – can't you fall in love with me?'

'Easily.'

'You – you can have me if you want, you'll be the only one.'

'I told you, lass, that's not love. Marry you, aye, then I'd have you.'

'Would you marry me?' breathed Alice.

'Easy enough to think on it,' said Ben, 'but you're young, lass, I'm a hundred. I've had my time.'

'Don't say such things.'

'I don't mean my number's up, only that my time's gone by for marrying someone as young as you.'

'Don't say that, either.'

'Good night, sweet lass,' he said, and away he went.

Alice was very emotional by the time she reached her billet.

Chapter Eleven

Sammy knocked on a door next to a shop and ten
seconds later it opened and Rachel showed herself
in a pearly-pink blouse with a lace collar, and a calf-
length skirt of maroon. Her black hair was dressed
in two pigtails, each ribboned in pink. Her brown
eyes looked velvety with pleasure.

'Oh, you've come, Sammy.'

'Well, I'm 'ere,' said Sammy, in jacket, jersey
and trousers, and a peaked cap on his head. He
raised it. 'How'd you do again, Rachel Moses, done
up to the nines, I see.'

'Oh, d'you like me skatin' outfit, Sammy?'

'Pretty,' said Sammy.

'Can you come up and say 'ello to my Daddy
before we go?'

'Mr Isaac Moses? Be a pleasure,' said Sammy,
and Rachel took him up to the living-room of the
flat, where her father greeted him solemnly, shook
his hand solemnly, and gravely requested him to
take care of Rachel. 'Well, Mr Moses,' said Sammy,
'I'm not gen'rally regarded as bein' careless, yer
know. I'm fairly certain I can get Rachel to the rink
and back without losin' 'er.'

'Thank you, Sammy.'

'Don't mention it, Mr Moses. Me mum sends 'er regards and says it's always been a pleasure doin' business at your Walworth Road pawnshop.'

'We do our best, Sammy,' said Isaac, smiling. He liked the look and character of Sammy, a tall, self-confident lad with a fund of mental and physical energy. 'You wish to be a friend to Rachel?'

That caught Sammy on the hop. Well, how much would it cost to be a friend to a girl who was obviously treated to a lot of coinage by her dad?

'Daddy, we're friends already,' said Rachel.

'Yes, Mr Moses, so we are,' said Sammy, and then realized that her dad's question was because Rachel was Jewish and he himself was a Gentile. That, actually, didn't bother him in the least. 'It's easy to be friends with Rachel, Mr Moses.'

'Well, I think we understand each other, Sammy,' said Isaac. 'Now go and enjoy yourselves.'

'Ready, Rachel?' said Sammy.

'Yes, I've only got to put me hat on,' said Rachel, and a round white straw one was sitting on her head when she and Sammy left to catch a tram, Sammy carrying the bag containing her boots and skates along with his own. The June day was warm but somewhere the elements had managed to put together a welcome breeze. It ran around the stationary tram and nipped in to flirt with Rachel's skirt as she mounted the stairs to the upper deck. The lace hem of a white petticoat took a coy look at the Saturday afternoon scene in Westminster Bridge Road before shyly hiding itself again. On the upper deck, empty of passengers, Rachel said, before seating herself, 'Oh, did me skirt blow up a bit?'

'A bit,' said Sammy, who'd been behind her. Rachel giggled. ''Old on, don't sit down yet,' said Sammy, and took out a man's large handkerchief and dusted the seat. Rachel blinked.

'Oh, you are gallant, Sammy,' she said, and she and he sat down together. Sammy thought what a nice smell she had, sort of clean and fresh and with a delicate hint of scent. And she looked clean and fresh herself. Bless me soul, he said to himself, it's a bit of luck she's a follower of Abraham, or I might get serious about her when I'm old enough, and blow the expense.

Up came the conductor, an old cove who looked as if he'd come out of retirement to do his wartime bit on the trams.

''Ello, just you two, eh?' he said. 'I suppose you couldn't 'ave sat downstairs to save me legs, could yer?'

'Oh, we didn't know about yer legs,' said Rachel, 'or we would 'ave.'

'I forgive yer,' said the conductor. 'Mind, don't get canoodling. It ain't allowed on the tramways.'

'Might I point out it don't say so?' said Sammy.

'Well, young 'un, you got my word for it. Still, while I'm down below and you're up 'ere, who's to know, eh?'

'Here, mind what you're saying,' said Sammy, while Rachel did her best to blush, as a girl of fourteen ought to. 'Kindly respect our ages.'

'Oh, beg yer pardon, me lord, I'm sure,' said the

conductor. 'Fares, if yer please. Where yer goin'?'

'Brixton roller-skating rink,' said Sammy.

'Right, two to Effra Road, is it? That's tuppence each, me lad. Still, yer young lady's worth it. 'Ere, wait a bit, what's this?'

'Fourpence,' said Sammy. 'Four farthings, four ha'pennies and a penny.'

'Found it in yer Ma's cocoa tin, did yer?' grinned the elderly conductor.

'No, in me pocket,' said Sammy, 'and all 'ard-earned.'

'Much obliged, I'm sure,' said the conductor, and clipped two tickets. 'When yer gettin' married?'

'When I've made me fortune,' said Sammy, with the tram heading for St George's Circus.

'Well, yer don't say, sonny.'

'Yes, I do,' said Sammy, 'marriage ain't cheap, yer know.'

The conductor winked at Rachel.

'Got yerself a real caution in this lad, young miss.'

'Yes, ain't he funny?' said Rachel, and the conductor departed with a grin and tested his ancient muscles going down the stairs. 'Sammy, fancy 'im talkin' about us canoodling,' said Rachel.

'Yes, at our ages,' said Sammy, 'and us just good friends.'

'Still, boys of sixteen do kiss, don't they?' said Rachel.

'What, each other?' said Sammy.

'Ugh, no, you silly, girls.' said Rachel, and the

tram rattled over the network of rails at the Elephant and Castle junction.

'I'm a business bloke meself,' said Sammy, 'I've got to keep me mind on me future, which'll start as soon as the war's over. Me brother Boots is in France, yer know, Rachel, doin' his bit with the Army.'

'Boots?' said Rachel, feeling happy about Sammy being beside her.

'He's always been called that,' said Sammy, 'and Lord Muck as well.'

'Why?'

'He grew up talkin' posh on account of 'avin' a grammar school education.'

'Oh, I'm goin' to start a college education next year,' said Rachel.

'What for?' asked Sammy.

'My Daddy wants to make a lady of me.'

'I suppose you'll be called Lady Muck then,' said Sammy.

'Oh, no, I won't ever be that,' said Rachel.

They chatted away the whole length of the journey to Brixton, the June sunshine bringing colour to shops, buildings, old three-storeyed houses and women's hats. When they reached the rink, Sammy gritted his teeth and paid the entrance fee for both of them. Inside, Rachel produced her purse and opened it. Silver glittered.

'No, that's all right,' said Sammy, manfully fighting the pain of having parted with two bob all at once.

'But, Sammy, if you're poor—'

'Well, it's 'ard on a bloke, Rachel, I can't say it ain't, but yer a nice girl.'

'Sammy, I do like you, you treat me lovely,' said Rachel, with young people swarming past them to get to the rink.

'Bless yer, Rachel, we're friends, ain't we?'

'Oh, yes.'

'Come on, then, let's get our boots and skates on.'

Rachel found the rink and the lively atmosphere generated by the young people utterly exhilarating. It was welcome escapism from a war that affected everyone, a war that was going on and on, with so many families losing loved ones. The knock on the door and the handing in of a telegram was dreaded by every family with a near and dear one at the Front or in the Navy.

Here at the roller-skating rink, such things could be forgotten for three hours, and Rachel took to it like a swan to a lake, her natural grace and equilibrium, together with Sammy's guidance, turning her from a novice into a skater within half an hour. He communicated confidence to her, and that, together with the music and the rhythm of her little boxwood wheels, put her where she wanted to be, among the flowing skaters and not with the nervous beginners skirting the sides of the rink. And Sammy's praise made her flush with pleasure. Some of the young people who knew him as a regular made the inevitable comments as they skated by.

''Ello, is that the lady I didn't see yer out with last night, Sammy Adams?'

'Who's yer good-looker, Sammy?'

'Crikey, you got a bit of all right there, Sammy.'

'How's your pocket feeling, Sammy?'

And, then, of course, there was the other kind of inevitable comment, from a young lout who skated straight at them, pulled up and stuck his nosy hooter close to Rachel's face.

''Ere, look what you got 'ere, Sammy Adams, a young Yid.'

'I ain't seeing what you're seeing, Gubbins,' said Sammy.

'Yer bleedin' blind, then. And it's Gibbons, if yer don't mind.'

'Well, you look like old Ma Riley's gubbins from where I'm standin',' said Sammy, 'so buzz off.'

''Oo's goin' to make me?'

A sturdy seventeen-year-old youth executed a swishing halt beside Sammy and Rachel.

'Want any help, Sammy?'

'Kind of yer, Phil, but I can manage,' said Sammy, with skaters in their scores skimming around.

'Just a tap on his hooter'll do it, Sammy.'

'I think I can manage that,' said Sammy, and the offensive lout faded away. The helpful youth smiled at Rachel, and left her in Sammy's care.

'Sammy, thanks ever so much,' said Rachel.

'Listen, Rachel,' said Sammy as they began to skate again, 'I don't want you takin' any notice of that sort of thing. As me mum says, if people can't live and let live, they ain't worth botherin' about. There's always some that can't see a kid wearin' glasses without callin' him "four-eyes", or "boss-eyes" if 'e's got a cast, or "bandy" if his legs ain't straight. On account of you bein' approvin' of fair profit, you're a girl after me own heart, and don't forget it. And don't let 'ard names ever make you cry. Well, yer see, Rachel, yer a sight better than anyone that calls you 'ard names. Rachel, yer a natural on a skatin' rink, did yer know that? Tell yer what, would yer like a cup of tea now and a fruit bun? I don't suppose there'll be much fruit in the bun, nor any butter or marge even, but I'm proud of yer natural talent and I'll treat yer with pleasure.'

Rachel, a young Jewish girl overcome, gulped.

'Sammy, I – I—'

'Come on, then,' said Sammy, and took her to the refreshment arcade adjacent to one side of the rink. He was quite reckless in the way he ordered the tea and buns, and in asking for butter, if there was any.

'Ever so sorry, love, but there ain't,' said the waitress who, like the venerable tram conductor, looked as if she had grandchildren.

'What, not for me one and only girlfriend?' said Sammy, using his cheeky blue eyes, and the waitress looked at Rachel.

'My,' she said to Sammy, 'you're doin' yerself a bit proud at your age, love.'

'It's me advanced charm,' said Sammy.

'You got yer share of that all right, me lad,' said the waitress. 'Still, I won't tell a lie, I'll see what I can do.' Away she went, plump and elderly and as goodhearted as any cockney ever born.

146

'Sammy, I'm ever so glad I met you,' said Rachel.

'Funny you should say that,' said Sammy, 'I just 'ad the same coincidin' thought.'

Rachel laughed. It was the best afternoon of her life, despite the uncomfortable minute on the rink. And when the waitress brought the tea and buns, she conveyed some good news.

'Not a word to Kaiser Bill,' she whispered, 'but I sliced 'em open meself and buttered 'em meself. Mind, it might taste a bit like marge, but better than dry buns, eh? Oh, and don't open them up, or they might get looked at.'

'Thanks ever so,' said Rachel.

'My, yer a lovely gel, you are,' said the elderly waitress. She smiled at Sammy. 'D'yer know that, me lad?'

'She's me fav'rite bun-eater,' said Sammy.

'That boy's a reg'lar caution,' said the waitress to Rachel, and went away smiling, having left the little bill on the table.

'Sammy,' said Rachel, 'would yer let me pay?'

'Well, I would,' said Sammy, 'but if I did, I'd be a disappointment to me whole fam'ly, and they'd talk about me be'ind me back. No,' he said, steeling himself to stand the pain, 'it's my treat, Rachel.'

They enjoyed the tea and buns, after which Sammy bore new pain stoically by giving the waitress a penny tip. She told him not to throw his money about like a reckless millionaire. Sammy said he was going to teach himself to be careful in future.

Rachel spent the rest of the session on the rink

with him, except for the occasional brief rest. Exhilaration prevailed, and when they finally left at six o'clock, she was flushed and glowing.

'Oh, I did enjoy meself,' she said.

'A natural, that's what you are, Rachel,' said Sammy.

Outside, Mickey Gibbons stood waiting.

'Still got yer female Yid with yer, I see,' he said to Sammy.

'I didn't hear that,' said Sammy.

'She's a bleedin' Yid.'

'I heard that,' said Sammy, and conked the lout's hooter with a balled fist. Down he went. 'Now you're bleedin' yerself,' said Sammy, 'all over yer face. Don't get lippy again, Gubbins, I ain't in favour. Come on, Rachel.'

On the home-going tram, Rachel said, 'I don't like bein' a trouble to you, Sammy.'

'Now, Rachel, didn't I tell you not to take any notice?'

'Yes, Sammy.'

'Gubbins won't come it again.'

'No, Sammy. Oh, my life, didn't you conk 'im a beauty? Can I feel yer muscle?'

'No charge,' said Sammy, and Rachel felt his biceps through his sleeve.

'Crikey,' she said, 'ain't you manly?'

Up came the conductor, this time a stout middle-aged bloke.

'Fares, hif you please, ladies an' gents.'

Buffalo Bill, thought Sammy, this is me most ruinous day in all me life. He dragged ha'pennies and pennies out of his suffering pocket.

'Two to Lower Marsh,' he said. 'Is there any discount?'

'Eh?' said Stout-and-Middle-Aged.

'We've already paid from Lower Marsh to Effra Road,' said Sammy, 'so is there any discount on the fares back?'

Rachel smothered giggles. Stout-and-Middle-Aged regarded Sammy with a grin.

'You're comin' it a bit, ain't yer, 'Oratio?'

'It's the war,' said Sammy, 'I'm makin' contributions, so I could do with a bit of tramways discount. Say twenty-five per cent, if I give yer thruppence instead of fourpence?'

'Just for yer cheek, I'll call it fourpence.'

'Thought you would,' said Sammy, and paid up with a faint sigh.

When they reached Lower Marsh, he saw Rachel to her front door at the side of the shop. Rachel let herself in, then turned in the passage.

'Sammy, I did 'ave a lovely time with you,' she said, 'I never met anyone nicer or kinder. Could I give you a kiss?'

'Well, Rachel,' said Sammy, 'I'm not much on kissin'.' Kissing could mean that the bloke let himself in for horrendously costly treats. 'Me female relatives go in for it a lot, yer know, so to stop 'em always kissin' me I charge 'em a penny a time. It don't always stop them—'

'Oh, I'll give you a penny for one, I'd like to,' said Rachel, and produced the copper coin in no time at all.

'Well,' said Sammy, stepping into the passage, 'I—'

'Here,' said Rachel, and pressed the penny into his hand. She put her arms around him, lifted her face and pursed her dewy young lips. Finally, she closed her eyes.

'Oh, well,' said Sammy, and kissed her. Her Cupid's bow quivered in bliss. A little sigh came from her as Sammy released her mouth. 'I 'ope that was worth a penny to yer,' he said.

'Oh, yes, thanks ever so much. Sammy, could I pay you for another one, just because you've been so kind?'

Crikey, thought Sammy, I think I might be on to something here.

'Well, all right, Rachel.'

Another penny changed hands, and another kiss landed very nicely on her rosebud lips, and another little sigh followed.

'Oh, 'elp,' she said.

'Was that one too many, Rachel?'

'Oh, no.'

'Well, I'd better get 'ome now,' said Sammy, 'you've got yer Sabbath evening to have with yer dad. Here we are.' He handed her the bag containing her boots and skates. 'It's been a pleasure, Rachel.'

'I never did 'ave such a lovely afternoon, Sammy.'

Sammy fell into a hole.

'Pick you up at two again next Saturday?' he said, his brain suffering temporary damage.

'Sammy, oh, yes, thanks ever so much.'

'That's all right,' said Sammy faintly, 'I'll scrape up the money some'ow.'

'Sammy, I'll pay, really I will.'

'I'll think about it,' said Sammy, and gave her hand a little pat and left.

Tommy and Lizzy were at home, and Emily too. She'd been invited to Saturday high tea. All three made a minute examination of Sammy when they learned how much he'd spent on Rachel Moses.

'He don't actu'lly look ill,' said Tommy.

'But 'e does look awful poorly,' said Emily.

'His eyes are all glazed over,' said Lizzy.

'I ain't surprised,' said Sammy, 'I'm near ruined.'

'Oh, you poor boy,' said Lizzy, 'give 'im a kiss, Em'ly.'

'All right,' said Sammy, 'but it'll cost 'er a penny. I ain't in the habit of lettin' anyone kiss me for nothing.'

'You Sammy,' said Chinese Lady, 'it's time you stopped talkin' about money.'

'Well, I ain't in favour of talkin' about old Mrs Purser's varicose veins,' said Sammy.

Emily giggled.

Chapter Twelve

The days out of the line passed peacefully for the West Kents in their farm billets. A Company under the command of Major Harris relaxed each day, and each evening passes were issued to the many men who wanted to go into town. There in the *estaminets* they raised Old Harry along with men of other regiments. The Military Police sorted out those who raised Old Harry above the rooftops, and took each man's name, rank and number. Major Harris, on receipt of the MP's crime sheets, dropped them into his wastepaper basket. Since he was going to be asked to take his men into hell, crime sheets could precede them there.

Boots was finding himself a favoured presence at the farm. Madame Descartes was giving in to the whims of her daughter and making him more than welcome. She even allowed him into her farmhouse kitchen to boil a kettle and to make tea for himself, English style. As for Cecile, she was giving in to the beguiling sounds of summer, discarding all the greys and blacks of widowhood and presenting herself in colourful raiment to Boots, never mind that a light dress was hardly suitable for farm work. She regularly prevailed on him to help her transfer the herd of cows from one field to another, or to the milking shed, and Boots came to know that lumbering cows had a wanderlust, or so it seemed. One knocked him over when his back was turned, and up came Cecile to laugh down at him.

'Clumsy, clumsy, aren't you?'

'Not half as much as these perishing cows of yours,' said Boots, propping himself on his elbows. Cecile went down on one knee beside him, her smile teasing. Her lips, lightly carmined, looked moist. There was a temptation to kiss her. Did she want that? She looked as if she did.

'You are bruised, yes?' she said.

'Numb,' he said.

'Oh, poor bloke,' said Cecile, and he laughed at the way she had taken to using the word. 'What is funny?' she asked.

'You are, Cecile.'

''Ow can everything be so funny to you, when you – when—' She stopped.

'When I've just been knocked over by one of your cows?'

'No, no, not that,' said Cecile, 'that is nothing.' She leaned to look into his eyes, her face close to his. 'You are wanting to kiss me? Why don't you?'

'Would that be a good idea?'

'Silly man, it would not be bad, would it?' she said, and made the move herself. Her mouth swooped and she kissed him with all the fire of a Latin. 'There, that is for saying unkind things about my cows,' she said, but her face was flushed, so perhaps there had been a different reason for the kiss. Boots saw the flush. It deepened. She dropped her eyes and put a hand on his right thigh. He thought here's a young woman, and a French one at that, who's been widowed for a year and spends all her time on the farm. I think this is what's called a meaningful moment. What would her parents say, I wonder? Well, they're as French as she is, so would they say get on with it? On the other hand, her father carries a gun around.

'D'you always kiss men who don't say the right things about your cows?' he asked, climbing to his feet.

'No, only you. And now look what you have done, they are all over the place.'

'Well, hard luck,' said Boots, now tanned to dark brown, the trench grey invisible, his eyes clear and unrimmed. Cecile let warm breath escape.

'Come, *cheri*, I don't mind,' she said.

'Don't mind what?' said Boots.

'That you 'ave fallen in love with me.'

'Who said that? Did you say that, Cecile?' he said. If he was in love with anyone, if he had ever been in love, it was with a close neighbour at home, a woman several years older than himself, Elsie Chivers, whose soft myopic eyes, gentle smile and equally gentle voice had fascinated him. Incredibly, she had been tried at the Old Bailey for the murder of her own mother, a harridan. Thankfully, the jury had found her not guilty.

He conceded Cecile Lacoste to be very attractive, very French and very tantalizing, but he could not say he was in love with her. She had become a very welcome and entertaining diversion from everything that was bloody grim. She was also beguiling into the bargain. 'Have I said—'

'The cows, *cheri*!' exclaimed Cecile, and they ran about, using sticks and slapping hands to get the herd moving together again. When all the brown-eyed animals were safely gathered in, Boots closed the gate. That left Cecile on the wrong side of it. 'Now you 'ave shut me in with them, you idiot.'

'You're safer there,' he said.

Cecile laughed and climbed the gate. Down she came in a rush, her dress running upwards above her boots and stockings. Creamy thighs flashed, but blushes were conspicuous by their absence. Well, she was very French and minded not at all at showing Boots she had very good legs.

'Now you may kiss me again,' she said.

The weather was still fine, little white clouds trailing, the fields under cultivation, lush with growth, the terrain soft with folds and undulations. The volunteer labour had returned to their billet, and the farm's few French labourers were hoeing fields on the other side of the distant farmhouse. Somewhere, very far away, the eternal guns were rumbling.

'Have I kissed you before, then?' asked Boots.

'Oh, I did not mind,' said Cecile, and wound her arms around his waist to bring her warm body close to his. 'See, if I could, I would keep you 'ere away from the war, and not let you go back to the trenches.'

'Cecile—'

'Why don't you kiss me?' she said, stretching her body until her lips were able to brush his.

Boots was far from being a man of wood, as a lady ambulance driver, one Lily Forbes-Cartwright, had discovered when she introduced him to a little bit of what a Tommy fancied and deserved, and Boots performed an encore, as he did the following night before they parted for ever.

He kissed Cecile, and Cecile stopped being a coquette, which she wasn't, in any case. She was in love, and knew it and showed herself so.

'*Cheri, cheri,*' she breathed in ardent syllables between kisses.

A dog barked somewhere, and somewhere was too close. Cecile unwound herself.

'One man and his dog,' said Boots.

'My father's dog,' said Cecile. 'Will you tell 'im?' She simply couldn't expel an aspirate.

'The dog?' said Boots.

'No, no, my father.'

'Tell him what?' asked Boots.

'That you 'ave fallen in love with me.'

'I wouldn't tell any young lady's father that while the war's still on,' said Boots. 'The war could muck it all up.'

'Muck it all up?' said Cecile.

'Spoil it,' said Boots. 'Front-line men can't afford to fall in love. Not fair to the women. Everyone knows it, the women as well. If it should happen to a bloke, he makes use of what sense he's got and keeps quiet about it and waits for the war to end.'

'Oh, but—'

Cecile's father appeared then, gun under his arm, his dog frisking at his heels. He smiled at Boots.

'The cows are home?' he said.

'Only after knocking me down,' said Boots.

'It's not meant,' said the farmer. 'They're playful, and like playful contact with humans.'

'Like dogs?' said Boots.

'And pigs,' said the farmer, and laughed. 'What do you think of Sergeant Adams now, Cecile?'

'I think he could be a very good farmer,' said Cecile.

'At first, Sergeant Adams, my daughter thought you an impudence.'

'I did not!' exclaimed Cecile.

'First impressions deceived her,' said Monsieur Descartes.

'I shan't worry about it,' said Boots. 'And it's time I left.'

'Perhaps it's time you had a few days to yourself.'

'No, no,' said Cecile, 'we still need his help.'

'Until tomorrow, then,' said Boots.

Reluctantly, Cecile let him go.

But the inevitable happened the following day, at the farthermost limit of the Descartes land, where a cluster of trees formed a secluded copse and Cecile wished him, she said, to bring to the farmhouse a wheelbarrow full of split logs. Boots said it was a long way to push a loaded wheelbarrow.

'This way,' said Cecile, and stepped over a large fallen branch. She caught her heel, but her fall was quite graceful. It did nothing injurious to her, but it did cause her skirt and petticoat to run up and for her legs to show. Boots, leaning, extended a helping hand. Cecile took it and pulled him down beside her. She turned and put herself into his arms.

It was very inevitable, what followed, and went a lot farther than kisses.

Much farther. All the way, of course.

Then there was the afterwards. She would cry, she said, when he went back to the trenches. Boots pointed out that that wouldn't do either of them any good. Cecile said she didn't expect it would, but she would cry all the same, and begged him to take very great care of himself, for her sake. Boots said he did that out of habit. Cecile said she would prepare herself for marriage. Boots, not expecting that prospect to be mentioned, since Tommies only had brief affairs with willing Frenchwomen, said circumstances were hardly in favour of weddings. Cecile said she hadn't meant this week or even next month, but as soon as the war was over. Everyone knew the Boches could not fight on for much longer. Boots said everyone might be making a mistake. Cecile said she would simply wait, then, and that she would not mind going to England with him as his wife if he did not want to help her father work the farm. Boots avoided the complications of a discussion on that by saying, well, as things were, he'd not propose marriage to any woman, especially one who had already been widowed by the war. A proposal, he said, would not be fair to her, and that he'd mentioned that point yesterday. Better to wait on events and to see how they both felt later on.

Yes, I have said so, I shall wait for you until the war is over, Cecile assured him. I know how I shall feel – as I do now. If the war is terrible, so is love when the guns are always in my ears, she said.

Boots felt that if he survived to the bitter end, he must at least come and see her. He also felt that by then she would have forgotten him, in which case his arrival would be an embarrassment to her.

'You must write,' she said.

The little trailing clouds ran away.

But in mid-Atlantic a huge depression was building up.

At his headquarters, far from the discouraging desolation of the trench systems, Sir Douglas Haig, Commander-in-Chief of the British Expeditionary Force, was finalizing plans for a huge Somme offensive with his opposite number of the French Army. It would be a combined effort by the British Fourth and the French Sixth, and both generals were prepared to hurl thousands of men into the storm of shot and shell.

Alice meanwhile was looking in vain each evening for Sergeant Ben Hawes. She was eating her heart out, and Polly was getting cross with her.

'Ye gods, Alice, if you've fallen in love, you're an idiot.'

'Well, I'm not made of upper-class unbreakable glass like you are.'

'Alice, I'll cut you dead if you ever say a thing like that again. That's hurt me, you rotter.'

'Oh, blow it, I didn't mean—'

'I hope you didn't,' said Polly. She had long chucked away any ideas that she was of a superior breed. Certain army officers, and the majority of staff officers, had inflated opinions of themselves, but in the field the commissioned men from company commanders down to young lieutenants knew the singular worth of the Tommies. And the Tommies knew the worth of the women ambulance drivers. Polly was one with these men, never mind their imperfections. 'We're all down to the lowest common denominator, Alice, we're all scruffy, smelly and lousy, you, me, the rest of the girls and the men, but we're the best the country's got. There's just one thing, old sport, don't fall in love.'

'Can I help my feelings?' said Alice.

'You can tread on them,' said Polly, 'best for you, best for Old Horse of the Northumberlands.'

'Polly, if he wants me, he can 'ave me.'

'Bloody hell, are you crazy?' said Polly.

'You've given yourself,' said Alice.

'Not out of love, out of sadness,' said Polly. 'You're different, Alice, and I won't let you do it.'

'Don't you think I feel sad?'

'We're all like that,' said Polly. 'Oh, all right, let your sergeant make love to you, then, but don't blame me if it destroys you when the Jerries finally blow him to hell. It's coming, Alice, a new offensive. Can't you hear it, can't you feel it? We're in the almighty calm before an almighty storm, and it's going to kill our souls.'

'You're a comfort, you are,' said Alice with a weak smile.

She asked around in the *estaminet*, she asked about the Northumberland Fusiliers until one evening a Royal Warwicks corporal came up with information.

'Their battalion moved out two days ago, Alice, they're up the line by now.'

Alice winced under the blow. Polly thought, poor Alice.

'Sorry, Alice,' she said a little later.

'Polly, I might never see 'im again.'

'That's the swine of it, don't you see, Alice? That's the permanent curse out here.'

'I'm goin' to get drunk,' said Alice.

'Good idea,' said Polly, 'I'll join you.'

'Sergeant Adams.'

'Sir?' said Boots, caught sluicing down under the cold tap after a day on the farm and another complicated and intimate interlude with Cecile way out in the fields. He should have said no to her, but damn it, what could a bloke do with such a passionate woman?

'A long day, Sergeant Adams?' said Major Harris.

'Long enough,' said Boots, towelling his wet chest.

'Exhausting exercise?'

'Not exhausting, no, sir.'

'Well, who won, you or the farmer's daughter?'

'Call it a draw, sir,' said Boots.

The bleak eyes glinted, and there was almost the hint of a smile.

'Have you eaten?' asked the Major.

'No, not yet, sir.'

'Well, when you have, report to me. By seven. Have you got that, Sergeant Adams?'

'Fairly clearly, sir. It's the reason that's a bit hazy.'

'Is that a suggestion you're entitled to one?'

'No, sir, it's—'

'If you come up with "yours not to reason why", I'll have your guts,' said Major Harris.

'Yes, a bit hackneyed that one, sir.'

'Seven o'clock,' said the Major, and left.

Boots finished his ablutions. Lounging members of his platoon were grinning. Up came Freddy Parks.

'You for the 'igh jump, Sarge?'

'Not as far as I know.'

'Done anything you shouldn't to the farmer's daughter?'

'Not as far as I know.'

'I thought 'er dad might've put in a complaint,' said Freddy.

'Not as far as I know.'

'D'you mind me sayin' you sound like a flamin' parrot?'

'No, I don't mind, Freddy, long-time-bloody-silly-volunteers-together.'

The time, seven-forty. The place, a narrow churned-up country road, the view one of grey ugliness in the immediate east, where the village of Becourt, a mile away, was no more than a jagged scar in a pockmarked landscape. Becourt, or what was left of it, was behind the German lines. The trench systems, British and German, were visible only as obscene patterns, and from this distance seemed like a merged oneness. Struggling patches of summer green showed through the grey here and there.

The battered old heap of an open army motorcar was stationary, Major Harris using his field-glasses to survey the unlovely scene. With other company commanders, he had been at battalion headquarters most of the day. He knew now precisely what the West Kents were in for.

'Well, that's for us,' he said, letting the glasses rest against his chest.

'That's where we're going in, sir?' said Boots. There'd been letters from home today, from Chinese Lady, Lizzy and Emily. Emily, the girl next door, was proving a godsend, according to Chinese Lady. Well, she'd always been greatly attached to the family, and as one of Lizzy's bridesmaids in March, she'd been in her element. Boots wondered what a man could say in reply to the letters without referring to the war as it affected the West Kents. Wish me luck as you wave me goodbye, we're going over the top again any moment? 'Doesn't look good for ground cover, sir.'

'What d'you want, Sergeant Adams, a suit of armour?'

'They're not army issue these days, are they?' said Boots.

Major Harris, in the passenger seat, produced a packet of Players Navy Cut. He took out two fags

163

and gave one to Boots. Boots struck a match, and the little flame steadied as he cupped it. Major Harris took a light, Boots followed. They sat smoking, saying nothing. They saw a plane then, low in the sky, the evening sun picking it out. Its red-painted wings dipped and flashed as it flew homeward towards the German lines.

'Albatros,' said the Major.

'Richthofen's going home to his supper,' said Boots.

'The air forces are fighting a war,' said Major Harris. 'Only God and the devil know what the armies are fighting.'

'Might be a good idea, sir, if we all packed up and took the first train home to Blighty,' said Boots.

'That's a good idea, is it, Sergeant?'

'It is as far as I'm concerned,' said Boots.

Major Harris regarded the grey wastes again. The trench systems showed not a movement, but he knew and Boots knew they were well occupied, by men, lice, rats and things that crawled out in the night.

They sat there, in the car, silent again. They smoked their cigarettes down to the butts and threw the butts away. France lay scarred under the evening sun. In Flanders, there was more fighting around Ypres, all for possession of piles of rubble. It would go on until the sun went down.

'Start the car, Sergeant Adams. Let's get back. I haven't eaten yet. It's a late mess tonight.'

Boots started the car, turned it and made for Albert.

'When's the push begin, sir?' he asked.

No answer. And he knew he wouldn't get one. Not yet.

When they got back to the farm cottage, Major Harris said, 'I've had a note from the farmer.'

'A complaint, sir?' said Boots.

'Does he have cause for a complaint, then?'

'No idea,' said Boots.

'If he might have, in respect of his daughter, I don't want to know about it,' said Major Harris, getting out of the car. 'The note is actually a reference in your favour. It could probably get you a post-war job on a French farm. How'd you manage this sort of thing? No, don't answer that, it's not necessary.' The familiar glint appeared in his eye. Boots wasn't always sure if it related to amusement or irony. 'Got your feet up in the farmhouse, have you, Sergeant Adams?'

'Too risky, sir,' said Boots.

'Too risky?'

'Well, when you act like one of the family, you could suddenly find you are one.'

'And that's not what you've got in mind?' said the Major.

'Home in Blighty, that's what I've got in mind most of the time, sir.'

Major Harris was silent for a moment, taking no notice of his adjutant, who had appeared at the door to the cottage.

'Sergeant Adams?'

'Sir?'

'Keep your head down,' said Major Harris, and entered the cottage.

Above the Atlantic, the huge depression was moving slowly but inexorably eastwards with the prevailing winds, light yet persistent.

Cecile took a snapshot of her English sergeant the following day, and he took one of her. She said she would sent her snapshot to him when he wrote to her. Boots said keep it until he next saw her. Then, because she was so ardent, he made love to her again.

It was two days later when Madame Descartes called out to her running daughter.

'Cecile! Where are you going?'

'To see what has happened! He hasn't turned up, nor any of his men!'

Madame Descartes sighed. Cecile ran, all the way down the lane to the barns. She stopped, aghast. Everything was empty of the men in khaki, everything. And everything was silent. Not even their ghosts whispered. She stood rigid with shock, disbelief and heartbreak.

A movement caught her eye down by the cottage. Out of it came old Jules. She ran to him.

'Ah, Madame Lacoste—'

'Where are they, Jules, where, where?'

'Gone, and before dawn,' said Jules.

'But no-one said anything, no-one spoke to my father or to me.'

'No-one is allowed to say anything of troop movements to civilians, Madame Lacoste, no, not even if one is living in the same house as the officers. They go when they must, and that is that. But here is something addressed to you.'

Jules gave her an envelope inscribed with her name. Cecile ripped it open and took out a brief note.

'Cecile, here is a hasty scrawl to say *au revoir* and to thank you and your family for my time with you. One day, if events let me, I'll come back and see you. You have been very sweet to me. For the time being, goodbye, Cecile. Kisses from your English sergeant, Robert Adams.'

Cecile could not believe her sense of desolation.

He was going back into that terrible war, and perhaps never coming out of it.

Chapter Thirteen

Round and round the rink the skaters went, the metal wheels of some skates rasping over the polished floor, boxwood wheels of others gliding smoothly. Speed skaters flashed by sauntering couples. The three-piece band in a little gallery above the alcoved restaurant played on.

It was Rachel's third visit to the rink with Sammy, and Rachel was a young girl light of heart and flushed with pleasure. It was all of a pleasure to be with Sammy. Imagine, he'd said she was his one and only. It could last until – well, it could last for three or four years. Just a nice happy friendship, that was all. Well, they were both too young to worry about anything else. How amazing to feel so secure in the company of a boy who was only sixteen. Someone had said he wasn't sixteen, not yet he wasn't. Rachel wasn't bothered. He looked sixteen and he had all the confidence that gave her this feeling of security and took away her sensitivity about being a Jewish girl among Gentiles. He took care of her and wouldn't stand for anyone calling her names.

'Sammy, it's got to be my turn to pay for tea and buns.'

'Well, Rachel—'

'You're spendin' so much money on me.'

'Well, Rachel—'

'I'm never 'ard-up, honest, Mother left me money of my very own and my Daddy sees I get a weekly allowance.'

'Crikey, are yer rich, Rachel?'

'Course not, you silly, not actu'lly rich.'

'Well, Rachel—'

'Sammy, will you stop sayin' "Well, Rachel"?'

'The point is, me fam'ly's a bit funny about fellers not lettin' girls pay. I ain't funny about it meself, except—'

'Oh, good,' said Rachel, 'come on, then, I'll stand treat.'

'Girl after me own heart, you are,' said Sammy, but he had this problem about what was right, not so much with Lizzy and Tommy as with Chinese Lady. Chinese Lady seemed to have ears and eyes that went everywhere, even if she was just sitting by the kitchen fire and doing some darning.

So, although it caused him the usual amount of grief and pain, he thwarted Rachel in her attempt to pay the bill, and settled it himself. However, he got fourpence back when he took her home and stood in the passage with her before saying good-bye.

Well, as soon as he stepped in with her, Rachel said, 'Sammy, you been awf'lly nice to me again, so can I kiss you?' This had happened on each occasion. The first time it had cost her tuppence for two kisses, the second time thruppence for three, and today she was willing to advance further.

'Well, it's no secret now, Rachel, that I 'ave to stick to me principles. I said to yer dad last week, didn't I, that a bloke that's got ambitions to be a businessman has to 'ave principles and stick to 'em, and yer dad said yes. So yer see, Rachel, I've got to charge a penny each for kisses.'

'Sammy, I like you 'avin' principles, it's only right,' said Rachel. 'Look, I've got four pennies in me purse today, I don't mind a bit payin' for four kisses.'

'All right,' said Sammy, 'I don't want to be unco-operative, not with a war on. Purse yer lips, Rachel.'

'Oh, my life,' said Rachel, but not in a shy way. More in the nature of can this be true? Sammy stood with his back to the closed door, and the light in the passage that led to the stairs was dim. Rachel lifted her face, pursed her lips and closed her eyes. Sammy gave her four very nice kisses, and she thought each one ever such good value for the money.

'There, 'ow was that for fourpennyworth?' asked Sammy.

'Sammy, you do kiss nice.'

'Kind of yer to say so, Rachel,' said Sammy, a born bliss to a girl, even at his age. 'Now, would yer like to come to Sunday tea tomorrow?'

'Me?' breathed Rachel.

'You can meet me fam'ly,' said Sammy. 'Well, me mum would like to see you, she thinks a lot of yer dad's Walworth Road pawnshop.'

Rachel's velvet brown eyes shone. Sunday tea with a Gentile family? Sammy's family?

'Sammy, I'd love to, ever so much.'

'Come at four, then. Mind, what with the war and all, it won't be like the Sunday teas we used to 'ave. Mum can't get the currants or sultanas for makin' a lot of fruit cakes, but it'll still be Sunday tea.'

'Thanks ever so much, Sammy.'

'Listen,' said Sammy, 'if you sort of happen to 'ave a tanner goin' spare next Saturday, I'll give you a baker's 'alf-dozen, if yer like.'

'Sammy, what d'you mean?'

'I'll give yer seven kisses for sixpence.'

'Sammy, seven all at once?'

'No, one at a time, Rachel. You're a nice girl, and you deserve a bit of a bargain.'

What a lovely girl, thought Chinese Lady over Sunday tea the following day. So well-behaved, and just the kind of girl who could improve Sammy by socializing with him. Of course, they were both young, but it didn't do any harm for a girl and boy to go about together, it would help them to grow up more sociably. Of course, it couldn't come to anything when they were older. Rachel being Jewish could only walk out formal with one of her own kind, but she and Sammy could get to be nice friends together.

Rachel met only Chinese Lady and Tommy over tea. Lizzy was out, first to visit Ned at the hospital and then going to her house again with Emily, but that didn't prevent Rachel thinking what a nice homely atmosphere there was. And Sammy's mum and brother were homely too, and so kind to her. It gave her such warm feelings to have a Gentile family accept her into their house, and to treat her just as if she was one of them. And when Lizzy and Emily came in later, the homely atmosphere became charged with liveliness. Lizzy and Emily both made a fuss of her, and Lizzy said crikey, no wonder Sammy's actually digging into his pocket. It's like the fall of the Bank of England, said Tommy. Sammy said he wasn't amused.

Everyone kept away from talking about the war, and Rachel didn't mention it. She knew Sammy's eldest brother, called Boots, was out there in France with the army. In a strange way, Rachel sensed this family of homely people were all too aware that one of them was absent.

The clouds came, light at first, then greyly spreading, and the weather in Northern France became pale and insipid. Here and there rain showers fell, dampening parts of the Somme sector.

But in the early hours before dawn on the morning of the first of July, the sky was clear, although there was mist in the valleys. The huge offensive began with a gigantic bombardment of the German defensive positions, and at dawn the first waves of men climbed out of their trenches.

The waiting Germans cut down the cannon fodder.

Ambulances from Albert were dispersed at

various points of the sector, and Alice and Polly were among the women about to face their most horrendous day of this horrendous war.

If the first day was hideous, so were successive days. Alice and Polly were appalled at the extent of the casualties and the ghastliness of wounds. They were operating in an area west of La Boiselle, where the sound of the guns bombarded their eardrums and stretcher-bearers and walking wounded created a slow-moving, never-ending picture of stained, torn and mutilated khaki against the distant background of smoke and carnage. Out of the hell on the seventh day of the vast labouring offensive came wounded Northumberland Fusiliers, along with casualties from other regiments. Medical Corps men and the ambulances were being stretched to the limit. Alice and Polly were close to exhaustion, eyes hollow, faces grey and teeth gritted, but they kept working. They helped to load the stretcher cases, knowing their duty was to get them to the field station for immediate treatment. They had lost count of the men who were dead on arrival, although each one was a bitter blow to them.

Alice spotted two Northumberland men, both with heavily bandaged heads and arms, the bandages blood-stained. They weren't ambulance cases. Like all others who could walk they were making their way to the station on foot, and on foot they were like zombies. Alice ran over to them. She had met them weeks ago in Jacques' *estaminet*.

'Have you seen Sergeant Hawes, have you seen him? Is he all right?'

'He's coming, lass, coming,' said one man and went on with the other.

Sergeant Ben Hawes appeared a few seconds later, his head bandaged, his face as grey as the clouds above, his waterproof trench cape worn over his shoulders, covering his body. The spitting rain was cold. July had turned wet and treacherous.

'Ben!' shouted Alice, and ran at him.

His fatigued eyes blinked.

'Well, it's nobbut you, lass,' he said, his face a grimace of pain, his voice tired out.

'Alice!' Johnny was calling her, her fully laden ambulance ready to be driven off. Polly was on her way, her ambulance vibrating over the torn road, and she was silently mouthing violent damnation on the generals.

Two German batteries began to return the British gunfire. Shells began to whistle, fall and explode, and the never-ending line of wounded men crumpled and collapsed as they dropped to the ground to find cover.

'Alice!' shouted Johnny again.

A shell struck ground and earth took fire and erupted and spewed. Alice and Sergeant Ben Hawes disappeared from Johnny's sight in a great gushing cloud of dirty smoke. The blast took the Medical Corps corporal off his feet and shook the laden ambulance.

Alice came to with the smell of fire and smoke in her nostrils, and with her left arm broken. Sergeant Ben Hawes lay close by, inert, his trench cape blown around his shoulders. Men were shouting, the German guns still firing. Alice drew a great painful breath, came up on her knees and edged herself forward.

'Ben? Oh, my God.' She saw then what the trench cape had covered. His left arm was a stump bound thickly, and the field dressing was dark with drying blood and wet with new. 'Ben?'

The Northumberland regular, the man of Mons, the Marne and the trenches, the sergeant his men called Old Horse, opened his tired grey-blue eyes again.

'That wor a nasty one, lass,' he sighed. 'You all right?'

The enemy's shelling stopped as the German batteries were found and caught by British heavy guns. The spitting rain turned into a sour downpour. Alice felt none of it. She felt the pain of a broken arm, and she felt for what Ben was suffering. But there was a light shining somewhere in her disordered mind.

'I'm all right,' she said, 'just a bit of a headache. You're the one, look what you've let them do to you, look—'

But Johnny arrived then, badly shaken and slightly concussed, but in automatic discharge of his duties. He took over. He brought Alice to her feet, discovered her broken arm and ordered her to get back to the ambulance. Alice refused unless he first put Sergeant Hawes aboard.

'No room—'

'Make room, d'you 'ear?'

'Alice, there's—'

'Make room! He'll die out 'ere, with all the others who can't get up. We can save 'im, can't we?'

'There's other ambulances comin'.'

'Do it!'

With the help of a slightly wounded stretcher-bearer, Johnny got Ben aboard the ambulance, squeezing him in over the floor. It was reliable old Johnny who then drove the ambulance to the field casualty station, Alice beside him, holding her broken arm, her mouth set, her teeth grating.

At the station, with the casualties unloaded, and Ben now lying on a stretcher, Alice went down on one knee beside him. His eyes opened yet again as she touched his shoulder.

'There you are, lass.' His voice was a tired sigh, his bandaged stump lying limply. 'Blew t' bloody thing right off, don't you see.'

'You've had the war, Ben Hawes, and you've had the army too.' It was the subconscious awareness of that which had sparked the little shining light. 'Somehow, some way, when you've convalesced, I'm never goin' to let you out of my sight again. D'you understand?'

'Tha's a sweet lass, Alice, fit for a better man than I am.'

'Blow anyone better, I want you,' said Alice. 'Now d'you understand?'

'Aye, lass, I understand.'

'Good,' said Alice, and kissed his lips.

She watched as orderlies took him up for treatment. By then, her eyes were wet, but the little shining light was still bright.

Her broken arm kept her out of action. Polly, however, continued to drive, to collect, to suffer and to swear.

It was on the 13th that the West Kents, after days of exhausting endeavour and heavy losses, were ordered to attack a German strongpoint in Trones Wood in support of the 7th Buffs. Major Harris, the eternal soldier, led his company in, Boots and his platoon not far from him.

'Stay on my immediate right with your platoon, Sergeant Adams,' he had said.

'What's left of it, you mean,' said Boots. Freddy Parks was among the absentees. But Freddy had been lucky. He was out of it only because of a badly wounded knee, a Blighty one. Others were dead and already buried.

'Do as you're told, you bugger,' said Major Harris. The only feelings he ever showed were those relating to disgust at the way the generals were fighting this war. All other feelings never reached the surface. Except now, when his orders meant he was going to keep his youngest sergeant in his sights.

The Somme offensive had been hell from the beginning. Trones Wood was a hell of its own. It erupted anew with flame, fire and shot as the West Kents went in. It was the last engagement Boots and Major Harris were to fight together. Close to the German machine-gun strongpoint, the Major went down riddled by bullets, and Boots fell beside him, the victim of the blinding flashing explosion of a German stick grenade.

On the 15th, Cecile Lacoste went to the British Army's area headquarters in Albert, where she made anxious enquiries about the casualty lists. It took some while to receive the information that Sergeant Robert Adams of the West Kents had fallen in action with his company commander, Major Harris. The news devastated Cecile.

She was not to know that on this particular day the complete casualty details relating to the battle for Trones Wood were not yet established. As far as the Albert headquarters staff were concerned, the initial report that Major Harris and Sergeant Adams had died together still stood as correct.

It was quite true that Major Harris, riddled with bullets, had died before stretcher-bearers could reach him amid the tempest of German fire. It was also true that Boots had fallen alongside his commanding officer, blinded by the searing flash of the exploding grenade and knocked out by its blast. It was hours before he was picked up. Hospitalized before being returned to Blighty for expert examination and diagnosis, his waiting days were spent in the knowledge that somehow or other he had to come to terms with the possibility of being permanently sightless. That and the death of Major Harris, a born soldier and the man he most admired, made those days the kind he never wanted to experience again.

He did not ask any nurse to write a letter for him to Cecile Lacoste. What was the point?

And when corrections had been made to casualty

lists, the entry concerning Sergeant Robert Adams recorded he had been wounded in action, not killed. No-one advised Madame Cecile Lacoste of the amendment. She was not his next of kin, or any kin.

Alice, given three months home leave, married her Northumbrian man in October. As a wife, she was then entitled to ask for work in Blighty, and the St John Ambulance Brigade found her a position at their London headquarters, while Ben was taken on by the Army Recruitment Board. Alice wrote to Polly, of course, and with the Somme offensive finally over, after a small amount of ground had been won at horrific cost, Polly wrote back to say well done, Alice, all the girls hope your future troubles will only be little ones. See you when the flags of victory are flying, ducky. Some bloody victory.

There was nothing that would ever bring Polly home until the war was over and she could part from her Tommies in the knowledge that she had done her full bit along with them.

Rachel and Sammy became almost inseparable, and her father, Isaac Moses, did not fail to note the simple unalloyed happiness she derived from the friendship, the happiness of a Jewish cockney girl accepted by a Gentile boy and his family purely for what she was, a warm-hearted and lovely young sprite. It cut her up when she met Sammy's eldest brother Boots, home from the war and blind, but such a fine-looking man. Sammy said not to cry, Rachel, Boots was going to marry Emily, and Emily would be Boots's own personal godsend.

Saturday afternoon roller-skating sessions continued, as well as the tram rides there and back.

'Sammy, later on, when I'm older and I – oh, you know.'

'Course I know, Rachel.'

'Well, we'll still be friends, won't we?'

'We'll always be friends, you and me, Rachel.'

'And we could still see each other sometimes, couldn't we?'

'Well, I don't know I'd like you bein' a perm-'nent absence in me life,' said Sammy, 'it might be a bit 'urtful.'

'Oh, I wouldn't want you ever to feel 'urtful about me,' said Rachel. 'I won't be a perm'nent absence, honest. Sammy, could I 'ave a penny one now?'

'What, 'ere on the tram, Rachel?'

'But there's no-one up 'ere with us.'

'All right, Rachel, a penny one, then.'

A penny changed hands, and Rachel did a little bit of a swoon as Sammy gave her a really lovely kiss, and then another.

'Sammy,' she breathed, when she'd recovered, 'you gave me two.'

'Did I? What, two for the price of one? That's only a ha'penny each. Blow me, Rachel, I'm sorry, but I can't lower me prices.'

'No, course you can't, Sammy, it's only right you shouldn't, and I'll give you another penny.'

'No, it's all right, Rachel. I don't mind givin' you one for free now and again.'

'Oh, thanks. Sammy, you remember you once give me a baker's 'alf-dozen?'

'So I did, Rachel, for a tanner. And I remember it didn't 'alf take a long time.'

'Oh, I didn't mind a bit, Sammy. Only what's a baker's dozen?' she asked, as if she didn't know.

'Usually, thirteen for a shilling. Sometimes, mind, a gen'rous baker'll make it fourteen. That's a baker's dozen and a bit, yer know.'

'Oh, my life, is it really? D'you think, then, that when me birthday comes round, I could give you a shilling and you could give me a baker's dozen?'

'Well, it's a lot and might take me quite a time,' said Sammy.

'Oh, I won't mind, honest.'

'You sure?'

'Honest, I won't mind how long you take,' said Rachel. 'I mean, you can only do one kiss at a time, can't you?'

'In that case, if time don't matter,' said Sammy, 'I'll give you a baker's dozen and a bit.'

'Sammy, fourteen? Fourteen kisses?'

'Just for yer birthday,' said Sammy, 'and if the war's over by then, I'll give yer one more for luck.'

'Oh, Sammy, ain't you kind to a girl?'

PART TWO

THE
RECKONING

Chapter One

It was in mid-July, 1934, that Boots dreamt for the
first time for many years of France, Flanders and
the sound of the guns. He dreamt of Ypres, of
Loos, of dead men and drowning ones. He dreamt
of the Somme and the storming of Trones Wood, of
the German strongpoint and its machine-gun,
and the fall at last of his hitherto indestructible
company commander, Major Harris. Then the
images of battle vanished in a flash of blinding light,
following which he fell headlong into a pit of darkness.

He jerked awake, perspiration damp on his
forehead. Beside him, Emily lay asleep, breathing
evenly. Emily, the family's godsend all through the
war, and his own help and strength all through his
four years of blindness. If he had good reason to be
thankful for Emily's part in his life, there was no
reason at all why he should have dreamt again of
Trones Wood. That was long past, for he'd seen
eighteen years go by since the Somme offensive.

He lay back again, thinking of the weeks before
the battle, when his battalion, the 7th West Kents,
was resting close to the French town of Albert, his
company of four hundred men billeted on a farm.

Memories flooded back, including an image of a young French war widow, the mettlesome daughter of a farmer. What was her name now? It took him a while to remember. Cecile. Cecile Lacoste. Just as it was many years since he had dreamt of the Somme, so it was many years since he had thought of Cecile. Well, his brief time with her had ended when his company left its billet on the farm to go up the line to the trenches with the rest of the battalion. The action in Trones Wood had brought the war to an end for him, and when it eventually ended for everyone else in 1918 and he recovered his sight two years later, he determined to put it all behind him and to live his life in the knowledge that survival had been his most precious gift. Live in thanks and without any song and dance, he decided, for no setback, however critical, could ever possibly disturb him as much as the sight, sounds and slaughter of the Great War.

He was wide awake now, damn it. He slipped silently from the bed. Emily turned over, but slept on. He put on his dressing-gown and went down to the kitchen to make himself a cup of tea. He had not awoken Emily, no, but his movements over the landing brought someone else out of her sleep.

He was standing by the kitchen cooker when Rosie entered.

'Daddy?'

He turned. There she was, his adopted daughter, just down from university, from Somerville College, for the summer vacation. In her blue silk dressing-gown, her fair hair unbound, her blue eyes wondering about him, all the advantages of being young were very apparent at three o'clock in the morning. At her age, nineteen, that ungodly hour wasn't in the least unkind to her.

'Rosie, what's got you up?' he asked.

'You,' said Rosie, 'I heard you on the landing.'

'I was as quiet as a mouse.'

'With squeaky shoes on its feet,' said Rosie. She closed the kitchen door. 'How about you, what got you up?'

'I was awake, Rosie, and thought I'd come down and make some tea.'

'Yes, but what brought you awake?' asked Rosie.

'Oh, this and that, poppet.'

Rosie smiled. He had always called her that. Poppet. She supposed he still would even when she was middle-aged.

'What was this and that?' she asked, and came to stand with him at the cooker, on the top of which the kettle was beginning to steam.

'Bits and pieces,' said Boots.

'You terror,' said Rosie. 'Nana's quite right. You've always got answers that don't tell us anything. You didn't have a nightmare, did you, at your age?'

'My age?' said Boots.

'You're lucky,' said Rosie. 'Men your age are always at their best. They can knock for six any female from the age of twelve upwards. Daddy, come on, tell me what brought you out of bed and down here.'

'I had an argument with the war, Rosie.'

'You mean you dreamt of the war after all these years?'

'Yes. Silly, of course.'

'Oh, dear,' said Rosie. 'Never mind, sit down and I'll make tea for both of us.'

'I can manage. You go back to bed.'

'No, I'm wide awake myself now. Go on, Daddy, sit down.'

Boots sat down at the kitchen table, Rosie made the tea and sat down opposite him. She filled two cups with the hot golden tea.

'Well, bless you, Rosie.'

'Bless you too, Daddy,' she said, regarding him in undisguised affection. He was her favourite person, the one she loved more than any other. He never seemed to look any different, he always had such a relaxed air, his smile quick to arrive. If Uncle Tommy was a handsome man and Uncle Sammy electric, her adoptive father was simply a man of instant masculine appeal. In a room full of people, good people, interesting people and ordinary people, he always stood out.

'Was it a bad dream?' she asked.

'Violent,' said Boots.

'Oh, poor old Daddy. Never mind, it's just you and me now, and I won't do anything violent. Are you really going to take me to the firm's Oxford Street shop on Saturday afternoon and let me loose on all the fabulous fashions? Oh, do you remember the story you've told about Mummy dragging you into ladies' underwear in Gamages before the war?'

'I should have kept that to myself,' said Boots, 'it was a young man's most disastrous first encounter with ladies' corsets. I didn't know where to look, but wherever I looked there was always one more poking me in the eye.'

'I think that's where you picked up the best part of your sense of humour, Daddy, in Gamages ladies' underwear.'

'What I picked up there, Rosie, was a sense of imagination.'

Rosie laughed, softly.

'Mummy said she was so nervous herself that she'd have run out if you hadn't been with her.'

'Believe me, poppet, I'd have beaten her to the exit. Tell me more about Somerville.'

'Oh, it's terribly educational and seriously devoted to making all its students very learned young ladies,' said Rosie.

'Good grief,' said Boots, 'how's this family going to cope with a very learned young lady?'

'You're the one who'll have to work that out,' said Rosie, 'it was you who made me go there.'

'Did I do that, poppet, make you go?'

'No, not really,' said Rosie, 'but you did say it was the chance of a lifetime for me. Oh, by the way, a young man might call one day.'

'A young man?' said Boots. 'A student?'

'No, he works in one of Oxford's bookshops. If he calls and tells you his name's Alexis Armstrong, that'll be him.'

'Alexis?'

'Yes, posh, isn't it?' smiled Rosie. 'He'll be on

holiday from his bookshop any moment. He's got digs in Oxford, but he'll be staying with his parents in Mitcham for a week. That's when he might call on me.'

'I see,' said Boots. Well, it had to come, the inevitable development that might lead to losing Rosie, the bright light of the family. He would miss her. He had missed her during her first terms at Somerville. But bright lights could not shine forever in family homes. They left to illuminate homes of their own. 'What's he like?'

'Talkative,' said Rosie.

'What else?'

'Political,' said Rosie. 'I'm not sure if you'll find him boring or stimulating.'

'How do you find him?' asked Boots.

'I find it best not to take him seriously,' said Rosie.

'Should I look forward to meeting him, then?' asked Boots.

'With luck, you might escape it,' smiled Rosie.

They drank tea and they talked, Rosie and her adoptive father, two people who were always in harmony with each other, and it was gone four before they went back to their beds, where they both fell instantly to sleep.

If Boots had had no real reason to dream about the war, Polly did. With her school having broken up for the summer holidays, she was free as a teacher to go to France for the funeral of Lucy Carpentier, formerly Lucy Chalmers, a long-standing friend who'd been at college with her and gone to France as a Red Cross officer. At the end of the war, she'd married a French officer from Amiens. She and Polly kept in regular touch, and Polly, during holiday visits to France, had visited her and her husband, a charming Frenchman. Lucy, vivacious and energetic, had done a splendid job for the Red Cross, and emerged in apparently fine fettle from the war. But it had taken its toll, and it was a heart attack that killed her before she was forty. The war had left many men physically maimed, and other people with scars that weren't visible. Polly felt a sadness, a touching remembrance of women like Lucy and of the wartime atmosphere of comradeship so prevalent in France and Flanders. She would go and see Lucy buried.

Because of Lucy's death, it was less surprising for Polly to dream about the war than for Boots. Hers was just as vivid. Ambulances, mud, wounded men, casualty clearing stations, *estaminets*, cursing Tommies, boisterous Tommies, and Alice and her Northumbrian sergeant. Alice, happily married now, and with children.

Polly, too, dreamt of the weeks before that first great battle of the Somme. She, too, crashed awake when the dream became a nightmare and she was driving her ambulance through a river of blood in which dead Tommies floated. Heart beating violently, she sat up in her bed, thinking of the Somme and the slaughter, and the fact that of all men, Boots had been there and come out blinded.

She could never help herself in her feelings for him, nor rid her mind of the conviction that if she had met him somewhere, anywhere, in France or Flanders, she would never have allowed any woman to have him except herself. The feelings never changed, even though he had always refused to make love to her. He remained the only man she had ever really wanted. And she was simply unable to understand what he had ever seen in Emily, a thin and plain woman. She conceded Emily had character, and an air of energy similar to Sammy's, but how she had come to win a man as distinctive as Boots for a husband was a teeth-grinding and frustrating mystery to Polly.

Polly, however, knew very little of Emily's steadfast devotion and loyalty to the Adams family during the war, something which Boots fully recognized and appreciated, and which he repaid with deep affection.

While he sat talking with Rosie, Polly's thoughts were reaching out to her time in Albert and why she'd been denied the chance then of running into him. She'd seen men of his battalion in the town, but never him. He had remained quite unknown to her until after the war.

She was nearly thirty-eight now. Perhaps that was a help, because at that age one did not fantasize quite so much about mad and abandoned weekends behind locked bedroom doors in South Coast hotels. 'Do Not Disturb.' One was almost mellow enough to settle for what one's father recommended. Boots, her father had said, is a man who, when he becomes your friend, will make that friendship last all his life. He'll always be there. Settle for that, Polly.

She was doing her best to, although Emily, of course, always had an eye on her. Strangely, Boots's incurably Victorian mother always gave the impression of being understanding and sympathetic. Polly didn't actually respond too well to sympathy. From an early age she had never wanted anyone to feel sorry for her.

With thoughts of those weeks in Albert still crowding her mind, she felt again, perhaps for the hundredth time, an urge to chuck bricks at a fate that had kept her from running into Boots. And she felt too the frustration of her relationship with him. What did a woman have to do to fall out of love with a man? Husbands and wives fell out of love. At least, they lost the heady flush of love and passion after a while, and settled for being companionable. One could meet another man, she supposed, and make a lover of him. She had no desire to marry. The only man she had ever wanted as a husband was Boots.

'Hello?' said Boots, picking up his office phone at mid-morning the following day.

'Hello, stinker.'

'Who's that?'

'You know who it is.'

'The switchboard girl told me a Miss Loveworthy wanted to speak to me about our Oxford Street shop,' said Boots. 'Is it a complaint you have, Miss Loveworthy?'

'I've got a hundred complaints,' said Polly.

'Have you seen a doctor?'

'No, you old po-face, I haven't. All my complaints are about you.'

'Well, Miss Loveworthy,' said Boots, 'since I haven't had the pleasure of meeting you, I fail to—'

'Don't get too funny,' said Polly, 'or I'll come and blow you up. D'you like my *nom de plume*, "Loveworthy"? Jolly appropriate, don't you think? Well, nobody's love is more worthy of a reward than mine.'

'Hold on,' said Boots, 'you're not a Miss Loveworthy?'

'Shut up, you idiot,' said Polly. 'Come and treat me to lunch today. Meet me at Romano's at twelve-thirty.'

'I think I'm talking to Polly Simms,' said Boots. 'Well, much as I'd like—'

'No excuses,' said Polly, 'take me to lunch or I'll ruin your life.'

'How would you do that, Polly?'

'I'll think of something,' said Polly. 'But I can at least give you a good reason for meeting me. My dear stepmamma is prepared to give Adams Enterprises a large order for new orphanage uniforms and athletic outfits.' Her stepmother was the chief patron and administrator of two orphanages. 'Boots, both orphanages now have the use of a sports field, by kind permission of the local council. I've got all the details and I'm to discuss them with you.'

'That's Sammy's province,' said Boots.

'Sammy's not available.'

'He will be for Lady Simms. Your stepmother's original business relationship with Sammy helped him enormously.'

'He's not available, not today he isn't, you stinker, if you can strain yourself to get my meaning. So meet me at Romano's. My time's my own and you can spare me some of yours. Boots, are you listening?'

'Fair do's, Polly, I'll meet you.'

'Listen, darling, you do understand, don't you, that sometimes I just have to have you to myself?'

'Sometimes, Polly, some feelings are mutual.'

'Well, dear old sport, it's quite elevating to have you say something nice to me once in a while.'

'It's no effort, Polly,' said Boots, and spoke to Emily a few minutes later.

'What?' said Emily, secretary of the company and comfortably accommodated in her own little office. 'Why can't Sammy meet her?'

'Prior lunch appointment,' said Boots.

'Oh, very convenient, I don't think,' said Emily, green eyes snapping a bit. 'Why can't she come to the office?'

'She's in town for the day.'

'Why can't she come in tomorrow?'

'Good question, Em.'

'So what's the answer?' asked Emily.

'Ask me another,' said Boots.

'Listen, my lad,' said Emily, 'is that woman goin' to spend all her life tryin' to get you into bed with her?'

'Well, we shan't know that, Em, until she's at the pearly gates,' said Boots.

'Ha, ha, very funny,' said Emily. 'Crikey, you and Sammy! I feel for Chinese Lady sometimes. I don't know any mother who's got two like you two when it comes to a gift of the gab.'

'I probably got mine from you, Em,' said Boots.

'Me? That's a laugh,' said Emily. 'Nothing comes out of my mouth that makes people scratch their 'eads or go cross-eyed.'

'Well, you've got your own kind of gifts,' said Boots.

'What gifts?' asked Emily.

'Oh, the usual,' said Boots, 'two of them. Twins, I'd say. Well, they're identical.'

'Well, fancy that,' said Emily.

'Just a passing comment, Em old girl.'

'Not so much of your "old girl,"' said Emily. 'It's Polly Simms that's gettin' on a bit. Crikey, she must be nearly middle-aged, poor woman. That's not your style, is it, takin' a middle-aged woman to lunch?'

'I did have tea at the Dulwich orphanage once with her stepmother, Lady Simms,' said Boots. 'Now there's a middle-aged woman with a great deal of style.'

'Don't be daft,' said Emily. 'How can a middle-aged woman 'ave a middle-aged stepdaughter?'

'It's possible,' said Boots.

'You sure Polly's goin' to discuss an orphanage contract with you?' asked Emily in dark suspicion.

'Quite sure, lovey,' said Boots. 'Lady Simms is

an old customer and a very nice one. And her middle-aged stepdaughter has all the details of the specific requirements.'

'I'm a lemon, I am,' said Emily, 'I still ask questions when I ought to know the kind of answers I'm goin' to get.'

'We all have our moments, Em.'

'You'd better not 'ave any, not with Polly Simms,' said Emily darkly.

When Polly and Boots entered Romano's in the Strand, the head waiter asked if they'd reserved a table.

Polly, who was at her most brittle, gave him a crushing look.

'Good grief,' she said, 'don't you know Lord Adams of Clapham Manor?'

'Ah,' said the head waiter.

'Any old table will do,' said Lord Adams of Clapham Manor. 'A corner one.'

Polly gave him a hard time over the lunch in the lush Edwardian atmosphere of the restaurant, popular for many years with young bloods and their damsels. Boots asked about the exact requirements concerning uniforms and athletic wear for the many orphans. Polly silently extracted a folded sheet of paper from her handbag and chucked it into his lap.

'It's all there,' she said.

'And you want to discuss terms, *etcetera*?' said Boots.

'Do I hell,' said Polly, 'I'm not a costing clerk.'

'What's up, Polly?'

'Is that a serious question?' asked Polly, playing about with a fish fillet. 'Here, wait a moment, what d'you think you're doing?'

'Running an eye over requirements,' said Boots.

'If you don't put that piece of paper away, I'll stab you to death with my fish fork,' said Polly. 'You're supposed to be drooling over my unblemished beauty. I could be lunching with Sir Claud Blenkinsop of Dulwich Court, you know. He nevers fails to drool.'

'Needs a bib, poor bloke,' said Boots.

'Do you ever think about my unblemished beauty, you stinker?'

'Frequently.'

'Do you ever think of doing something about it?'

'Well, I could put a roll of film into my camera and photograph it,' said Boots.

'In my undies, of course?' said Polly.

'In a punt with a parasol,' said Boots.

'Ye gods, just a parasol? What happens afterwards?'

'I pass,' said Boots.

'Listen, d'you realize I'm thirty-five?'

Boots, who knew she was close to thirty-eight, the same age as himself, said, 'I realize you don't look a day over thirty.'

'Eureka!' murmured Polly to what was left of her fish, 'he loves me. Listen, old darling, I had horrible dreams about the Somme last night.'

Boots let his eyes rest on the bodice of her stylish dress, much as if he was making a guess at her measurements, which quite pleased Polly.

'H'm,' he said.

'Darling, anytime you like you can conduct a private examination,' murmured Polly. 'Honest to God, lover, you won't be disappointed.'

'Tempting,' said Boots. 'Did you say you dreamt about the Somme?'

A waiter removed their plates. Another waiter served them their main course. The silver cutlery glittered with light, and the little green velvet bow on the front of Polly's hat danced as she looked at the food and then at Boots.

'Yes, I did say so.'

'It was a long time ago,' said Boots.

'I was in Albert before the storm broke,' said Polly.

'I know, Polly, you've said so before.'

'You were there too.'

'On a farm, outside the town,' said Boots.

'Yes, you've said so too. Why didn't we meet?'

'You've asked that several times, Polly.'

'I'd be Mrs Robert Adams now, mother to your children, four at least,' said Polly, knowing that would touch him, knowing how much he liked young people, and how much he would have liked a sister and brother for Rosie and Tim.

'It couldn't have happened, Polly. I had nothing then, nothing, except my uniform.'

'You'd have had me and everything that's made you the man you are today. It should have happened.' Polly looked almost melancholy. Her eyes, as grey as his, were dark with lament for the lost opportunities of those weeks in Albert. She had identified so closely with the fighting men that she had never been able to see herself marrying a man who had not known France and Flanders, and so often she had felt that among those thousands of men there was one made for her alone. And there had been. Sergeant Robert Adams of the West Kents. But she'd been robbed by Emily.

Boots really was touched then, for the mournful darkness of her eyes was so unlike her.

'Polly—'

'Oh, I'm sorry.' Polly picked up her knife and fork. 'Here we are, having a lovely lunch, and I'm no better than a wet blanket. But—' She stopped.

'But what?'

'I do love you, you know.'

'Well, you know, Polly, love doesn't always have to relate to the physical. There's the urge, we both feel that, I daresay. But there's always something else, there's always the permanent pleasure of knowing that certain of our friends are very special to us.' Knowing just what her time as an ambulance driver had meant to her, Boots said what he felt would mean most to her now. 'We may not have met during the war, but that doesn't alter the very special fact that we're old comrades, Polly, that when I was doing my bit you were doing yours.'

'Oh, my God,' said Polly, 'are you trying to break my heart?'

'Not consciously,' said Boots.

'I'm going to France tomorrow. No good asking you to come with me, of course, so that we can be very special together? No, silly of me. I think I'll get drunk.'

'Help yourself, Polly, I'll drive you home.'

'Same old friendly pal,' said Polly.

'Same old Polly,' said Boots.

Chapter Two

Polly attended the funeral of her old school friend and wartime colleague. She was in what she herself conceded was a funereal mood, and was veiled and in black. She thought of the Lucy she had known before and during the war, a character who flung herself as cheerfully and breezily into her war work as she had into jolly hockey sticks. Polly watched the coffin being lowered before the eyes of the bereaved husband. Women were weeping. Polly was sad at this loss of a wartime friend. The friends she most cherished were those who had shared with her the years in France and Flanders. Oh, my God, they were long gone, those years, and she would be old all too soon, she would be over forty and on her way to fifty. She wanted every year back, she wanted to be in Albert again, and to know Boots was there.

She left Amiens the following day, saying goodbye to the widower, the Frenchman who had understood the extrovert nature of Lucy. Restless, melancholy, she would not stay, she had to go and to be by herself. She got into her car and left, without having the least idea of where she was going or where she wanted to go.

It was morbid, perhaps, and even stupid, but two days later she knew where she wanted to go, and so she began a tour of the battlefields. She avoided the places which she knew drew tourists from the countries that had sent their fighting men to the war. Australians, New Zealanders, South Africans and Canadians made visits, and their old soldiers sometimes made pilgrimages.

Polly kept to herself and went her own ways, to the silent and ghostly battlefields, recalling memories of a kind that fitted her emotional mood. The guns that had never been silent were silent now, and the quiet of it all in the brightness of summer wrenched at her heart. She was never going to be able to forget her times among the Tommies who, caustic and earthy though they were, could nevertheless fill the *estaminets* with laughter and go over the top again and again because their generals told them to. Boots had been one of them. Perhaps that was why she was here. Which woman was it who had run off lines about those men? One of the ambulance women whose sentimental side had not yet perished at the time. And what were those lines?

Polly remembered.

> *When it is over, this war,*
> *I shall come again to these places*
> *And stand in the silence of peace*
> *To listen once more for the sound of the guns*
> *And for the laughter of those*
> *Who died.*
> *Let it come again, their laughter,*

For they brought it out of battle with them
And shared it with us.
They failed no comrade, nor their country,
Nor us, their women.

She motored slowly each day over roads that had once been full of craters and mud, causing her ambulance to shake, rock and skid. Those ambulances and the women who had driven them, dear God, who could ever forget?

Take her up to Hellfire Ridge, girls,
Give the old bone-shaker a go,
Let her jump all the craters and bumps, girls,
Let her gaskets gurgle and blow.

And so on.

She had recited that many times to hundreds of men and heard them roar with laughter at the final line. 'To pick up what's left of your boots.'

Boots.

He was constantly on her mind, and it was a compulsive journey she made to the village of Guillemont. From there she walked to Trones Wood in the region of the Somme, where Boots had fought his last battle for the West Kents, and where he lost the man he admired above all others, his company commander. Trones Wood, still no more than a place of scarred stumps, amid which green summer growth was sprouting, was eerie in its silence. But she was not a gawping visitor looking for gruesome souvenirs of the horrendous first battle of the Somme. She was here because of her mood and emotions.

In its silence and its scarred reminders of battle, the place to Polly breathed of the men who had fallen, the men who had miraculously survived, and the incomparable comradeship of all of them. Was there anything in the world she would ever value more than having been part of that comradeship, the only worthwhile thing to have been born in that hell of a war?

Having been so close to the front line many times, having seen the men going up to the trenches, tramping, marching and with rifles slung, it was not difficult for Polly to conjure up a vivid mental picture of the storming of Trones Wood by the West Kents and the great flash of the exploding German grenade that had blinded Boots, and left him blind for four years. Thank God that that was all it had done. In her persistence, she had dragged from him more anecdotes than anyone else had, and she always thought, whenever he spoke of Major Harris, that it was his company commander who had turned him, a young volunteer, into the man he had become.

She wandered around the scarred stumps, treading, she supposed, in the long-vanished footprints of Boots and his West Kents, and at no time did she feel she was indulging fanciful sentiment. The moment was real for her, and she would not have been surprised to have looked up and seen her mud-splashed ambulance close by.

'Madame?'

She turned and saw an elderly French farmer in his black beret. She mentally winced. He had noted, of course, that she was not young, and assumed she was married.

'Good afternoon, m'sieur,' she said in French, the language she had perfected, as Boots had, because of being among the French during the war.

'This was once Trones Wood, madame.'

'Yes, I know, m'sieur.'

'You lost someone here, madame?'

'I lost comrades, m'sieur. Tommies. They were all my comrades. I drove an ambulance, you see.'

'Ah, then you are a brave woman, madame.'

'A frightened one many times, m'sieur, believe me.'

'But still brave. You are English?'

'Yes,' said Polly.

'My son, a soldier, was also a comrade of your Tommies.' A little smile creased the farmer's brown face. 'For once, the English and French fought together, not against each other. But it was a terrible war. Madame, if you would like to come to my farmhouse, my wife will make you some English tea.'

Polly hesitated. In her mood, she knew she was best by herself. But the farmer had kindness and sympathy written all over him.

'Thank you, m'sieur, I should like some English tea.'

'Come, then, madame.'

'I'm not married, m'sieur.'

'What does that matter, ma'moiselle? You are still welcome.'

'Thank you,' said Polly, and accompanied him to his farmhouse. It was not far, no more than a quarter of a mile, and there she was introduced to his grey-haired but rosy-faced wife, who happily set about making the pot of tea. When she was filling the pot, the son arrived, a man of forty and an ex-soldier of France. Handsome, smiling, he was delighted to meet Polly, and was at once extravagant in his compliments. Over the tea, which Polly found execrable because of its biting strength and its massive foundation of tea-leaves, the farmer, his wife and his son all bombarded her with comments and questions. They all talked at once and across each other, and the son smiled at her, looked at her legs, smiled again and looked again, and the low ceiling of the farmhouse living-room bore down on Polly and made her feel suffocation was on its way.

In their hospitality, the family offered her a room for the night. Polly said thank you, but she was going to put up at a hotel somewhere. They expressed disappointment, and the son took another look at her legs. It was he who saw her to the door of the farmhouse when she said goodbye. However, he made no move to open the door for her. Instead, he smiled again.

'Come, let me show you the room you can have,' he said. 'You will like it, it is next to mine.' He put a persuasive hand on her arm.

'Let go, if you please, m'sieur,' she said.

'Come,' he said, and smiled yet again, keeping hold of her arm.

Ye gods, what a glutinous cretin, thought Polly, and socked him one in his breadbasket. He let go and she escaped.

On her way back to Guillemont, she thought again of Boots, son of a cockney mother, and in making her comparisons between him and the smiling son of a French farmer, the latter came nowhere. He was bound to, in any case. Polly had become a one-man woman years ago.

She could not return to England, not yet, not in her present mood. In her present mood she was quite capable of confronting Boots and raising the roof a mile high unless he became her lover. She drove to Bapaume and took a room in a hotel there.

Chapter Three

Annabelle Somers, elder daughter of Lizzy and Ned Somers, called on Boots and his family on Friday evening, bringing her young man, Nick Harrison, with her. Annabelle, in her eighteenth year, was like her mother in her rich brunette colouring. Bubbly of personality and slightly precocious by nature, she was in the throes of her first serious relationship. It was very serious, actually. Well, what else could it be when Nick, a tall and very personable bloke of twenty-one, made her pulse jump about all over the place whenever he looked as if he was going to kiss her? And when he did, oh, crikey, she actually went swoony like modern girls weren't supposed to.

She threatened to tell her dad about him.

'Why?' asked Nick, saying goodnight to her at the time.

'Why? Why? You're not supposed to make me nearly faint when you kiss me. You don't want my dad to come to blows with you, do you?'

'No, I don't,' said Nick, 'I like your dad.'

'Well, then, you'd better try again,' said Annabelle.

So Nick gave her another goodnight kiss as they

stood on the doorstep. Annabelle's knees simply went all wobbly again, but she decided not to make any further complaints.

They were all in the garden on this warm July evening. Chinese Lady, her husband Edwin Finch, Emily, Boots, Rosie and twelve-year-old Tim, together with Annabelle and Nick. They were talking about their forthcoming summer holiday. The senior Adams family and the Somers family were spending it together in Salcombe, Devon, taking over the whole of a guest house for a fortnight, commencing the last week in July. Annabelle had spent a little while persuading Nick to get his holiday dates changed to coincide with hers so that he could join them. Nick said that as he'd only started with his present firm in March he might have a job getting the dates changed. Annabelle said she'd ask her Uncle John to come down heavy on him if he didn't try. Her Great-Uncle John was Nick's previous awesome boss, with a lot of influence in the City. Nick asked if that was fair. Annabelle said what's that got to do with it? I thought I'd ask, said Nick. He managed to get the dates changed, and Ned and Boots both said there was always room for one more if one more happened to be the lovelight in Annabelle's eyes. Annabelle said having a daft dad was something most girls had to put up with. Having a daft uncle as well was a bit trying.

Boots had ideas of everyone doing some sailing. Salcombe was a favourite place for mucking about in boats.

'Can you sail a boat, Nick?' asked Rosie.

'Never had the chance,' said Nick.

'That's done it,' said Tim, 'none of us can, Nick.'

'The idea,' said Boots, 'is that we all take lessons from an expert.'

'All?' said Chinese Lady, as straight-backed as ever. She associated a straight back and a firm bosom with respectability. That is, she hadn't anything to be ashamed of. 'If you think you're goin' to get me in some boat out at sea, you've got another think comin'. I've never been out at sea in a boat in all my life, and I'm not startin' now.'

'Don't worry, old lady,' said Boots, 'we'll put you and Edwin in charge of the oars.'

'You won't,' said Chinese Lady.

'Wait a minute,' said Emily, 'you used to sail the seas in a merchant ship, Dad, so you can probably sail a boat, can't you?'

'Probably in a rusty fashion,' said Mr Finch.

'That'll do,' said Boots, 'we'll hire a sailing boat and you can polish off your rust, Edwin.'

'I'll need a crew,' said Mr Finch.

'That's us, Grandpa,' said Tim, 'after you've helped us learn.'

'That sounds all right,' said Boots.

'That's it, be airy-fairy about it,' said Chinese Lady. 'Nobody's goin' out to sea in any boat except over my dead body, unless they know what they're doin'.'

'Good point, old girl,' said Boots.

'I'm not old yet,' said Chinese Lady, who wasn't going to concede she was until she was ninety.

'Well, as an alternative we'll buy some shrimp nets, roll our trousers up, tuck our skirts up, and catch shrimps,' said Boots.

'Fun,' said Rosie.

'Edwin,' said Chinese Lady, 'is that son of mine expectin' me to tuck my skirts up and catch shrimps?'

'I think he's saying you're not old yet, Maisie,' said Mr Finch, his mind, as it often was, on Hitler's Germany and the recent horrifying massacre of Brownshirts by the SS under the command of Goering and Himmler, an event that had shocked the world. Nazi Germany had issued a communique for international consumption, detailing criminal treason of a kind that had necessitated the execution of a hundred or so traitors. But reports from reliable sources inside Germany spoke of far more than that. Mr Finch, knowing Germany and knowing Hitler's excessive attachment to Prussian militarism, was sure that the Nazi leader would eventually lead Germany into war.

With an effort, Mr Finch brought himself back into the atmosphere of the moment, into the animated discussion on sailing boats. Chinese Lady was saying donkey rides were a lot more enjoyable than being in a boat going up and down on the sea.

'Do they have donkeys at Salcombe?' she asked.

'I don't think we've got any information about Salcombe donkeys,' said Boots.

'I had a donkey ride at Southend once, with your late dad,' said Chinese Lady. 'My, I never knew anything more lively. Your dad laughed his 'ead off.'

'Why, what happened, Nana?' asked Tim.

'Yes, what did?' asked Nick.

'Yes, what, Nana?' asked Annabelle.

'Never you mind,' said Chinese Lady.

'I think we can guess,' smiled Mr Finch.

'I don't want anyone guessin', thank you,' said Chinese Lady.

'Nana, I bet you showed your legs,' said Tim.

'Em'ly, box that boy's ears,' said Chinese Lady.

'But, Nana,' protested Tim, 'I only said legs, I didn't say—'

Emily's hand over his mouth stopped him mentioning what he shouldn't have.

'It seems to me,' observed Boots, 'that going up and down on a donkey could be more spectacular than going up and down in a boat.'

'What's that mean?' asked Chinese Lady.

'Nana,' said Rosie, 'it means that if your only oldest son tells you, you'll want someone to box his ears too.'

'I thought as much,' said Chinese Lady.

'Here, the doorbell's ringing,' said Tim, and away he went to answer it. He came back to deliver a message to Rosie. 'Rosie, there's a bloke says he's come to see you.'

'Tim, you mean Rosie's got a visitor,' said Chinese Lady.

'That's right, Nana, a bloke. He says his name's Armstrong.'

'Oh, that's Alexis,' said Rosie, and up she got and off she went, a smile on her face.

Annabelle, who knew about Rosie's interest in an

Oxford bookshop assistant, said, 'I can't wait to see what he's like.' She thought he had to be pretty special and dynamic, because Rosie had been immune until now.

'What was 'e like, Tim?' asked Emily.

'Like one of those blokes who stand on soap boxes by Hyde Park,' said Tim, who'd been taken by Boots to Speakers Corner a couple of times.

'Like what?' said Chinese Lady, taken aback.

'Yes, that's right, Grandma,' said Tim.

Rosie reappeared, and with her was the young gent in question, lean, lanky and rakish. He was hatless, his black hair thick and smooth, his complexion slightly pale. His jacket was black, his grey gaberdine trousers fashionably baggy by Oxford standards. Just as fashionably he wore no waistcoat. His flannel shirt was striped, his bow tie a brilliant red. With a lock of his hair falling over his forehead, and his pale complexion accentuating the darkness of his eyes, he reminded Boots of James Maxton, the Scottish MP who was a radical member of the Labour Party and a virulent opponent of capitalism.

Rosie, not at all fazed or sensitive about having Chinese Lady blinking at the sight of the bright red bow tie, introduced her Oxford friend to everyone in turn. Twenty-four years old, the young gentleman shook hands all round. Annabelle hid her surprised reactions by delivering a lovely smile. Heavens, who'd have thought Rosie would fall for someone with a pale hungry look?

'Hello, how'd you do, nice to meet you.' That was how he greeted each of them in turn. Then he stood back and smiled, showing two rows of white teeth. 'So you're all Rosie's kith and kin,' he said. 'I argue a lot with Rosie about kith and kin, has she told you?'

'I daresay she might in time,' said Boots. 'Pull up a chair and sit down. And would you like a drink?'

'A nice cup of tea, say?' suggested Chinese Lady, deciding it wouldn't be right to be put off by the glaring bow tie.

Alexis said he wasn't a great tea drinker. Beer was more his style, he said, if there was any going. Boots said there'd been some going a little while ago, but it was as good as gone now, judging from the nearly empty glasses on the table.

'The bottles aren't empty, Dad,' said Tim.

'So they're not,' said Boots. 'How about fetching another glass, Tim?'

'Got you, Dad,' said Tim, and went to fetch one.

Alexis received his beer, saying it was the drink of the proletariat, of which he was one. Rosie was watching him with a little smile, and Annabelle was wondering if he knew what his bow tie did to people's eyes. He went on to say it was odd about kith and kin. You were born, he said, but not until you reached the age of reason did you realize what kind of kith and kin you were stuck with. It could be a shock. He'd had a shock himself, he said, when he realized his parents and his closest relatives were all middle class. They drank sherry, he said. By the way, he said, I always speak frankly.

'So do I,' said Annabelle.

'And as Rosie knows, I don't go in for small talk. I regard small talk as a reflection of people's ignorance about this country's deplorable social conditions.'

'What brought this on?' asked Boots.

'I told you Alexis was talkative, Daddy,' said Rosie.

'So's Nick,' said Annabelle, 'he's turning me into a dumb listener.'

'I bet,' said Tim. 'Crikey, Annabelle, you can talk the hind leg off a donkey, specially over the phone.'

'Now then, cheeky,' said Annabelle, and looked at Nick, who at once put his grin away. 'Yes?' she said.

'I'm keeping quiet,' said Nick.

'Wise man,' said Mr Finch.

'I always think anyone that's got something to say, should say it,' said Chinese Lady. 'Mind, I sometimes feel it's best if Boots doesn't say too much, what with his habit of not always saying what he means.'

'And not always meanin' what he says,' remarked Emily.

Alexis looked slightly pained.

Rosie, still showing a little smile, said, 'I think there's some small talk going on.'

'Oh, I can sit through a middle-class gathering,' said Alexis, speaking frankly as was his wont and preference, 'I survived a surfeit when I lived at home.'

Boots, not a man of prejudices or fixed first

impressions, nevertheless took a sudden dislike to the idiot. If Rosie's serious about this politically-minded adolescent, he thought, I'm going to suffer a father's worst headache.

Chinese Lady asked, 'What does Mr Armstrong mean by what he just said, Rosie?'

'Oh, he means he'll be happy ever after when the middle classes have been done away with and everyone goes to work in a flat cap and we all earn the same as each other,' said Rosie.

'But what's he saying it to us for?' asked Chinese Lady.

'Well, we don't wear flat caps, Nana,' said Rosie. 'Mind you, all kinds of other people would say things if we did.'

'Did he say some people ought to be done away with?' asked Chinese Lady.

'Yes, it's all part of the grand design,' said Rosie.

Alexis said conditions of desperate deprivation, deliberately brought about by capitalists and their governments, could only be alleviated by the destruction of the class system, the setting up of workers' councils and central governmental control of all industry and all resources.

Alas for the sociable nature and the summer evening peace of Chinese Lady and her kith and kin, and Nick too, for once fully mounted Alexis Armstrong could not be pulled from his saddle or held back from his gallop. On he went, his flaming red bow tie his badge of uncompromising revolution, and eventually, when Annabelle had a glazed look and Tim was thinking Rosie had really done it on the family by letting a crackpot into the house, he reached out for the spirit of Lenin and planted it figuratively on the table.

'Lenin knew he couldn't compromise; the corrupt bourgeois had to be swept away by a total revolution. But look what that and his pure socialist teachings have done for Russia, and consider what they might do for this country.' He paused for a bit of breath and to finish his proletarian beer.

No-one said anything. What could be said when the talking gasbag was Rosie's young man? If he hadn't been, someone could have hit him over the head, of course. Nick glanced at Boots, a man he had come to know and like. Usually, whatever was being said, he looked as if a smile was about to surface. He had a wicked sense of humour. But for once he didn't seem at all amused, there was almost a look of irritation on his face.

The gasbag was off again.

'There's no argument, you know, this country needs a revolution to clean it up. If only—'

'Stop,' said Chinese Lady.

'Oh, he can't stop, Nana,' said Rosie.

'If only the workers can be given the right kind of leadership and the right kind of incentives to bring down the forces of oppression represented by the monarchy, the capitalists, the middle classes and the parasites—'

'Stop,' said Chinese Lady.

'Then the revolution would be victorious, and the Utopian nature of Lenin's Soviet Russia could be enjoyed by the workers of this country, and bread and milk brought into the mouths of their starving children—'

'Stop!' Chinese Lady smacked the table with the flat of her hand. Glasses jumped. Alexis stopped, glancing at her with a frown, his lock of hair going almost stiff with annoyance.

'You have a point to make?' he said.

'I think my grandma has several,' murmured Rosie.

'I never heard the like in all my life,' said Chinese Lady. 'I've heard a lot from my only oldest son, Rosie's dad, and most of it misunderstandable, but I never heard more downright foolish talk than now. Nor such bad manners. I don't know what your parents were about, young man, lettin' you teach yourself to come into people's 'omes and tell them that if you don't like their faces or their way of livin', you're goin' to do away with them. Young man, all I know about Lenin is that his Bolshevists went about killing everyone who didn't agree with him so that he could sit in his Bolshevist castle bein' Lord-I-Am. The last thing me and my fam'ly will stand for is havin' Lenin walk into our parlour and start doin' away with us—'

'Be of good cheer, old lady, he's been long dead,' said Boots.

'Well, no-one told me, and don't interrupt, and don't call me old lady in front of strangers,' said Chinese Lady. Strangers. That was it. Whatever Rosie's feelings were for this tiresome young man, he was never going to be allowed to darken Chinese Lady's doorstep again. 'I should think it's a good job Lenin is dead, 'e was a lot more trouble than he was ever worth, and if you go into any more homes, Mr Armstrong, and talk about doin' away with people you've never met before and other people you never will meet, you'll be so much trouble to yourself you'll come to a sorrowful end. People that do away with other people get done away with themselves. And I don't know what you mean about middle classes and workers and para-what-was-it?'

'Parasites,' murmured Mr Finch, now thoroughly enjoying himself.

'I informed everyone at the beginning I always speak frankly,' said Alexis, 'and I claim the right of a free man to—'

'Stop,' said Chinese Lady.

'I won't be—'

'Never mind what you won't and will,' said Chinese Lady. 'I don't know what all that meant about middle classes and workers and parasites, whatever they are. There's aristocrats, yes, but all the rest of us are workers. My fam'ly's been down to the soles of their feet, I'll have you know, and why you've got the impertinence to call us a middle-class gatherin' because we've now got our own 'ouse and garden, I just don't know. I never heard anything more daft. And it's not your place to do away with our King and Queen, we don't hold with people takin' it on themselves to chop other people's heads off.'

Alexis, glancing at Rosie, looked as if he thought she should have told him her grandmother was due to be certified.

'Oh, dear,' said Rosie, 'I think it's your turn again, Alexis.'

'Well,' he said, 'consequent on a successful revolution, we the workers will decide the question of—'

'I wouldn't let anyone who works in a bookshop decide things for anyone in this fam'ly,' said Chinese Lady.

'By the way, Mr Armstrong,' said Mr Finch, 'Lenin never did a day's manual labour or held down any kind of job from the day he was born until the day he took office. He lived on what he could scrounge. He was, alas, a parasite, never a worker.'

'I'm used to misguided remarks of that kind,' said Rosie's talking gasbag.

'Well, you've made a very good speech, Alexis,' said Rosie, 'and I think you can say goodbye to everyone now. Then I'll see you to the door.'

'I'm willing to throw open the subject for discussion, Rosie.'

'Not now,' said Rosie, 'I think you've come a bit of a cropper. Never mind, I'll still come and buy books from you. Say goodbye now.'

Mr Alexis Armstrong, accepting that he was probably among people with the fixed minds of potential counter-revolutionaries, said his goodbyes and Rosie walked back into the house with him to see him out.

'Excuse me a moment,' said Boots to Emily.

'Boots, you'd best leave those two to each other,' said Emily.

'Shan't be a tick,' said Boots.

He caught Rosie in the hall. She had just closed the door on the departing revolutionary.

'Hello, Daddy,' she said brightly. 'My word, I bet you thought he was a caution, didn't you? And didn't Nana let fly?'

'I'd have let fly myself if he hadn't been your guest,' said Boots.

'Daddy, are you grumpy?'

'Yes, I am. He's an idiot.'

'But I thought you'd laugh at him.'

'Because he's your idiot, Rosie, we all bit our tongues, except your grandmother.'

'Stop being cross with me.'

'Rosie—'

'It hurts,' said Rosie.

'Well, I'll suffer fifty painful fits myself if you've got serious feelings about that political clown,' said Boots, and Rosie stared at him, astonishment showing in her blue eyes. Then she smiled and shook her head.

'Daddy, you silly, you don't really think I'd fall for someone like him, do you? Heavens, when he was doing all that fiery talking, weren't you glad, as I was, that all our families don't go in for using dotty politics to upset our friends? Look, I use his bookshop, that's all, like other students. I'm not saying he doesn't have ideas about making me his own Comrade Adams when the revolution arrives, but those aren't my ideas. He said he'd call on me during his holiday, and I told him he might get a flea in his ear. He's got two, one from Nana and another one from me. I gave it to him on our doorstep. So there.'

Boots looked wry, inwardly acknowledging he'd shown the fault of a father wanting too much of a say in the affairs of his daughter. But in his relief at the dismissal of the political animal as suitor, he was able to laugh.

'Well done, poppet. Let's rejoin the others, but get your fiddle first.'

'My fiddle?' Rosie had a violin, which she could play with a fair amount of talent. 'What for?'

'A celebratory jig,' said Boots, and Rosie, laughing, went to fetch her violin.

'Have you been talkin' to Rosie?' asked Chinese Lady when Boots reappeared.

'Yes,' said Boots, 'and we've no worries. As far as Rosie's concerned, that young man is a freak.'

'Well, I've never heard a more relievin' piece of news,' said Chinese Lady.

'Nor me,' said Annabelle. 'Crikey, I had a feeling I was one of those he wanted to do away with. Me, imagine. I mean, is there anyone nicer?'

'There's me,' said Tim.

'And me,' said Emily.

'I'll pass,' said Nick, 'I think I'd better.'

Out came Rosie with her violin and bow

'What's this for?' asked Chinese Lady.

'Well, old love,' said Boots, 'as you're one of the workers of the world and the effective voice of the family, I'm going to take you for a celebratory jig on the lawn while Rosie fiddles.'

'Yes, up you get, Nana,' said Rosie.

'Yes, up you get, Maisie,' smiled Mr Finch.

'I'll do no such thing,' said Chinese Lady, 'I've never done any jig on a lawn in my life, and I'm not startin' now.'

'Come on, Mum, up you get,' said Emily.

'Certainly not,' said Chinese Lady, but Boots took hold of her hands and drew her to her feet. 'Listen, my lad, if you think at my age I'm doin' any jig with you—'

'Go on, Dad,' said Tim.

'What tune?' asked Rosie, cradling her violin.

'Try "One Man Went To Mow",' said Boots, 'that should be lively enough.'

Rosie laughed and began to scrape. Tim, Emily, Annabelle, Nick and Mr Finch all began to sing.

One man went to mow, went to mow a meadow,
One man and his dog, went to mow a meadow!

Boots began a jig over the lawn with Chinese Lady.

Two men went to mow, went to mow a meadow,
Two men, one man and his dog, went to mow a
*   meadow!*

Rosie's laughing eyes were alight. Chinese Lady was doing little galloping jigs with her only oldest son.

Three men went to mow, went to mow a meadow,
Three men, two men, one man and his dog, went to
*   mow a meadow!*

A woman's voice sailed over the hedge from the garden next door.

'What's going on over there?'

'Just a bit of a jig, Mrs Fletcher,' called Tim.

'Can we join in?'

'Yes, come round,' called Boots, 'and bring your dog, if you like.'

'Boots, if you don't stop gallopin' me about, I won't be responsible for me actions,' gasped Chinese Lady.

'Leg it, old girl,' said Boots.

Six men went to mow, went to mow a meadow,
Six men, five men, four men, three men, two men,
    one man and his dog, went to mow a meadow!

Mr Finch smiled.

Chinese Lady was laughing.

Chapter Four

Polly, still maudlin, still with the years of war on her mind, had made slow progress from one place to another, each place known to her. She arrived, inevitably, in Albert. She drove into the town, its war-damaged buildings rebuilt or repaired. She parked outside the *estaminet* run during the war by Jacques Duval, and where, during the run-up to the Somme offensive, it had been full each evening of Tommies due to go over the top and run into a merciless German fire. She went in, and the first person she saw wiping a table top clean was Jacques himself, now stout and balding. Behind the wine counter was a girl. She was polishing glasses, and Polly supposed she had replaced Helene. She smiled at Polly. There was only one customer present, an old man sitting at a corner table with a glass of cognac in front of him. He was talking to himself, as some old men do.

'Jacques?' said Polly.

The proprietor turned and looked at her, seeking recognition.

'Madame?' he said.

'You don't remember me, Jacques?'

Jacques searched her face again.

'Ah, wait, wait,' he said. 'Once in a while someone comes back, to visit the cemeteries, to look for the graves of their old comrades – wait, yes, I know you. Let me think.'

'Think of ambulances,' said Polly.

'Ah,' said Jacques, and smiled then. 'Now I know. Ma'moiselle Polly.'

'Just Polly, Jacques.'

'Not married?' smiled Jacques.

'No, not yet,' said Polly, 'the right gentleman has eluded me. Will you serve me a coffee with cognac and perhaps have a cognac yourself?'

'A pleasure,' said Jacques. 'And a little conversation before my evening customers arrive?'

'Then I must go to the hotel and book myself a room,' said Polly.

'For some of those who come back, there's a room here, ma'moiselle, with breakfast.'

'Jacques, how kind, it would suit me very well for a night or two,' said Polly, and sat down at a table with the amiable proprietor.

'Eloise,' said Jacques to the girl, 'coffee for – ah, already, my chicken?'

'Yes, I heard what was wanted,' said Eloise, smiling, and brought two coffees and two cognacs to the table. Brown-haired and with a fair complexion, she had the fresh look of the young. Seventeen, thought Polly. God, less than half my own age. 'You are English, ma'moiselle?' said the girl, eyeing Polly with interest.

'Yes, one more of those who sometimes come to visit the wartime places,' said Polly.

'I am half English myself, am I not, Uncle Jacques?' said Eloise.

'So you are,' smiled Jacques. 'Eloise, alas, has lost both her parents,' he said to Polly. 'Her mother was a cousin of mine. Now she lives with us and works with us.'

'For hardly any wages,' said Eloise, and laughed. Jacques grinned, sipped coffee and took a little mouthful of the cognac. 'But who would ask for big wages when one is looked after so well? Ma'moiselle, you were here during the terrible war?'

Polly said she had been an ambulance driver and stationed in Albert for many months in 1916. Eloise said many brave Englishwomen drove ambulances according to her Uncle Jacques, and that he had known many because they drank their wine here with the English Tommies.

'Yes, I was one,' said Polly, 'which is why your Uncle Jacques managed to recognize me after he'd looked at me long enough. Do all my extra years show, Jacques?'

'No, no, Ma'moiselle Polly,' protested Jacques, 'I recognized you because although there have been several years—'

'Eighteen,' said Polly.

'Several or eighteen, what does it matter when most of them have passed you by?' said Jacques.

'Eloise, you have a very gallant uncle,' smiled Polly, letting the warming fire of cognac linger in her mouth and throat.

'Oh, he is always bowing and nodding to ladies

good-looking,' said Eloise. 'Did you know many English soldiers, ma'moiselle?'

'All of them except one,' said Polly.

'All of them?' said Eloise in astonishment.

'Well, perhaps not all,' said Polly, 'although I sometimes felt it was like that.'

'But who was the one you did not know?'

'Oh, that's a very long story, Eloise.'

'I should like to hear it,' said Eloise.

'Ah, stories,' said Jacques, 'who does not have some to tell?'

Three patrons arrived then, all talking together, and Jacques excused himself to Polly. Polly finished her coffee and cognac, then collected her luggage from the car. Eloise took her up to the room Jacques had offered her. It was clean, comfortable and adequate, and Polly assured her it would do very well.

She unpacked and freshened up. She wondered what she was doing, lingering in France and in this strange, lamenting mood. She stretched out on the bed and read several chapters of the book she had brought with her. *All Quiet On The Western Front*. It was a bitter, satirical and truthful book, written by the German author, Remarque, and it looked at the war from the point of view of the ordinary German soldiers, whose disillusionment was no different from that of the Tommies.

She went out later and dined at a restaurant. If other diners wondered what she was doing by herself, she gave their glances hardly any consideration at all. She still did not need company. Her own was enough for her at the moment. Nevertheless, when she returned to the *estaminet* it wasn't long before she was sitting at a table with several of Jacques' patrons, some of whom were old soldiers. Very quickly they began to exchange wartime reminiscences with her. Polly stood treat, and Eloise brought the ordered bottles of wine to the table.

'Here we are, ma'moiselle,' she said.

'Thank you,' said Polly, looking up at the girl. Eloise smiled, and Polly thought then that her brown hair, oval features and fair complexion were more Anglo-Saxon than Gallic. Grey eyes held a little hint of blue. 'I see now,' said Polly, 'yes, you are half English, Eloise.'

One of the old French soldiers laughed.

'So are many children of France,' he said, and they all laughed.

'That isn't funny,' said Eloise, and did to the joker what Helene before her had done to more than one Tommy. She hit him over the head with her tin tray, then laughed herself as she went back to the bar.

'Ah, but there it is, ma'moiselle,' said the joker to Polly, 'some men arrive to make war, and make love instead.'

'Was Eloise's father a British soldier, then?' asked Polly.

'That is so, ma'moiselle, but he fell in action before she was born,' said another man.

'No woman should have married a front-line soldier during the war,' said Polly, forgetting that she would have married Boots only a day after meeting him.

The Frenchmen looked at each other.

'There was no marriage, ma'moiselle, the war did not give them time,' said one.

'So Eloise herself has said,' nodded another.

Polly, with her brittle smile, said, 'Well, at least, whoever the man was, he has left France with a flower.'

'An English rose, ma'moiselle.'

'Yes, perhaps you could call Eloise that,' said Polly.

She spent the following morning wandering around Albert, taking in a visit to the building which the Red Cross and St John Ambulance Brigade had used for their headquarters. It was still standing. With the help of her Northumbrian sergeant, Alice had pinched silk stockings from the Commandant. But neither she nor Polly had made any immediate use of them. The Somme got in the way, and when Alice was given Blighty leave, Polly gave back the pair Alice had pinched for her. She knew by then that Alice was going to marry Sergeant Ben Hawes. Two pairs are better than one for a bride, Alice, she had said.

Polly lunched in the town and returned to the *estaminet* in the afternoon. The place was quiet then, and Jacques and Eloise were pleased to see her and to have time to talk to her.

'Ma'moiselle, would you like some tea?' asked Eloise.

'Don't think me ungracious, Eloise, but—'

'Oh, it will be English tea, made with boiling water and with milk,' said Eloise. 'My mother watched my English father make it in her parents' kitchen, and told me about it. Coffee, yes, he would drink her coffee, but he always said the most refreshing hot drink was tea.'

'I'd love tea in the way your father made it,' smiled Polly, who had taken to the girl.

'Ah, *très bien*,' said Eloise, and disappeared.

Jacques smiled and said, 'When she brings the tea, she will ask if you knew her English father and where his grave is, as she asks all the English who come back here to visit because of the war.'

'Oh, it's true I knew a great many of our men, Jacques,' said Polly, 'but not every name.'

'It will make no difference,' said Jacques, 'she will still ask. She sees herself as a child of love, which perhaps she is.'

'Sometimes, Jacques, it wasn't like that,' said Polly. 'I'm afraid many of our Tommies scattered their seed about very casually.'

'Don't tell Eloise that,' said Jacques.

'I wouldn't dream of it,' said Polly.

'She's quite sure her father would have married her mother if he hadn't perished on the Somme,' said Jacques.

'Jacques, I think the very best of our world perished there,' said Polly.

'Ma'moiselle,' said Jacques gently, 'does it haunt you?'

'Sometimes, Jacques, sometimes.'

232

'You are not alone,' said Jacques. 'As for Eloise, she'll certainly talk to you again about her father. She cannot help wondering what happened to him after he fell in action. He was lost in the mud, perhaps, for neither she nor her mother ever found his grave in any of the Somme cemeteries. Yes, she'll talk to you again.'

Sure enough, when Eloise brought a pot of steaming tea, with milk and sugar, and placed the tray before Polly, she said, 'My father was an English soldier, ma'moiselle, who lost his life before I was born. Perhaps you saw him somewhere, perhaps you knew him. See, look, this is his photograph, which I've kept since my mother died a year ago. Would you have known him?' She placed a framed sepia-tinted photograph, a snapshot, on the table in front of Polly. 'There, ma'moiselle, that is my English father. He looks a nice man, don't you think? Would you have met him, ma'moiselle?'

Polly smiled at the girl, at her grey eyes bright with the hopes and optimism of the young, the eyes of a girl wanting to know all she could about the man who had loved her mother.

'Well, let me see,' said Polly, and looked down at the snapshot of a man standing by a farm gate, a man in the peaked cap, shirt and trousers of a British soldier obviously out of the line for a while, the sleeves of the shirt rolled up and a large bucket depending from his right hand. He had a smile on his face. Polly stared, her eyes opening wide, her body suffering the shock of incredulity. It couldn't be, it was too unbelievable. But there was no mistake. Polly of all people knew there wasn't, despite her incredulity. It was Boots as a young man, a soldier of the trenches, yet already no longer young. Boots had been twenty at the time of the Somme, a few months older than herself, she knew that, but it wasn't a young man in this well-preserved snapshot, it was a veteran of France and Flanders, a sergeant. Polly knew what so many others knew, that it was the sergeants who were the backbone and strength of the British Army. She could not take her eyes off the snapshot, nor detach her mind from all it meant. She heard Eloise say something. 'Excuse me, Eloise?'

'Ma'moiselle, did you perhaps meet this soldier, my father? See, if you drove an ambulance, perhaps you know where his grave is. My mother went to the British town headquarters after the first weeks of the battle, to find out what had happened to him, and they examined the casualty lists and said he had fallen with his company commander in Trones Wood.'

He had fallen, yes, Polly knew that. He had fallen blinded and unconscious, alongside Major Harris, and perhaps the mistake of placing him among the fatal casualties had been all too easily made at the time, although it would have been rectified later in the regimental records of the West Kents. But this girl's mother, a Frenchwoman, had not been advised of the mistake. And why should she have been? She was not married to Boots, she was merely a woman who had asked after him, and perhaps at the time she did not even know she was expecting his child.

Drawing breath, Polly said, 'When were you born, Eloise?'

'At the end of March in 1917,' said Eloise, and Polly thought, yes, that would be right. The West Kents had been billeted near Albert for the first three weeks in June, 1916, and gone up to the line a week before the offensive began. She looked again into the girl's grey eyes with their hint of blue, and saw the eyes of Boots there. Boots had a hidden streak of steel, and when it surfaced it showed, it put a faint blue into the grey.

So, he was the father of this bright young girl. Polly felt the worst kinds of emotion stir: anger, jealousy and even bitter envy. The Frenchwoman in question had known him in a way she herself never had. He had given the woman an enchanting daughter. Who was going to tell him? The mother was dead, but the daughter existed, his natural daughter. Must I tell him? Should anyone tell him, when it was all so long ago? What would it do to Emily, to Tim and to Rosie? What would it do to Boots himself?

One could say nothing because, after all, it was only one more story similar to many others relating to a traumatic yesterday.

'It's right, your mother died last year, Eloise?'

'Yes, ma'moiselle, and her parents, my grandparents, died earlier, leaving their farm to my mother's brother, a hard man. I did not get on with him, so when my mother died I came to live with Uncle Jacques and Aunt Marie.'

235

Jacques' wife Marie appeared then. She was a peaceful-looking woman who liked to keep herself in the background with her housework, her cooking and her cats. She smiled vaguely at Polly, picked up a bottle of wine from the counter, and returned to her quiet anonymity.

'Your father spent time on the farm with your mother, Eloise?' said Polly. Boots, you swine, she thought, you've never said a single word to me about your Frenchwoman. No wonder I never had a chance to meet you, you were spending all your time with her. 'I mean, this snapshot looks as if it was taken on the farm.'

'Oh, yes, his company was billeted in the long barn,' said Eloise, 'and Mama took the snapshot a few days before he left. Ma'moiselle, the photograph is interesting you? Do you think it's of a soldier you knew? If so, perhaps you could help me find out if he has a grave somewhere. I should so like to visit it and place flowers there sometimes. See, he was such a fine-looking man, don't you think? Mama loved him very much.'

My God, thought Polly, what am I to say and do?

'For how long did your mother know him, Eloise?'

'Oh, only for a few weeks,' said Eloise, 'while his company was at the farm. She always said it doesn't take a lifetime for a woman to fall in love. Ma'moiselle, you haven't said, did you know him?'

'No, I never met him while I was in Albert, Eloise.'

236

'But might you have heard of him? His name was Robert Adams, and he was a sergeant.'

'I can truthfully say, Eloise, that all through my time in France, I never came across Sergeant Robert Adams.'

'Eloise,' said Jacques, 'he was only one of many thousands of British soldiers.'

'Yes, but one has to ask about him, Uncle Jacques. Someone might know if he has a grave in one of the cemeteries. It's only right to try to find out, and only right too that his daughter should visit it and place flowers there in remembrance of him and his love for my mother.'

Oh, my God, thought Polly, what would this girl do if she knew he was alive?

'Many soldiers have no known grave, my chicken,' said Jacques.

'That's very true, Eloise,' said Polly, and wondered if she should leave immediately and put all this behind her. If she told Eloise her father was alive, and exactly what he was like, the girl would probably go rushing off to England. Should she tell her? Could she do so without speaking to Boots first? She must think about it, if she could clear her mind of all its confusions. She must think about it long and hard, which meant she could not leave, not yet.

The entrance of patrons brought relief. They took Jacques and Eloise away from her. She went up to her room, paced about and then came down again. She left to go to her car, and in it she drove out of Albert in a new kind of emotional state. Oh, bloody hell, she said to herself, what a swine you are, Boots, you've made love to other women but always turned me down.

What would he say if he knew about Eloise? What would he do? He would have his family to think about, Emily especially. Oh, damn Emily.

On she went, driving with no clear objective guiding her, but she ended up in the village of Guillemont as if drawn by a magnet. And from there she walked again to the remains of Trones Wood, though the new growth springing up amid the scarred and lifeless trunks, and where Eloise's mother thought, because of incorrect information, that Boots had died. She halted and she stood in long and silent reflection. She was quite alone, except for the ghosts of the fallen, and because of that and all her new emotions, she heard again the sound of the guns.

Meanwhile, Boots and his family, together with Lizzy and Ned and their four children, and Nick, were holidaying at Salcombe for the last week in July and the first week of August. Everyone except Chinese Lady was involved with a hired sailing boat, and all were under the instruction of Mr Finch who in his youth had known the sailing waters of the Baltic with his German family. Hilarious was the fun, and vivaciously alive was Annabelle, either in her bathing costume or her shorts and shirt. She dazzled Nick. Rosie dazzled all the other young men there. Women looked at Boots in his summer drill slacks rolled up above his knees and his open flapping shirt.

'Come here, you,' said Emily once.

'I'm needed?' said Boots, arriving at her side.

'Yes, you're needed so I can give you an earful,' said Emily. 'Stop talkin' to all these women who keep edgin' up on you. You're a husband and father, and you're out of circulation, and Chinese Lady says you're not decent showin' your legs and chest the way you do when you're talkin' to women you 'aven't ever met before.'

'All right, Em, tell Chinese Lady I'll put my raincoat on.'

Up came Rosie in shorts, shirt and bare feet, hair tied with a ribbon and face turning golden brown.

'What's going on?' she smiled.

'I'm givin' your dad an earful on account of him lettin' women come up and rub elbows with him,' said Emily.

'Oh, that's not his fault,' said Rosie, 'it's his sex appeal.'

Emily blinked.

'Sex appeal, what's that?' she said. 'It don't sound nice to me, Rosie, nor half decent.'

'Oh, it's the latest thing among Hollywood film stars,' said Rosie. 'All the film magazines talk about them having sex appeal now.'

'Well, I don't like the sound of it one bit,' said Emily, 'and nor will your grandma. And I don't want to hear you saying your dad's got some – here, where's he gone?'

'Oh, just to share some of his sex appeal with the lady in that posh yacht,' said Rosie.

'Well, you can just go and tell 'im to bring it back

239

here,' said Emily. 'I never heard of anything more – more—'

'Improper?' said Rosie.

'Well, whatever it is, you tell your dad to get rid of it or cover it up.'

Rosie shrieked.

'Mum sweet, you can't cover it up.'

'Well, it ought never to 'ave been invented,' said Emily, 'so you make sure your grandma never gets to hear about it.'

'Bless you, no, never,' said Rosie, 'and I'll tell the lady with the posh yacht that Daddy's sex appeal is all yours, Mum, and that he's got to bring it back here so that you can put it somewhere safe.' Away Rosie went, laughing.

Emily couldn't help smiling. That young lady had her own appeal. And she was so like Boots, she had the same sense of humour, the same way of enjoying life, and she could easily have been his natural daughter. Emily sighed a little then. She'd done her best in her marital relationship with Boots, but she'd only produced one child, their son Tim. She knew he'd have liked more, he was always at his best with young people, and always specially good fun when in company with Tim and Rosie and his nieces and nephews.

Look at some of them now. Annabelle, Bobby, Emma, Edward, Tim and Rosie, all clambering around the hired boat, all having fun with Boots. And with Ned too, wearing summer trousers down to his sand-shoes to hide his artificial leg, with Lizzy watching him to make sure he didn't fall over the oars or something. Lizzy, her oldest friend, had a really good marriage, being the boss and Ned not minding it that way. It was a bit more difficult for herself to be boss with Boots, he just didn't take her seriously enough, he'd say something to make her giggle when she didn't want to giggle.

Nick was down at the boat as well, a lovely young man and a firm friend to Boots, as well as being such a good companion to Ned and Mr Finch. He was also Annabelle's one and only. She had given the push to all her other boyfriends. Look at her, what a picture she was, all colour and sparkle, and such a teasing minx to Nick. But you could tell how she felt about him by the way she responded to him and the way she provoked him into tickling her. She went mad with shrieks and laughter, and then came back for more. It was what you felt when you were in love, you wanted to be touched. Oh, the years when she herself would have died with bliss to have Boots tickle her, only she'd been such a skinny thing and nowhere near as pretty as Lizzy had been.

'Come on, Aunt Em'ly,' called Bobby, 'come and help push the boat. Grandpa's going to sail it with some of us in it.'

'Comin', Bobby,' said Emily, and down she went to help push and launch the hired yacht, her skirt tucked up, her slim legs shining in the sunlight. And as she went she thought of her years in Walworth and the poverty, and the blessings of having lovely neighbours like the Adamses, who'd been even poorer than her mum and dad. Imagine, out of that hard life had come a summer day with poverty far behind them, and the young people actually enjoying all the wonders of messing about in boats, like only rich people used to do.

Chinese Lady, seated in a deckchair and under an old-fashioned parasol, watched them all as the boat was pushed into the water, then she returned to the book she was reading, a holiday novel bought for her by Boots. It was by Ethel M. Dell, and Chinese Lady was deep into the author's detailed description of the hero. She was trying to work out what it all meant.

Rosie could have told her it meant the hero had sex appeal.

Chapter Five

Polly found herself staying on. If Jacques was kindness itself, Eloise was happy each day to serve her French breakfast and to have her around to talk to. And there were always questions.

Where would I begin, ma'moiselle, if I wanted to find out if my father had brothers and sisters? Do you think, ma'moiselle, it's foolish perhaps to want to know about his family, to find out if I have English uncles and aunts? Ma'moiselle, I must stop talking like this, don't you think? Only I think you very English, and attractive in a very English way, and I keep saying to myself, ah, Eloise, you are English too but in a French way, do you think so, ma'moiselle?

Polly answered all questions in oblique fashion, and put together comments that made Eloise smile. Jacques spared the girl from her work one day, when the weather was particularly fine, and Polly took her out into the countryside for a picnic lunch. Eloise was delighted, and said how kind English people were, and with such good manners. She liked ma'moiselle very much, she said.

'For my good manners, Eloise?'

'For how nice you are, and for your sense of

humour. That is sometimes the best thing for people to have, a sense of humour, don't you think so?'

Boots has his share of that, thought Polly.

'If one has no looks, Eloise, and no fine hat and dress for Sunday Mass, a sense of humour would be a great help.'

'Oh, yes, one could laugh away one's liabilities,' said Eloise.

On the way back, the girl asked Polly if she would like to see the farm which once belonged to her mother's parents and where her mother met her English sergeant. Polly, traumatized, said yes in a hollow voice, and Eloise directed her there. She showed her where to park the car, beside a gate in a leafy lane. Out of the car they stepped, Eloise opened the gate and they entered a farm lane.

'What's that?' asked Polly, pointing.

'Oh, that's the long barn where the soldiers of my father's company were billeted, and see, there's a smaller barn farther on, which he and the other sergeants used. And look, down there is the cottage used by the officers. My mother told me all this.'

'Yes, Eloise, of course,' said Polly, and bit her lip. The scene was so peaceful, so rural, and it was painfully easy to visualize how like paradise it must have seemed to the trench-weary West Kents. And what would the addition of a farmer's daughter have done for Boots, if not to keep him here and out of the town's *estaminets*? No wonder she herself had been robbed of the chance of meeting him.

The summer insects winged, the sun laid its heat on the barn roof, and such was the country quiet that she was sure she would hear the sound of the guns yet again any second.

'Ma'moiselle?'

'Excuse me?'

'Ma'moiselle, you look so sad.'

'Well, you see, my young friend, they were here and then they went, and so many of them died. They had faults, Eloise, the faults of men, but even so they were the best of men, with so much courage, as your soldiers of France were. Your father was a volunteer—'

'A volunteer? Ma'moiselle, how did you know that?'

Polly, biting her lip again, said, 'Well, you see, Eloise, Britain didn't begin conscription of men until 1916, and as your father was a sergeant he must have enrolled with the Army long before service became compulsory. Do you see?'

'Yes, ma'moiselle. You have very deep feelings about your Tommies. That is what the French and Belgians called them, Tommies. Ma'moiselle, do you find it hard to forget them?'

'Hard? No. Do you think I try to? No, never. In four years I lived a lifetime with them, Eloise, and can never forget them.'

'I think that is a proud and precious thing, ma'moiselle. See, if we walk down this lane we shall come to the farmhouse. It's the lane my father walked every day to see my mother before the war took him.'

Oh, God, I shall come hopelessly apart, thought Polly, as they began the walk. I'm crazy. One should never go back to one's yesterday, not when yesterday is so emotionally painful. What am I doing now if I'm not walking in his footsteps again? What help is that to me?

Her legs moved stiffly. Eloise swung along beside her, a girl not of sadness or maudlin sentimentality, but a girl who seemed to take pleasure in being the daughter of a man she had never known. There was an eagerness about her in her wish to show Polly where he had met her mother.

'That is the farmhouse?' said Polly, as it loomed up solid and enduring.

'Yes, and that is the dairy,' said Eloise. The stone-built dairy was as enduring as the farmhouse. 'See, it's where they met, just outside the dairy, and would you believe, ma'moiselle, my mother chased him with a pitchfork, thinking he had come to steal the chickens. She shook her fist at him, told him many things to his discredit, called him many names, and in the end he laughed, yes. He thought her very amusing, you see, and he wasn't at all afraid of her tongue or her fist or her pitchfork. Oh, she told me this many times, how he laughed at her, so of course, she fell in love with him there and then. Is it easy, ma'moiselle, to fall in love with men who laugh at you?'

Polly remembered the moment when she had finally met him, in 1920, and in a dreadfully grotty shop by Camberwell Green, full of army surplus. She had gone there to deliver an order for her

246

stepmother, already involved with Boots's brother
Sammy in respect of blankets and so much else for
a new orphanage. Only Boots had been there, and
she could hardly believe that such an arresting man
could be in charge of a stupid shop. She lingered,
however, her whole being disturbed, and she told
him eventually to close the shop and come up to
town with her. More or less, he laughed at her, and
she stormed out with insults on her lips. But she
went back on another day, she had to, and from
then on she made a place for herself in his life.
Compulsion drove her, and how bitter she was
when she found out he was married, for she knew
he had been the one man in France she had
subconsciously looked for.

'It's very easy, Eloise, to fall in love with a man
whom you feel is meant for you alone.'

'What are you doing here?' A man barked the
question and they saw him moving towards them
from the farmhouse. He was short, squat and very
dark, his old felt hat pulled low, a black moustache
sitting thickly on his upper lip, his expression ill-
tempered.

'That's my Uncle Petrie, my mother's brother,'
whispered Eloise. 'Don't let him upset you.' She
lifted her head as he rapidly advanced on them.

'What are you doing here?' he asked again, looking at Eloise and ignoring Polly. Polly thought him
a mishap of nature, a squat black beetle masquerad-
ing as a man by standing upright.

'I've only brought an English friend of mine to
see the farm,' said Eloise.

247

'Well, you're not welcome, and nor is she, or any damned English people. Clear off, both of you. I know what you're after, brat, you're after half of the farm. You'll not get it, you've no claim, you're illegitimate.'

'And you, m'sieur, are the ugliest and most unpleasant creature in a country made for cultured and civilized people,' said Polly, 'and I count it a sad misfortune to have met you.'

'Get off my land, English whore!'

'M'sieur, I would not stay here, no, not for all the gold in the Bank of England,' said Polly. 'Come, Eloise, leave him to his pond, his frogs and his mud.'

He stood roaring after them as they went back down the lane, Eloise holding a hand to her mouth to stifle laughter. When they were out of sight and hearing of her uncle, she spoke.

'Ma'moiselle, how brave you were, and did you see his face when you said to leave him to his frogs and his mud?'

'Well, I should think he's first cousin to a frog, wouldn't you, Eloise? Except, perhaps, that's unkind to frogs, for I'm sure frogs aren't nearly so ugly and have far better manners.'

Eloise burst out laughing.

'Ma'moiselle, oh, I do like English people, and am proud my father was English. I will find his grave one day, I'm sure, and then I will tell him so.'

* * *

248

That night, restless in her bed, Polly made her decision. She did not say so to Eloise when she left two days later. She said nothing at all about the fact that she was going to tell Boots he had left a flower in France.

'Ma'moiselle, oh, I'm so sorry you are leaving. Uncle Jacques and Aunt Marie are also sad. It's been so much pleasure, and you have put up so well with all my talk and questions. Perhaps you will visit us again one day?'

'I think we shall see each other again, Eloise. Yes, I do think so, and perhaps before very long.'

'Ma'moiselle Polly, you will always be welcome,' said Jacques.

'Always,' said Eloise. Polly kissed her, then Jacques, and slipped into her car. They waved to her from the doorway of the *estaminet* as she drove off. '*Au'voir, ma'moiselle, au'voir!*' called Eloise.

And Polly called back, in English, wartime variety.

'Cheeri-oh, old things, toodle-oo!'

'Oh, she is so English, isn't she, Uncle Jacques?'

'They were all like that, Eloise, when they were comrades of France. Cheeri-oh and gawd blimey, you know.'

'Excuse me?' said Eloise, watching Polly's car turning and receiving a last wave from her.

'Yes, cheeri-oh and gawd blimey,' smiled Jacques.

'What does it mean?'

'It means the English Tommies are about.'

'I'm half-English, Uncle Jacques.'

'Yes, we've agreed on that many times, my chicken.'

'And I'm about.'

'So?'

'Cheeri-oh and gawd blimey, Uncle Jacques.'

Chapter Six

'Well, dear old thing, what d'you say, then?' said Polly. She was sitting on the garden terrace with her father at their Dulwich home. Below them, the lawn, perfectly patterned by the gardener's mower, stretched green and smooth. 'I have to tell him, don't I?'

'Have you asked yourself what Boots himself would want?' said General Sir Henry Simms, spruce and iron-grey.

'Yes, a dozen times, until my own answer was positive. Boots would want to know, and he would want his child. You know what he's like about young people. And I have a feeling, a very sure feeling, that Eloise would want him to want her.'

'And Emily?'

'Emily's not important,' said Polly brusquely.

'Emily is very important,' said Sir Henry.

'Emily is in my way, and always has been,' said Polly, and took a long swallow of her cool gin and tonic. 'Oh, look here, old thing, it's Boots's decision and no-one else's.'

'But his decision could affect Emily seriously. Suddenly, she'll find herself a stepmother, suddenly she'll find that before Boots married her he'd loved another woman. Incidentally, why didn't he return to France when the war was over, why didn't he contact the Frenchwoman again?'

'You're forgetting something, aren't you, old scout?' said Polly.

'Yes, of course, so I am,' said Sir Henry. 'He was sightless for four years.'

'He didn't know the woman, Cecile Lacoste, had had his child. If he had, that would have made things difficult for him. As it was, I imagine he made the very reasonable decision that a blind man had absolutely nothing to offer a woman. And in any case, when the war ended he was already married to Emily.'

'Who took him on without knowing he would recover his sight, Polly.'

'My God, don't you think I would?' said Polly.

'Polly, all these years—'

'I know,' said Polly, 'I know. I should have found someone else. Well, I haven't been able to do that, have I? I'm an idiot, aren't I?'

'Not to me, Polly,' said Sir Henry. 'You've stuck to your guns, by George.'

'Some guns,' said Polly, 'they haven't fired a single shot, old love. The target's always been out of range. My God, Emily's still got him, and Cecile Lacoste had him, and how has that left me? Deprived.'

'Boots cares for you, Polly, damned if he doesn't.'

'That's the swine of it,' said Polly. 'Why the devil didn't he do to me what he did to Cecile Lacoste when we were both in Albert at that time? Ye gods, old sport, we were almost within touching distance. Now I have to tell him what happened when he placed himself within definite touching distance of Cecile Lacoste.'

'And what will he say, I wonder?' mused Sir Henry.

'Oh, he'll say something like "Is that a fact, Polly old girl?" And I daresay he'll then ask who's going to tell Emily while he catches the boat train to France. If I know him, it'll be something like that, but of course it won't represent what he feels. He's got this devilish ability never to give anything away. If I ever stood on Putney Bridge and threatened to jump into the river unless he became my lover, I think he'd say, hold on a tick, Polly, while I take my shoes off, and then I'll jump in with you, it's a nice day for a swim.'

'I doubt if he'll react quite like that when you tell him he has a daughter in France,' said Sir Henry.

'Perhaps not,' said Polly, 'but I'm suffering all the sarcastic prejudices of a woman livid with jealousy, so I have to speak like one, don't I?'

'Understood, Polly. But you and Boots share a very special friendship. Don't tear it up. When will you speak to him?'

'Tomorrow afternoon,' said Polly. 'Emily always goes shopping on Saturday afternoons, and I need to speak to Boots alone.'

The family had been back a week from Salcombe, and, after Saturday lunch, Emily and Rosie departed for the Streatham shops. Tim went out to play cricket for his school team, Mr Finch took a walk to the Herne Hill hardware shop, and Boots began to mow the lawn.

Chinese Lady answered the doorbell.

'Oh, it's you, Miss Simms,' she said. 'My, don't you look nice and summery?'

Polly, in a cool white linen dress and a light brimmed hat that circled her head, smiled and said, 'Hello, Mrs Finch, did you all enjoy Salcombe?'

'Come in, come in,' said Chinese Lady, always well aware that Emily considered Sir Henry Simms's daughter a threat. She herself considered the threat could be yoked by maintaining close ties with Polly, who had indeed become a long-standing friend of the family. Closing the door as the visitor stepped in, Chinese Lady said, 'Well, I must say Salcombe was nice. I used to like Margate and still do, but a change is good for all of us, I always say. But that Boots and the sailin' boat he hired, well, you never saw such a hullabaloo day after day with all the young ones, and that son of mine in the middle of it with me husband, and even takin' his shirt off at times, and of course he wasn't wearin' any vest. Em'ly spoke very strict to him once about the way he was showin' himself off, but you know what Boots is – it's like talking to a puff of air. Oh, I forgot to ask what you've called for and if I can 'elp.'

'Is Boots at home, Mrs Finch?' asked Polly. She and Boots's mother had a strangely compatible relationship. Chinese Lady, always very admiring of Polly's war record, couldn't help liking her. And Polly, who saw Chinese Lady almost as a caricature of a cockney Victorian, nevertheless held her in almost affectionate respect. And why not? Polly had no social prejudices, and she recognized without reservation that Boots's remarkable mother had brought up three sons and a daughter in a way that had made them assets to the world.

'Boots is in the garden,' said Chinese Lady, 'he's mowin' the grass. Oh, lor', if he's got his shirt off—'

'I'm very broadminded, Mrs Finch, and I shan't run for cover,' smiled Polly.

'Well, I suppose it could be a bit hot out there, but all the same it's not what I like, men takin' their shirts off in public. Of course, a garden's more private, but there's still proper ways to behave. I'm sure you wouldn't ever do what you know wouldn't be proper.'

'I could be trusted not to take any of my clothes off in public, Mrs Finch,' said Polly, who knew, of course, that that wasn't what Boots's mother meant.

'My, the very idea, I'm sure you wouldn't,' said Chinese Lady. 'You're a born lady, Miss Simms, and you always behave like one. You can go through.'

'Thanks,' said Polly, 'I do have something I need to talk about with Boots.'

'I'm sure,' said Chinese Lady, who could keep an eye on things through her kitchen window if she felt she needed to.

Boots, running the mower over the lawn, had indeed taken his shirt off. The August afternoon was very hot. Polly, emerging from the kitchen on to the flagstones, saw him in the golden light in just a pair of old brown slacks and shoes. His dark brown hair, thick at the temples, needed a brush. His bare chest was brown from the Devon sun and sea air, his long legs executing a kind of lazy amble behind the mower. Polly winced. There he was, a man smug with self-satisfaction, no doubt. Smug, though? No, that was her sour grapes surfacing. No-one could ever call him that. But he did at least always have the air of a man who never allowed problems to disturb him. They might rack other people, but not him. Well, perhaps for once he would be racked.

'Boots?'

He stopped pushing the hand-mower and turned.

'Hello, Polly old girl, where did you spring from?'

Ye gods, the casualness of him.

'From a French cowslip,' she said.

'French?' said Boots, picking his shirt off a garden chair on his way over to her. Slipping it on, he said, 'Have they got cowslips in France, then? I can't remember seeing any.'

He stood before her, a half-smile on his face, his eyes trying to read hers. He was very brown. So was she. They had both been in the sun.

'You're a devil, aren't you?' she said.

'Well, I suppose there's always something wrong with most of us,' he said.

'Well, how about doing wrong for a whole weekend, a whole year?' said Polly, her piquant looks favouring her thirty-eight years. 'Say in a country cottage?'

'Happy thought, Polly. Shall we sit down? Then you can let me know why you're here.'

'You're not going to like it,' said Polly.

'Why, are you going off to Africa again?'

'How can I?'

'Can't you?'

'No, I damn well can't. It's too bloody boring.'

'Who's been upsetting you?' asked Boots.

'You have. You specialize in that.'

'How have I managed it this time? I haven't seen you for nearly a month.'

'I'll tell you. Yes, we'd better sit down.'

'Would you like a drink, Polly?'

'Not yet,' said Polly, 'but I think you'd better help yourself to a large whisky, I think you'll need it.'

'I'll make do without it,' said Boots, as they sat down at the garden table. 'In any case, I fancy my mother will produce a pot of tea in ten minutes.'

Tea. Cecile Lacoste had watched him make it in her parents' farmhouse kitchen.

'Listen very carefully, Sergeant Robert Adams,' said Polly, and began to recount the events of her recent weeks in France. In painful control of herself she told him how she had attended the funeral of an old friend in Amiens, and that afterwards she had given in to a need to visit the silent places that had once known the hideous clamour of the war.

She explained how she had arrived at Trones Wood. Boots, listening with interest, but with a slight frown, searched her face. 'Don't say anything, not yet,' she said, and went on to describe what Trones Wood was like now, and how it had affected her. Boots shook his head. Polly went on, explaining quite clearly and in fine detail how she had finally arrived at an *estaminet* in Albert run by Jacques Duval. During the war, she said, his daughter Helene helped him. Now, she said, a niece of his worked and lived there. Her name was Eloise, and she was the daughter of a Frenchwoman who had had a mad, reckless and brief love affair with an English soldier.

'Not uncommon, Polly,' said Boots, but his eyes were very searching now. He knew she was not recounting all this merely to pass the time.

'No, not at all uncommon,' said Polly. The girl's mother had died a year ago, she said, and her father had died on the Somme according to original casualty reports. Eloise had tried many times to find his grave in one of the Somme cemeteries, but without success. She wished to find it, to visit it and take flowers, because her mother had loved him very much.

'Polly, what are you up to?' asked Boots.

'I speak with feeling,' said Polly. 'That English soldier never made love to me, never gave me the chance to have his child, never even troubled to meet me.'

'Who the hell are you talking about?' asked Boots.

'Are you sure you can make do without a whisky?' asked Polly.

'Get on with it,' said Boots.

'Eloise showed me a framed snapshot of the man, one her mother had taken before he left for the Somme.'

'Polly?'

'My God,' said Polly, 'how could you do it to me, make love to that Frenchwoman when I was close by, in the town itself, waiting for you, waiting to meet you?'

Boots was silent, remembering. When had he last thought of Cecile Lacoste, the young French widow? A month ago. After he had dreamt of the Somme for the first time for many years. An engaging, teasing and attractive young woman, eager to have him make love to her. As Polly had said, it wasn't an uncommon thing, not in that world of the dead and the dying.

'Polly, are you telling me the girl Eloise is my daughter?'

'What else? Boots, oh, the hell of it, sitting there, listening to Eloise, with that snapshot of you in front of me.'

'Polly, you should long ago have found someone suitable.'

'I don't want someone suitable. Suitable? Ye gods, how boring. I've settled for friendship, haven't I? And I'm not going to lose that. Why aren't you up on your feet, pacing about and rending your garments? You've got a daughter, a flower of France, who thinks you're dead, and you've got a wife and a son, and Rosie too, and they've all got to know about Eloise, because you can't keep her out of your life now, can you? Do you still not need a whisky?'

'No,' said Boots.

'Well, d'you want to see what your natural daughter looks like?'

'Yes, Polly, I do.'

Polly looked at him and saw the dark greyness of his eyes, and the memories there, and the ghosts of the Somme, the ghosts that were hers too. During the fourteen years she had known him, he had never in her presence let those ghosts surface. He had always kept them hidden, always told her it did no good to live in the past. She knew now that, like herself, and so many other men and women of France and Flanders, he could not forget all that the war had meant, the mud, the slaughter, the guns, the comrades, and particularly, perhaps, those who had been outstanding: men like his company commander, Major Harris.

'Boots darling, I'm sorry. Oh, I'm such a bitch, aren't I?' She put her hand over his and pressed. 'I'm so sorry, but I was shattered and so damned jealous. Did you love her, the Frenchwoman?'

'I made love to her, yes,' said Boots, still remembering, 'but I don't think I was madly in love with her. Had I been, I should have thought about her a lot more than I did, and written to her. As it was, I came out of the Somme not much good to any woman. Emily, fortunately, didn't see it like that. As for the town of Albert, how was I to know you were there when I hadn't even met you?'

'You should have known, you should have had a feeling, you should – oh, it's all perverse ifs and buts, isn't it? There, the worst is over, dearly beloved, for you know now, and I shall show you a snapshot of your charming young daughter.'

From her handbag Polly extracted the snapshot, given to her by Eloise because they'd become such good friends. She passed it to Boots, and he examined it, seeing a girl with the same engaging prettiness as her mother, but fair where her mother was Latin-dark. A smile peeped at him.

'I see,' he said, and she thought that a typical understatement of what his real feelings must be.

'You can be proud, darling, she's a lovely girl, and fun,' said Polly.

'Is that a fact, Polly? Well, someone's going to have to tell the family, aren't they, and I'm going to have to slip off to France, aren't I?'

Polly stared at him, then laughed.

'Boots, oh, you old darling, what woman would want anyone else if she could have you? I knew you'd say something like that.'

The kitchen door opened and Chinese Lady appeared.

'I'm just makin' a nice pot of tea,' she said, 'would you both like a cup?'

'Very much, Mrs Finch,' said Polly, 'and I know Boots would.'

'Would he? Well, yes, he does like his tea. I'll be pourin' in a bit and I'll bring it out. And I must say

I'm pleased you haven't taken your shirt off, Boots, seein' we've got Miss Simms visitin'. Well, I'll be out again in a minute with the tea, then I'll be doin' me Saturday bakin'.'

Chinese Lady, holding back her curiosity, disappeared and the kitchen door closed.

'Your mother's always herself,' said Polly. 'Boots, when will you go to France?'

'I've already thought about that,' said Boots. 'I'll catch a car ferry on Tuesday and head straight for Albert.'

'Then I shall go on Monday,' said Polly.

'Will you?'

'Yes, I must. Eloise must be told first. You can't simply land on her doorstep, darling. She must be given time to prepare herself for your arrival. After all, it's going to be very emotional for her, and she'll need all of twenty-four hours to think about what it will mean. You'll want to bring her home with you, you'll want her as part of your family and to have her adjust to English life. I thought myself that that was what she'd want too, but since returning, I've had second thoughts. Boots, you have to face the possibility that while I know she'll be very happy to see you, she may feel she'd rather stay in France with her Uncle Jacques and his wife. She has very deep feelings about you, because of her mother, but you'll actually be a stranger to her. So I must go in advance of you and talk to her again. Perhaps if I can catch a ferry tomorrow, I'll go then and not wait until Monday.'

'Do that, Polly, and thank you.'

'Darling, I'd do anything for you, don't you know that? Except tell your family. That's your cross.'

Chinese Lady brought the tea out then.

Chapter Seven

Mr Finch came back from his little excursion, and, later, Emily and Rosie returned from their shopping expedition. Boots then asked everyone to gather around the garden table, as he had something to tell them. Only Tim was absent. He rarely got back from his afternoon cricket match before six-thirty. Gathered together, then, by what Emily said was the summons of their lord and master, she and Chinese Lady, as well as Mr Finch and Rosie, all gazed at Boots in expectation. Rosie's little smile was showing. Whatever Boots was going to say, she was sure it would be either entertaining or eye-opening.

'What's this about?' asked Chinese Lady.

'The family,' said Boots. He was over his ghosts. He never let them linger. They were best kept in limbo. He was purely concerned with Eloise. 'We're one short,' he said.

'Yes, Tim's not here,' said Mr Finch, 'but I thought you mentioned you'd speak to him by himself.'

'I think I should, he's only young,' said Boots.

'Then why did you say we're one short, Daddy?' asked Rosie, eyeing her father with a sudden certain feeling that something extraordinary was going to be expounded. She could read Boots better than anyone except perhaps Mr Finch.

'We may stay one short, Rosie. It depends on very personal feelings. Or we may have an addition. You'll have to forgive me, all of you, if what I tell you isn't easily acceptable, and I'd rather tell you all together than one at a time.'

'All right, lovey, get on with it,' said Emily, 'I just hope you're not talkin' about that woman with the posh yacht who kept bumpin' into you at Salcombe. She's got wrinkles.'

'It's a little more personal than that, Em,' said Boots, and told them about his time on the farm before the battle of the Somme and his meeting with a young French widow called Cecile Lacoste. Chinese Lady began to look darkly suspicious. Emily sat up. Mr Finch's eyes flickered. Rosie gazed in a kind of mesmerized fascination at Boots, who could do no wrong in her eyes. He spoke quite candidly about his feelings for this young French woman, feelings affectionate but short of actually being in love with her. Even so, it led to him making love to her.

'I knew it,' said Chinese Lady, 'I knew goin' to France wouldn't do you any good. I mentioned a hundred times that Frenchwomen don't 'ave any respectability, I said to all our neighbours that they'd lead our soldiers on.'

'It wasn't quite like that, old lady,' said Boots. This particular Frenchwoman, he said, spoke of waiting for him, of waiting for him to come back to her after the war ended. But how could he? He hadn't committed himself, he hadn't proposed to her, and he was blind, anyway. There was no point in going back to her. And the fact was, of course, that Emily was the only one he needed, and Emily came up trumps.

'Well, you said that very nice, Boots,' said Chinese Lady.

'Yes, you did, love, and just in time,' said Emily, who wasn't so simple as to have ever believed nothing happened to the soldiers of the Great War outside of either sitting in the trenches or going over the top of them. Boots had always been attractive to women, even as a very young man. There'd been times when Emily thought Elsie Chivers wouldn't have minded having him to herself in her parlour, even if she was years older than him. Poor Elsie. She was now in one of those places where understanding men and women in white coats looked after people who weren't quite right in the head. She and Boots sometimes went to see her. It all flashed through Emily's mind as she accepted what had happened in France eighteen years ago, that Boots had had a very brief love affair with a young French war widow. 'But wait a minute,' she said, 'you're not tryin' to tell us this Cecile or whatever is goin' to come and join us, are you? I'm not 'avin' that.'

'Nor over my dead body, either,' said Chinese Lady.

'It's not that, Nana, it's something else, something much more dramatic,' said Rosie.

'Rosie, how d'you know that?' asked Emily.

'You can tell from the look of Daddy,' said Rosie.

'That son of mine has always got a look I don't trust,' said Chinese Lady. 'I might of guessed he'd do things he knew I wouldn't approve of while he was in France and out of my sight. I hope there's not worse to come.'

Mr Finch smiled. He thought he knew what might be coming, and it wouldn't, in his opinion, be of a worse nature. And it did come, the revelation that Boots had fathered a daughter called Eloise. This was followed by the information that the mother had died last year. With Chinese Lady sitting straight up, her bosom stiff, Emily emotional, and Rosie wide-eyed but already forgiving, Mr Finch put a question in.

'How did you get to know this, Boots?'

'I'll come to that later,' said Boots.

'I don't know I want to listen,' said Chinese Lady, 'I don't know I haven't already heard as much as I want to.'

'Go on, Boots,' said Emily quietly.

Boots informed them that Eloise was presently living with an uncle and aunt who ran a wine bar in Albert, and that, because of misinformation about Somme casualties, she thought her father was dead. Accordingly, Boots was going to France to see her and to talk to her.

'Well,' breathed Chinese Lady, 'it's come to something, a son of mine responsible for a child born out of wedlock. Boots, I never should of let you go off to France behind my back. Now look what's happened, it's a disgrace to the whole fam'ly, a girl without a mother and never havin' had a father.'

Emily looked at her husband. He smiled, asking for her understanding, asking for her help, asking for her to accept Eloise.

Lord above, she thought, I'm mother to Tim, adoptive mother to Rosie, and stepmother to a French girl. I never heard of any other woman being put into that kind of position in all my life. I don't know it wouldn't be in order to have a fainting fit or hysterics. Blow that, I hate fainting as much as hysterics.

She caught Rosie's glance. Rosie mutely appealed for family togetherness. Rosie, of course, would always want everyone to stand with Boots.

'Emily?' he said.

She shook her head at him, the late afternoon sun putting dark fire into her auburn hair.

'Boots, you shockin' man,' she said, 'doin' that with a Frenchwoman behind all our backs and gettin' her in the fam'ly way as well. I don't know I'd 'ave married you if I'd found out.'

'Mum love, of course you would,' said Rosie. 'We've all got to forgive what our soldiers did when they were out of the trenches, we've all got to stay loving them, even the ones who lose their jobs because they still get drunk and pick fights. Daddy, we all understand. You might be a bit of a shocker, but you're ours and we'd never swap you for anyone else.'

'I suggest there's really very little to forgive,' said

268

Mr Finch, whose liking and admiration for Boots never wavered.

'I don't know,' said Chinese Lady, shaking her head, 'it's not what I ever brought him up to be, I've always been against any of my sons goin' round shockin' people and their own fam'ly too.'

'I'm not actu'lly shocked, Mum,' said Emily, 'I'm just flabbergasted that my husband had got the devil in him while he was still a young man. No wonder when we got married he—' Emily stopped before she made the blushing mistake of informing the family that, even though he was blind, Boots knew exactly what to do when their wedding night began. 'Rosie, are you laughin'?'

'Goodness, I should say not,' said Rosie, 'I'm flabbergasted too. Heavens, what a real shocker. But what a silver lining, Mum. Well, I mean, who's going to complain about Daddy providing Tim and me with a sister? I'd much rather have a sister than the revolution my bookshop friend is so keen on.'

'I'm prepared for slings and arrows,' said Boots.

'Daddy, don't be like that, you silly,' said Rosie, 'we all still love you.' She had felt from the beginning that Boots was going to deliver extraordinary news.

'This is Eloise,' he said, and handed the snapshot to Emily to look at and to pass round. Heads craned.

'Oh, my shakin' knees,' said Emily, torn between forgiveness and a painful feeling that the girl should have come from her, not from some other woman.

'I can't hardly believe this. Oh, she's pretty, isn't she? Boots, she's yours all right.'

'She's ours, Emily, if she'll let us have her. She's the family's.'

Chinese Lady and Rosie studied the snapshot together, Rosie's hair brushing her grandmother's cheek.

'Daddy, she's lovely,' said Rosie.

'Well, much as I'm shocked out of my being,' said Chinese Lady, 'you'll have to bring her home, Boots.'

'You're sure, old lady?' said Boots.

'She's an Adams,' said Chinese Lady with a firmness that discouraged any attempt to follow revelation with argument, never mind if Boots had been disgraceful.

'Yes, you're the father, Boots old chap,' said Mr Finch, taking his turn to examine the print. 'When do you go to France to see her?'

'Tuesday,' said Boots.

'Wait a bit,' said Emily, 'you haven't come yet to tellin' us how you got to know about the girl.'

Chinese Lady glanced at her son. She was sure she knew then why Polly Simms had called to see him. But she kept her peace. It was up to Boots.

'Polly dropped in earlier this afternoon,' said Boots. 'She's just got back from France.' He explained in detail. Oh, blow that, thought Emily, that woman's never going to get out of Boots's life, especially now she's found his natural daughter.

'Well,' said Chinese Lady, 'I must say Miss

Simms did the right thing in accidentally finding out for us that Boots has got a daughter in France. Mind, I'm not saying I like her bein' born out of wedlock, but it can't be helped, not now.'

'It happened too many years ago for us not to accept it, Maisie,' said Mr Finch, 'and it happened in the kind of circumstances we can only guess at. Further, in this family, as Boots himself would say, there's always room for one more. And Polly, I think, deserves a commendation.'

'Yes, eureka for Aunt Polly,' said Rosie.

'Blow your Aunt Polly,' said Emily, but under her breath and only to herself.

'She's going back to France tomorrow or Monday,' said Boots, 'to talk to Eloise before I get there myself. I think that's right, I think Eloise should be told before I arrive.'

'Yes, and I think Miss Simms did right, not tellin' the girl about Boots until she'd spoken to him first,' said Chinese Lady.

'Bear in mind that we can't be certain Eloise will leave France,' said Boots.

'I'm going to come with you,' said Emily. If that Polly was going to be there, waiting for Boots, and in a French town of all places, something had got to be done to see Boots didn't do more disgracing of the family. He had acquired a joint passport a few years ago, having in mind an overseas holiday for the family sometime, and so Tim and Rosie also had theirs. 'Oh, no, I can't, I've got to be with my mum when she goes into hospital on Tuesday.' Her aged and very stout mother was to have an operation, and she wasn't taking too kindly to the idea. She wouldn't move one step out of her home unless Emily was with her.

'Rosie,' said Boots, 'would you like to come instead of your mother?'

'Daddy, oh, would I!' said Rosie. Despite being a very promising undergraduate of Somerville, with a host of new friends who had very little in common with the cockney elements of Chinese Lady's extensive family, Rosie showed delight. Heavens, a Channel ferry and a journey through France to meet the girl Eloise? 'Daddy, utter bliss.'

'Yes, you go, Rosie,' said Emily, 'you can keep an eye on your dad. We don't want him disgracin' us again in France.'

'Boots, might I suggest no attempt at persuasion, no pressure?' said Mr Finch.

'There'll be none,' said Boots, 'I'll talk to her and see how she reacts. She may not like me, and she may not like the fact that I didn't go back to her mother.'

'Boots, of course she'll like you,' said Emily.

'And I think by the time you get there, Polly will have fully explained why you didn't go back,' said Mr Finch.

'Daddy, we'll all understand if she doesn't want to leave her uncle and aunt, if she doesn't want to come to England,' said Rosie. 'It won't be anything to do with not liking you or being angry with you, only to do with feeling her aunt and uncle are her family. You'll understand too, won't you?'

'Yes, of course, poppet,' said Boots, 'but I must

go and I must talk to her. Does everyone understand that?'

'Yes, of course we do, lovey,' said Emily, putting
aside all feelings except those relating to what was
expected of her as his wife. 'Tell her she's got a
second mother waitin' for her.'

'And aunts and uncles and cousins,' said Chinese
Lady. 'Lord, my goodness, what's your sister Lizzy
goin' to say, Boots?'

Boots smiled. It had been delivered, the astonishing news, it was off his chest. And his family had
not stoned him.

'I'll come to that later,' he said.

'I think I need a drink,' said Mr Finch.

'I'll be startin' supper in a few minutes,' said
Chinese Lady. The discussion was over, everyone
had had their say, and it had all boiled down to one
fact as far as she was concerned. Despite Boots
having disgraced himself, and the family, the
motherless girl was an Adams. Her place was here.
That accepted, Chinese Lady did not think the
usual preparations for supper need be affected.

'I'd still like a drink,' said Mr Finch.

'I need a pot of strong tea,' said Emily.

'I think I'll have a whisky,' said Boots.

'Well, you get the drinks, Edwin,' said Chinese
Lady, rising, 'and I'll make the pot of tea before I
start the supper.'

'That's fair,' said Mr Finch, getting up. Rosie
followed him into the house.

'Grandpa?' she said, as he opened the door of the
drinks cabinet.

'Yes, Rosie?'

'What d'you think?'

'About this girl?'

'Yes.'

Mr Finch smiled.

'We've an addition to the family, Rosie,' he said.

'You wouldn't say Daddy's chickens have come home to roost?' said Rosie.

'I'd be the last one to say so.'

'It's really quite exciting,' said Rosie.

'It's your mother's feelings that count the most, Rosie.'

'Yes, I know,' said Rosie, 'but she's come up trumps, Grandpa, and you're for Daddy, aren't you?'

'Rosie, my dear girl, I'll always stand with your father.'

'Well, that makes two of us,' said Rosie.

Chapter Eight

Chinese Lady and Emily both said all the family had got to be told, so Boots began by phoning Lizzy and giving her an outline of the situation.

'What?' gasped Lizzy over the line. 'What did you say?'

'I thought I'd let you know,' said Boots, 'and I'll have to talk to Sammy and Tommy as well.'

'Wait a minute, I've not taken it in yet,' fumed Lizzy. 'Have I actu'lly been listening to you tellin' me you fathered a daughter before you got blinded on the Somme?'

'Afraid so, Lizzy love, although I didn't know it at the time.'

'Don't call me love, you – you – oh, my own brother doin' this to his fam'ly, a fam'ly that gave him a good education and all. It wasn't so that you could go off and take advantage of some poor French lady and leave her expectin'. You ought to be downright ashamed.'

'Well, I am, of course, Lizzy, and I'm going to try to redeem myself in my penitence.'

'Stop usin' educated words,' said Lizzy, who felt she was suffering undeserved upsets, what with this news and the fact that Annabelle had obviously fallen in love with Nick Harrison, a young man whose father had spent time in prison. Lizzy had had to come to terms with that, and could only hope Nick hadn't inherited any of his father's taking ways. 'Tell me what Chinese Lady said. I bet she went for you, didn't she?'

'Not really, apart from calling me a disgrace to the family and telling me she hadn't brought me up to be a shocker.'

'You're a shocker all right. Oh, that poor girl, her mother dead and thinking her father dead. What're you goin' to do about it?'

'Try to redeem myself, as I said. I'm going to see if I can bring her home with me.'

'Well, thank goodness for that,' said Lizzy. 'You've got to bring her, if she's really yours. You're sure she is?'

'Yes, I'm sure, Lizzy. Everything she said to Polly fits, and so does the snapshot of me.'

'Well, then, you've got to make it up to the girl by bein' a good and lovin' dad to her. D'you hear me, Boots?'

'Yes, Lizzy, I hear you.'

'And don't you ever do anything like that again.'

'No, Lizzy.'

'Well, you're old enough now to know how to behave yourself, I hope.'

'I hope so too, Lizzy.'

'I don't know how I'm goin' to tell Ned and the children.'

'Shall I come over and talk to them?'

'Not likely,' said Lizzy, 'I don't want them dyin'

of shame in front of my eyes at hearin' you tell them what you've just told me. Somehow I'll have to make it sound not so bad. What did Em'ly say?'

'That she couldn't hardly believe it.'

'Oh, I'd better come and see her as soon as I can. Poor Em'ly, has she taken to her bed?'

'Not yet. She'll wait till bedtime.'

'I mean, is she ill with shock?'

'No, she's bearing up, Lizzy.'

'Well, I'll still come round and help her to bear up. What about Rosie?'

'She's tickled.'

'She's what?'

'Well, she's singing "Any Old Iron" at the moment. I can hear her.'

'Boots, if you're tryin' to make out there's something comical about all this, I don't think much of it. Rosie singing "Any Old Iron"? I don't believe you.'

'Sorry, Lizzy old girl, but Rosie's tickled about suddenly finding she has a sister, and a French one at that. Well, half-French. She's coming with me to France, and we're leaving on Tuesday.'

'Well, the sooner the better, I suppose,' said Lizzy, 'we don't want that poor girl to be without a mother and father for the rest of her life.'

'She might not come, of course.'

'Might not come home with you?'

'She might not, Lizzy, she might prefer to stay living with her aunt and uncle.'

'Well, me and Ned are her aunt and uncle, and so are Vi and Tommy, and Susie and Sammy. She

277

belongs with us. You've got to bring her home, specially as you're her father.'

'No, I shan't pressurize her, Lizzy. It's got to be what she wants.'

Lizzy was quiet for a moment. Then she said, 'Yes, I suppose so. Well, as she's yours, let's hope she comes. But what about all your friends and neighbours and everyone, are you goin' to tell them you've adopted her, like you did with Rosie?'

'No, I don't think so, Lizzy, I don't think she'd like that.'

'No, perhaps not,' said Lizzy. 'I suppose we'll all get over the shock by Christmas. What was she like, by the way?'

'The girl's mother?'

'Yes.'

'Very French,' said Boots.

'H'm, no wonder,' said Lizzy. 'Oh, well, never mind, lovey, I understand. I know what it was like over there from what I've been able to drag out of Ned. You're forgiven. I couldn't go to church without forgivin' you.'

'Well, bless you, Lizzy.'

'Which reminds me, what's the girl's religion?'

'Same as her mother's was, I imagine,' said Boots.

'Don't be airy-fairy,' said Lizzy, 'religion's important, you ought to know that. Have you thought she's probably Roman Catholic and we're all Church of England?'

'With luck, she may be a Huguenot,' said Boots.

'A what?'

278

'You did history at school, Lizzy.'

'I don't remember doin' you-go-knows.'

'They belong to a French reformed religion, and they're closer to Protestants than Catholics.'

'Well, aren't you the clever one?' said Lizzy. 'What a sauce you've got, showin' off your education at a time like this. Didn't you ask that poor French widow what her religion was before you went and made love to her?'

'Alas, Lizzy, I—'

'Alas? Alas? Stop talkin' like some archbishop. Boots, you get worse as you get older. All you 'ave to say is no, you didn't ask what her religion was. You don't have to say "alas" as if you've got the Bible in front of you. Just remember you've probably got a lot of work to do if the girl does come home with you. Well, I'm goin' to have to tell Ned now, and then he'll have to tell our children. Yes, and you've got to let Tommy and Sammy know.'

'Well, bless you, Lizzy, and thanks for being understanding.'

'Well, I don't see tellin' you off is much good,' said Lizzy. 'Now I'm goin' to give Ned the news.'

Ned, when given it, didn't blow a fuse. He actually smiled.

'It's not funny,' said Lizzy.

'And I don't suppose Boots thinks it is, either,' said Ned. 'On the other hand, nor will he think it a disaster. If I know him at all, he'll be shaking hands with himself.'

'Doing what?' said Lizzy.

'He's a family man,' said Ned, 'he'll be liking the idea of one more. I'll wager that one of the first things he'll do will be to teach the girl – what did you say her name was?'

'Eloise.'

'That's French all right,' said Ned, 'and one of the first things Boots'll do with her will be to teach her how to play garden cricket.'

'Ned Somers, d'you think this is all a joke?' asked Lizzy.

'Not a bit,' said Ned, 'but it's still a feather in Boots's cap.'

'I might 'ave known you'd be on his side,' said Lizzy, 'two old soldiers together, you are. What about Em'ly's feelings?'

'She'll come round,' said Ned. 'After all, it happened well before she was even engaged to Boots. She'll see that. Emily's got her share of sense.'

'Supposin' Eloise doesn't want to leave France, what about that?' asked Lizzy.

'Mm, that's a point,' said Ned.

'You'll have to tell your children the news as soon as they're all in,' said Lizzy.

'That's another point,' said Ned. 'I think we'd better tell 'em together. Annabelle won't need an explanation, but how'd you explain the sudden existence of a seventeen-year-old French cousin to youngsters like Bobby, Emma and Edward?'

'Don't ask me,' said Lizzy.

The subsequent reactions of her sons and daughters were all different when Ned told them in simple fashion that their Uncle Boots was the father of a

French girl, that the mother was dead, and that Uncle Boots hoped to bring her home to England. Annabelle said well, saucy old Uncle Boots, what a surprise and what a performance. Lizzy said it shouldn't be spoken of like that. Annabelle said well, credit where it's due, Mum, but you can still knock me down with a feather. Bobby asked how Uncle Boots had managed it, wasn't he in the trenches? Lizzy said he was having a rest behind the lines. Annabelle said you sure you mean rest, Mum? Don't ask those kind of questions, said Lizzy. Bobby asked was there a wedding? Ned said there hadn't been time. Well, it beats me, said Bobby. Still, as it was Uncle Boots, he said, I suppose it's all right. Emma said how was Uncle Boots supposed to have a French daughter when he was married to Aunt Emily? He wasn't at the time, said Ned. Oh, I don't suppose she minds, then, said Emma, but I think I'll have to talk to Uncle Boots about it to resolve my curiosity. You're showing off, said Bobby. Edward, a mere nine, simply stood about looking puzzled. I'm tickled, said Annabelle, I'm going to phone Rosie. Which she did, and they had a long chat about Boots and the French war widow and the girl called Eloise.

Consequent on this, Annabelle told her parents she didn't mind Uncle Boots having a bit of the devil in him, it sort of suited him.

'Now just look here, Annabelle,' said Lizzy, 'it's men with a bit of the devil in them that can make a lot of problems for themselves and their fam'lies.'

Annabelle, who knew her mum was taking the

opportunity to point her finger at Nick's father, said, 'Yes, I know, Mum, but nice families just make sure afterwards that a bit of the devil is kept in a pot with the lid on.'

'Well, listen to that,' said Lizzy. 'Did you hear what your daughter just came out with, Ned?'

'Yes, I think she means that all Emily has to do now is keep Boots under lock and key,' said Ned.

'There's other men besides Boots,' said Lizzy. 'Anyway, as far as Boots is concerned, it's too late.'

'Yes, I think the horse has bolted, don't you, Dad?' said Annabelle. 'But the problem's a kind of happy family surprise. Well, I think so.'

'I don't know that your Aunt Em'ly does, poor woman,' said Lizzy. 'I'm goin' round to see her now, she's probably ill with shock.'

Emily wasn't, however. She was already reconciled. Still, she and Lizzy had a lengthy gossip by themselves, and shared a pot of needful tea as well. Lizzy mentioned about Annabelle saying Boots had a bit of the devil in him, and that Annabelle had actually said it suited him.

'I expect it suited that French widow,' said Emily. 'But him at his age, he was only twenty.'

'Oh, the devil was hanging about in 'im when he was only sixteen,' said Lizzy.

'Oh, me sad past,' said Emily.

'What d'you mean, your sad past?' asked Lizzy.

'Well, if I'd been more like that French widow, instead of all skinny and aggravatin', Boots might 'ave tried a bit of his devil on me,' said Emily.

'What, before he joined the Army and you were only sixteen?' said Lizzy.

'Well, I had me dreams, didn't I?' said Emily.

'Em'ly, you shocker,' said Lizzy.

Boots also phoned Tommy, and Tommy's initial response was just like Lizzy's.

'What?' he said. 'What?'

'Yes, it's a fact, Tommy.'

'I'm fallin' about,' said Tommy.

'Well, mind your head,' said Boots.

'You old bugger,' said Tommy.

'Can't be helped,' said Boots.

'Has Em'ly chucked you out?'

'Not yet.'

'What's she said?'

'That she didn't know I was going to turn her into a stepmother. I didn't know myself until Polly delivered the news.'

'Was that all that Em'ly said?' asked Tommy.

'More or less,' said Boots.

'Well, good old Em'ly and lucky old you,' said Tommy. 'And I'll probably feel better meself by next week when me head stops 'urting and me ears stop ringing. Vi's goin' to faint, of course, and what your Aunt Victoria's goin' to say when she gets to know might make the vicar faint as well. She's against skeletons risin' up out of fam'ly cupboards. Still, this one is out now. What 'appens next?'

'Rosie and I are going over on Tuesday in the hope that Eloise will come and live with us, if not immediately, then in a month or so, perhaps.'

'Good on yer, mate,' said Tommy. 'You tell her there's a lot of open arms over here.'

'Thanks, Tommy. Now I'll ring Sammy.'

'Yes, you'd better,' said Tommy, 'it's his turn to be hit by a coal bucket. Still, knowin' Sammy, I daresay he won't be unconscious for long. And I'd better tell Vi and let 'er have her faintin' fit.'

Vi, however, apart from losing her breath for a minute or so, came nowhere near having a fainting fit when Tommy informed her what had happened after Boots had done a young French war widow wrong in 1916.

'I bet it was the other way about,' she said.

'Beg yer pardon?' said Tommy.

'Well, a French widow, I ask you,' said Vi. 'Mind, now that she's dead, I wouldn't want to miscall her.'

'Vi, you sure you don't feel faint?' said Tommy. 'I mean, d'you want to sit down for a bit?'

'What for?' asked Vi.

'Well, it's an all-round fam'ly shock, ain't it?' said Tommy.

'It's not goin' to make me faint,' said Vi. 'Bless me, our Boots, what a dark horse, and he couldn't 'ave been more than twenty at the time. Still, the war and all, we can't blame him. What's goin' to happen about the girl?'

'Boots and Rosie are goin' to France on Tuesday. Boots hopes to bring the girl 'ome.'

'Crikey,' said soft-eyed Vi, 'it'll be like bringing home a special Easter present for the fam'ly.'

'Easter's gone,' said Tommy.

'Well, Harvest Festival present, then,' said Vi. 'Did Boots mention if the news upset Em'ly a bit?'

'He did say she's not breakin' up the furniture.'

'Oh, that's good,' said Vi, 'I don't like ructions in the fam'ly.'

'Well, I'm not goin' to 'ave any with you, Vi,' said Tommy, 'I'm goin' to 'ave a glass of beer and you can 'ave a nice drop of port. Might as well call it a celebration weekend and not a wet one.'

'French one, I'd say,' smiled Vi.

'French what?' said Tommy, pouring the port.

'French weekend,' said Vi. 'Well, French widow and French daughter, and a 1916 French haystack, probably.'

'Well, you're a cool one, Vi, blowed if you ain't,' said Tommy. 'But good on yer, I'll treat yer.'

'What to, another drop of port?' asked Vi.

'No, a French weekend,' said Tommy.

'What, at my age?' said Vi, thirty-four.

'Yes, and mine as well,' said Tommy.

It was Sammy's turn next to receive a phone call.

'Are you listening, Sammy?' asked Boots, after an unusual silence from the other end of the line.

'I'm listening,' said Sammy, 'but I'm goin' to have a fit if I'm hearin' right. Boots, you sure you said what I think you just said?'

'Yes, I said it, Sammy, all of it.'

'Well, I'll grant there was a lot of it,' said Sammy. 'Mother O'Reilly, Chinese Lady never brought any of us up to enjoy the patterin' of tiny feet out of wedlock. It's against her principles, and what God ordered.'

Susie, having overheard, intervened.

'What's that, Sammy?' she said. 'What's that about out of wedlock? Who's out of wedlock, who's that you're talkin' to?'

'Hold on, Boots, me married wife is musclin' in. Susie, I'm havin' a private phone conversation with Boots, if you don't mind.'

'Well, I do mind,' said Susie, 'you can't have private phone conversations that leave me out, especially not with Boots.'

'Well, Susie, the conversation is also embarrassin', Boots havin' just said things that've made me hard of hearing.'

'Hard of hearing? Embarrassing? Sammy, give me the phone.'

'Now, Susie—'

'You go and sit down, Sammy, your hair's standin' on end. There, I'll talk to Boots. Boots?'

'Susie?'

'What've you been sayin' to my better half?'

'Well, it's like this, Susie,' said Boots, and put her in the picture. It took quite a few minutes, and Susie, after listening without interrupting, let him know her reactions were in his favour.

'Well, I think that's wild,' she said. 'Aren't you thrilled that you've got another daughter? Don't take any notice of Sammy talkin' about out of wedlock, he's old-fashioned. These things couldn't help happenin' over there in France. The girl, my goodness, just wait till she knows her English soldier dad is alive and wants to bring her home. Boots, you did sow a wild oat, didn't you? My dad told me once that lots of the Tommies did, but he didn't tell me you were one of them. What did Emily say?'

'She said I was a shocker for being one of them.'

'I bet the girl's mother didn't say so, I bet she liked havin' you as her soldier lover, and Emily won't hold it against you, not when it was all those years ago, will she?'

'No, we're still friends, Susie.'

'You'll have to excuse Sammy actin' as if he was fallin' apart. It's his old-fashioned prudery.'

'You Susie,' said Sammy, standing by, 'I'm listenin' to you, and me prudery's climbing up the wall.'

'Boots?' said Susie.

'I'm still here, Susie.'

'Don't worry about me and Sammy, we're on your side, and it's right you goin' to France to bring the girl home. Sammy says blow the expense.'

Sammy rolled his eyes.

'I'm hoping she'll come,' said Boots.

'Oh, yes, and thanks for telling us,' said Susie. 'And lots of good luck when you go to France. It's sensible that you're takin' Rosie with you. The girl – what did you say her name was?'

'Eloise.'

'Yes, well, she'll like meetin' a sister. I'm sure she'll want to join the fam'ly. Bless us all, isn't it excitin'? 'Bye for now, Boots.' Putting the phone back, Susie turned to Sammy. 'What were you embarrassed about, Sammy Adams?'

'Me embarrassment, Susie, was on your behalf, your mum havin' brought you up delicately and not lettin' you read the *News of the World* or show your knickers.'

'Do what?'

'Yes, when Boots was givin' me the horrendous news, I said to myself, Sammy Adams, I said, you've got to break this gently to Susie on account of sparin' her blushes. I don't want her jumpin' out of her knickers and dyin' of embarrassment, I said to myself. That would be something else to worry about, I said.'

'Sammy love, Boots has found a new daughter, which means we've got another niece, so don't let's have any old-fashioned stuff about it bein' unmentionable or blush-makin' to me or the fam'ly. Boots is head of the fam'ly, and we've all got to stand by him. So would you like to say something more appropriate than me jumpin' out of my knickers?'

'Yes, I'd like to, Susie.'

'Well, then?'

'Well, it's me fixed opinion, Susie, that there's always room for one more Adams.'

'That's my Sammy,' smiled Susie, and gave him a teasing little touch where she knew he would feel it most.

'Oh, me gawd, you Susie.'

'Don't mention it, Sammy love.'

Finally, when Boots spoke to Tim of Eloise, and Tim realized there was a sister in the offing, he asked if she'd been mislaid or something until now.

Boots said, no, she'd just been out of sight. Tim said, well, he didn't suppose it would interfere with his Saturday afternoon cricket, although according to what some of his friends had told him, it wasn't an advantage to have more than one sister, and he'd already got Rosie.

'Would you mind one more, if she didn't mind herself, Tim?' asked Boots.

'Well, Dad, I've heard about wartime babies,' said Tim, nearly thirteen, 'and if our family's got one, I daresay I could soldier on.'

'Good man,' said Boots.

'Bit of a palaver, though, Dad.'

'They happen all the time in most families,' said Boots.

'What do?' asked Tim.

'Palavers,' said Boots.

Chapter Nine

Chinese Lady invited everyone to Sunday tea. She had no intention of sitting in a corner with her knitting. Although she had accepted the disgrace herself, the whole family had to be faced, and anyone who wanted to say something had better say it and get it over with. Then she'd know where everyone stood in regard to the wartime goings-on of her eldest son. Mind you, she said to her husband when they were on their way to church on Sunday morning, I'm not having anyone saying too many hard things about Boots. After all, he only went to France to do his duty to his King and country. He's given me a lot of double-Dutch talk in his time, even when he was still at school, but he was never the sort to let the family down. It was mixing with fast Frenchwomen that did it, and all that parley-vooing.

'Parley-vooing, Maisie?' said Mr Finch, keeping his face straight. Living as he did with her and Boots's family had perfected the necessary art of a straight face.

'You know what I mean, Edwin.'

'I think you're worrying too much, Maisie,' said Mr Finch, lifting his hat to passing neighbours. He cut a distinguished figure. Chinese Lady was her usual upright self, never having lost the habit of presenting a firm and proud front to friends and neighbours, and to the One Above for that matter. 'I don't think anyone in the family is going to say hard things about him.'

'Still, I want to know how everyone stands,' said Chinese Lady, 'I don't want anyone always givin' the girl sly looks if Boots brings her back to live with us. Those that do won't be allowed past our front door in the future.'

'Maisie, can you really think of anyone in the family who'll turn their noses up at the girl?' said Mr Finch.

'Well, you never know,' said Chinese Lady.

If she had anyone in mind, thought Mr Finch, it would be Vi's mother, known as Aunt Victoria to everyone. He actually thought his resilient cockney wife was bringing the whole tribe together in a challenging way, as if she meant to establish an acceptance of Eloise from the beginning by making it known that that was her wish, which everyone had better bow down to, or else.

In the event, after expecting every grown-up to participate in an argy-bargy about an illegitimate Adams offspring, Chinese Lady could hardly believe what happened. Certainly, the young children were all spared by being despatched to the front room to amuse themselves harmlessly or to sit on each other in rowdy fashion, but the men and the older children, well! They just sidled off to play cricket on the lawn, Boots among them, as if an argy-bargy was the last thing they had on their minds, and even as if a family get-together wasn't necessary. Boots, Sammy, Tommy, Tim, Rosie, Ned, Annabelle, Bobby, Emma and Edward, they all simply took themselves on to the lawn, set up the stumps and played cricket.

Not only that, but Ned and Lizzy's four all fussed around Boots as if he were some sort of hero. On top of which, Uncle Tom, Vi's dad, slipped cagily away from Aunt Victoria's elbow to join the game. Finally, Edwin himself disappeared, and the next Chinese Lady saw of him was as one of the fielders at the far end of the lawn.

That left her with just Emily, Vi, Susie, Lizzy and Aunt Victoria, and Aunt Victoria was doing all the talking.

'Everyone knows I've always held Boots in fond regard, I've always felt no-one was more of a born gentleman than him, and I hope I'm not hurtin' anyone's feelings by saying this sort of behaviour's not what I ever expected of him. Goodness knows, as I said to Vi's dad last night, we've all thought a lot of him as his mother's eldest son and a credit to you, Maisie, and it's very saddening to know what he got up to in France.'

'Oh, I don't feel sad, Aunt Victoria,' said Susie.

'No, well, we've all got to put on a brave face,' said Aunt Victoria, 'and I'm makin' a start by not saying anything to my friends and neighbours.'

'Are you sure that's a brave face?' asked Emily.

'I'm doin' it for the family's sake,' said Aunt Victoria.

'Well, you needn't,' said Chinese Lady. 'Boots's French daughter is an Adams, and no-one has to keep that quiet. Mind you,' she added, frowning a little, 'it might be best, if she comes home with Boots, to do what we can to make her more English. Just in case she's a bit too Frenchified.'

'Frenchified?' said Vi.

'Fast,' said Lizzy.

'Well, yes, it's born in most of them,' said Chinese Lady, then realized she had given Aunt Victoria another carpet to beat.

'Yes, we've all heard stories that don't bear repeating,' said Aunt Victoria, who was actually addicted to repeating everything scandalous over a cup of tea with a neighbour, but only in a shocked and confiding whisper, of course.

'Oh, you can tell us, Aunt Victoria,' said Susie, 'we're all married women.'

'No, it wouldn't be right,' said Aunt Victoria, 'but I will say it's hard to believe that Boots of all people has a French daughter.'

'No, she's half-English,' said Emily, 'seeing that her father is all English. Come to that, she doesn't look a bit French in the snapshot.'

'Or fast,' said Vi.

'Lots of men have French daughters, especially Frenchmen,' said Susie. 'Anyway, we all mean to stand by Boots, don't we, Aunt Victoria? We'll all be very nice to her, won't we?'

'We've got to for Boots's sake,' said Vi.

'And the fam'ly's sake,' said Lizzy.

'Well,' said Aunt Victoria, 'I should think everyone knows I'm willing to do all I can to help Emily get over what must have been a painful shock.'

'I've already done that,' said Lizzy, 'over a cup of tea last night. And afterwards we had a drop of port to cheer us up.'

'That's funny,' said Vi, 'Tommy gave me some port last night.'

'Well,' said Aunt Victoria, 'while I've always been Christian-minded, I don't hold with anyone being born out of wedlock.'

'Tommy mentioned we ought to celebrate a sort of French weekend,' said Vi, 'so he gave me another port at the end of dinner today, and 'ad one himself.'

'Does that make a French weekend?' asked Susie.

'Well, not just the port,' said Vi.

'Vi, you're giggling,' said Lizzy.

'What, me at my age?' said Vi.

'I don't know anyone should be giggling,' said Aunt Victoria.

'Sammy's never given me a French weekend,' said Susie.

'I've had all kinds of weekends with Boots,' said Emily.

'I don't think we'd better hear about them, Em'ly,' said Chinese Lady.

'No, not likely,' said Emily, 'not in my state of 'ealth.'

'Emily,' said Aunt Victoria, 'I'm sure your Uncle

Tom and me understand the shame you must be feelin'.'

'I suppose it's not really the best time to talk about French weekends,' said Susie, 'but couldn't you bring yourself to tell us something about all kinds of weekends with Boots, Emily?'

'Em'ly, don't you say another word,' admonished Chinese Lady.

'But we're dyin' to hear,' said Vi.

'Vi, I'm surprised at you,' said Aunt Victoria.

'I'll write it all down in a book in me old age,' said Emily.

'Em'ly, now you're doing some giggling,' said Lizzy.

'It's me memories,' said Emily. 'Mum, d'you remember the time Boots came 'ome on leave for Lizzy's weddin' and gave us all presents he'd bought in France?'

'I 'ope you're not goin' to write down in a book what he gave you,' said Chinese Lady. 'I was never more embarrassed by that son of mine.'

'Come on, Emily, I won't be embarrassed,' said Susie.

'Would anyone like me to talk to Boots about his shameful behaviour?' asked Aunt Victoria.

'Come on, Emily, what did Boots bring you back from France?' asked Susie.

'Go on, tell, Em'ly,' said Lizzy, and laughed.

'French cami-knickers,' said Emily. 'Me, would you believe? Me that was all soppy, innocent and romantic, gettin' French cami-knickers from me fav'rite soldier.'

'Help,' said Susie.

'Yes, someone hold me up too,' said Vi.

'I didn't know what to do with me rapturous blushes,' said Emily.

'You're giggling again,' said Lizzy.

'So am I,' said Susie.

'That Boots of yours, Maisie,' said Aunt Victoria, 'it's an alarming surprise to me, him havin' that much of the devil in him when he was in France.'

'Yes, even my Annabelle said he's got a bit of the devil in him,' said Lizzy.

'It makes it hard for your family to hold its head up, Maisie,' said Aunt Victoria.

'It's not hard for me,' said Lizzy, 'he's always been a surprise packet.'

'I'm keepin' quiet about Sammy,' said Susie.

'Yes, and Tommy's earned medals,' said Vi.

'I don't think I want to hear any more about them sons of mine,' said Chinese Lady.

Susie, Lizzy, Emily and Vi laughed. Just the faintest smile touched Chinese Lady's firm lips. Her daughter and her daughters-in-law had all been telling her in their own way that the family wasn't in crisis as far as they were concerned. Boots was to be forgiven. They were closing ranks around him, around the family, and they'd close them around the girl Eloise if she came home with Boots. Even Aunt Victoria looked as if she accepted that what had been done couldn't help having been done at the time.

'Boots,' called Susie, 'could you spare a minute?'

Boots, keeping wicket, came over to the ladies of

the family, who were sitting around the table on the flagstoned area outside the kitchen. He looked a little wary.

'Well, Susie?' he said.

'We've got something to say to you,' said Susie.

'What?' said Boots.

'You're a surprise packet,' said Susie.

'Am I?' asked Boots. 'Who said?'

'Aunt Victoria,' said Lizzy.

'Oh,' said a flustered Aunt Victoria, 'I meant it nice, and we're all standin' by you, Boots.'

'Well, good on you, Aunt Victoria,' said Boots, and planted a warm kiss on her forehead.

Aunt Victoria went quite pink and sort of coughed.

'Crikey, Mum,' said Vi, 'now you're giggling.'

'It's this French weekend,' said Susie.

That brought shrieks of laughter, and it meant that by the time tea was being enjoyed in the garden, Chinese Lady knew no-one was going to fall out of line, that her wish for Eloise to be accepted without question would be observed.

A little while after tea, when many hands had helped to clear up and wash up, Lizzy called Annabelle in from the garden and took her into the empty dining-room.

'What's this for, Mum?' asked Annabelle.

'Nick's just arrived,' said Lizzy, 'and he's in the sitting-room.'

'Oh, yes, we were going to meet this afternoon,' said Annabelle, 'but when he phoned me this morning to arrange the time, I told him there was a family get-together here and that he could only call for me after tea.'

'Annabelle, you're already seein' so much of that young man that I don't know why you had to have him call here this evening,' said Lizzy, showing that she still wasn't completely happy about Nick's background. To Lizzy, his background was dubious because his father had done time in prison, and although she couldn't help liking Nick, she still wished Annabelle's first serious relationship had been with someone who didn't have that kind of a father. 'Your dad and me haven't put anything in the way of you goin' out with Nick, but I do think you could have put him off this evening when the whole fam'ly's here on account of the awkward problem your Uncle Boots has given us. The evening ought to be just a fam'ly one.'

'But, Mum, the problem's not awkward any more,' said Annabelle, 'everyone's accepted it, everyone's had their say.'

'No, they haven't,' said Lizzy. 'Most of you just sneaked off to play cricket when we should all have been talkin' about the best thing to do.'

'But everyone agrees the best thing to do is to see if the girl will come home with Uncle Boots,' protested Annabelle.

'I don't like you bein' so casual about it,' said Lizzy. 'It's not the time to have outsiders here, it's for the fam'ly alone.'

'Mum, that's not fair, Nick isn't an outsider. You're just saying that because of his dad.'

298

'Annabelle, I won't have any sauce from you, d'you hear?' said Lizzy. 'It's natural for your own fam'ly to want the best for you.'

'Well, Nick's the best,' said Annabelle. 'I'll never meet anyone better, I know I won't, so that makes him the best.'

'I hope he hasn't said anything about gettin' engaged to you,' said Lizzy, frowning.

'No, he hasn't,' said Annabelle, 'and I'll be eighteen soon. I won't ever forgive you if you put him off asking me.'

'Annabelle!'

'He knows you disapprove because of his Pa, Mum, you show it nearly all the time.'

'Annabelle, I won't 'ave you talk like this to me. You've been brought up, like I was, to honour your parents, like the Bible says. The trouble with you, my girl, is that you want your own way too much. You're precocious.'

'Oh, Mum.' Annabelle regarded her mother in dismay. They were so alike, this mother and daughter, both vividly brunette, chestnut hair and brown eyes identical. Lizzy at thirty-six was quite beautiful in her looks and her hour-glass figure, the latter sustained by the lightest of modern corsets. Annabelle, nearly eighteen, was lovely. Nick was utterly gone on her, and she knew it, and revelled in it. 'Mum, don't say things like that – oh, lor', I'm not selfish and precocious, am I?'

Lizzy perceived her dismay, the little shock in her expression, the shock of a young lady almost certainly thinking that perhaps her young man saw her like that. While Lizzy would have to admit her first-born was at least a little precocious, she was far from being selfish or demanding.

'Annabelle lovey, no, of course you're not. I shouldn't have said that. I suppose it's Boots, that brother of mine, that's put me out a bit.'

'Mum, he couldn't have helped doing what he did, I'm sure he couldn't. We all know what our soldiers went through, I'm sure that when they were out of the trenches none of them could have resisted French war widows who wanted some love themselves.'

'I think we all realize that,' said Lizzy, 'it's why we've forgiven Boots.'

'Well, we should,' said Annabelle. 'Mum, you don't suppose Nick thinks I'm a bit spoiled, do you?'

'I'm sure he doesn't, because you're not,' said Lizzy, and found a smile for her daughter. 'Me and your dad are proud of you, lovey. There, go and see Nick, he's waitin' in the sitting-room for you and will be wondering what's keepin' you. And I want you to know I think him a very nice and upright young man.'

'Bless you, Mum,' said Annabelle, and went to find the light of her life. Nick, seated, got up as she entered.

'Hello, Sleeping Beauty, someone kissed you awake?' he said.

Annabelle was still a little uncertain about herself, still wondering if it was true she liked her own way too much. She knew she liked having her own way with Nick. Not that he always gave in to her, far from it. It was in her favour, wasn't it, that she didn't throw tantrums whenever things went his way and not hers? There he was, and really a very nice young man without being boringly nice. There'd been a lot of laughs over tea, all about her Uncle Boots having a bit of the devil in him. Annabelle thought he'd always had that, and she also thought Uncle Sammy had his share, and from what Aunt Vi said, Uncle Tommy wasn't dull, either. Annabelle saw Nick in those terms, she saw him as a young man with a lovely bit of the devil in him. It was that which made her pulse rate jump about sometimes, that which made him exciting to her. She'd known him for ten months now, she'd been his one and only for seven months and she thought it was time he said something to make their relationship more definite. After all, as she'd reminded her mum, she'd be eighteen later this year. But Nick knew her mum still had reservations concerning whether or not the son of an ex-convict was right as a prospective son-in-law, and he probably wouldn't commit himself until those reservations went and lost themselves somewhere.

'Hello,' she said, 'what makes you think I've been kissed awake? Oh, you mean the time I've taken to get here. Well, there's been a bit of a discussion.'

'Yes, you mentioned on the phone this morning about a big family get-together,' said Nick, thinking her delicious in a summer dress of apricot. She made a little face. 'What's up?' he asked.

'Nick, you don't get fed up with me sometimes, do you?'

'Fed up?'

'Yes, you don't think I'm a bit spoilt, do you?'

'What's brought this on?' asked Nick.

'I think I've lost a bit of belief in myself,' said Annabelle.

'Well, I haven't,' said Nick, 'I'm living on top of the world about you.'

'You really like me just as I am?'

'I don't want you any different,' said Nick. 'The family discussion wasn't about you, was it? I mean, has one of your aunts or uncles put you down?'

Annabelle let a little breath of relief escape. She knew Nick, she knew he'd have been frank if he'd thought she was a little spoilt.

'No, it was nothing like that,' she said. There was no point in not telling him, because everyone close to the family would know about the girl Eloise eventually. Annabelle didn't doubt she would come to England sooner or later. 'Nick, it was all about my Uncle Boots having discovered he was the father of a French girl.'

'Come again?' said Nick.

'Yes, what an eye-opener,' said Annabelle. 'He was billeted with his company on a farm just before the battle of the Somme began, and the French farmer's daughter was a young war widow. It must have been love at first sight. Anyway, Uncle Boots, having been blinded in the battle, was sent home to a hospital and never went back to France. He had no idea his French lady love had had a daughter by

302

him. He's just found out, and, as the mother is dead, he's going over to France with Rosie in the hope he can bring the girl back home with him. What d'you think of that as a fascinating piece of news?'

'Bit of a family shock, I should think,' said Nick.

'Oh, it was at first, but all is forgiven,' said Annabelle. 'Well, Uncle Boots isn't the sort of man anyone wants to chuck bricks at. He's a sort of institution.'

'Well, I like him myself, and that's a fact,' said Nick, 'and I'd certainly like to meet his French daughter. How old is she?'

'Ten,' said Annabelle.

'Ten?' said Nick. 'I can't work that out.'

'You don't have to,' said Annabelle, 'you're not going to meet her. I don't trust French girls.'

'I don't trust you saying she's ten,' said Nick. 'From what you've just told me, she must be all of seventeen.'

'Yes, that's why you're not going to meet her,' said Annabelle. 'No, seriously, don't you think it's fascinating?'

'What does everyone else think?'

'That Uncle Boots didn't half get up to something when he was in France,' said Annabelle.

'Mother O'Grady,' said Nick, 'what a hot potato to land in his family's lap after all these years.'

'Excuse me,' said Annabelle, 'd'you mind not referring to my French cousin as a hot potato? I might tell you everyone's dying to see exactly what the girl is like. No-one's mentioned anything about a hot potato.'

'Slip of the tongue,' said Nick. 'What about a shadow out of your uncle's French past? How does that sound?'

'Oh, I'll allow that,' said Annabelle. 'By the way, I'll be eighteen quite soon.'

'By the way,' said Nick, 'I—'

'You can't say by the way when I said it first and when you haven't made any comment on my remark.'

'No, I suppose not,' said Nick. 'What was your comment?'

'I'll be eighteen quite soon.'

'No, is that a fact?' said Nick. 'You're growing up.'

'Your tongue's slipped again,' said Annabelle.

'By the way, my salary's been increased to twelve pounds a month,' said Nick.

'Twelve pounds? Three pounds a week?' Annabelle was all attention then. 'Nick, that's smashing.'

'It's a useful leg-up,' said Nick. 'D'you think your mother will like it?'

'What's it got to do with Mum?'

'Well, I think she's still giving me funny looks about Pa.'

'Mothers are like that,' said Annabelle. 'We just have to work round them with the help of dads.'

'Well, do me a favour,' said Nick, 'you work round yours with the help of your dad, and then find out if I could come and ask her if three pounds a week would be enough.'

'Enough for what?' asked Annabelle.

'Four pounds would be a lot better, of course,' said Nick.

'Better for what?'

'Roses round the door?'

'Nick?' Annabelle's colour sprang, flushing her face. Her brown eyes swam with light.

'Well, I like the sound of it myself, don't you? It's an old saying, of course, but it still sounds all right. If your mum thinks three pounds is enough as a starter—'

'Never mind my mum, what about me? Say it to me.'

'Well, I'm asking you, Annabelle, would three pounds a week be enough for someone special? You're very special.'

'Oh, I do agree, Nick, I am.' Annabelle laughed. 'But so are you. Are we going to be very special together?'

'I thought if we could get officially engaged on your eighteenth birthday, and married in five years when I'll probably be earning a fiver a week, which is a lot of oof—'

'Five years? Blow that for one of your funnies,' said Annabelle, 'it's going to be early next summer. You mean it, don't you?'

'Yes, seriously.'

'Oh, that's nice, isn't it nice? Love me, do you?'

'Yes, seriously,' smiled Nick.

'Well, seriously,' said Annabelle, 'on twelve pounds a month we could get a mortgage on a lovely little house.'

'And you wouldn't mind about my Pa's unfortunate record?'

'Nick, I've told you and told you, that's got nothing to do with you and me,' said Annabelle. 'It's his problem, not ours.' In any case, Nick's father was doing an honest job now, and Mrs Harrison always said he wouldn't have gone off the straight and narrow if he hadn't unfortunately got himself mixed up with common miscreants. He was never common himself, she told Annabelle, just unlucky. And then, Annabelle quite liked him, he was a real charmer. Her mum would come to like him too once she'd accepted Nick as a son-in-law.

'Nick, can I have a forthcoming engagement kiss?'

He gave her one, a warm and lingering one. Her knees went wobbly, so he gave her another to help her recover, but it didn't do a great deal for her knees. Still, he did help to keep her on her feet. She made a faint-voiced suggestion that he'd now better face up to the whole family.

'Face up to them?' said Nick. 'Why, are they going to chuck things at me, then?'

'If they do, I'll chuck them back,' said Annabelle. 'No, you silly, you've first got to speak to my mum and dad and ask them if they mind you marrying someone very special. Me. My dad won't give me away as if I'm a set of cigarette cards, you know. Tell them about your rise, that you'll be able to afford a mortgage on a nice house, that you'll jump off a bridge if you can't marry me, and – oh, yes, tell them we want a knees-up.'

'A knees-up? Now? Tonight?'

'No, at the wedding reception, you silly. It's a family tradition.'

Nick laughed, put his arm around her waist and they went to find her mum and dad.

Lizzy gave in gracefully. Ned didn't have to give in. He'd accepted months ago that Annabelle wasn't going to have anyone but Nick.

Chapter Ten

It was late Sunday afternoon and cloudy when Polly arrived in Albert, having caught a morning ferry out of Dover. She pulled up outside the *estaminet*. Patrons sitting at the outside tables glanced at her with interest as she alighted.

'Bonjour, messieurs.'

'Bonjour, ma'moiselle.'

She was known.

Entering, she saw Eloise, serving a customer with coffee. The girl glanced and an immediate smile danced.

'Ma'moiselle! You are back so soon?'

'It seems so, doesn't it?' said Polly.

'Uncle Jacques, see who is back already!'

Jacques came out from behind the bar and shook hands with Polly.

'To stay a little while with us again?' he said.

'No, no, I won't impose on you this time Jacques, it wouldn't be fair,' she said. He and his wife did not run an inn or a *pension de famille*, only their wine and coffee bar. 'I've reserved a room at the town hotel.' She had decided, in view of Boots's arrival on Tuesday, that the hotel would suit her better. Exciting things might happen, for she had

308

also reserved a room for him, by arrangement.

'You are as welcome to stay here as before, ma'moiselle.'

'I know, Jacques, and thank you,' said Polly, 'but this is a rather special visit.'

'How special, ma'moiselle?' asked Eloise.

'Special for me, and perhaps for you and Jacques,' said Polly.

'Ah?' said Jacques.

'I'll speak to you sometime this evening, Jacques,' said Polly. 'Now, if you please, I'd like some coffee.'

'Yes, ma'moiselle,' said Eloise. 'Have you come back to tell me you've found out who my father was and if I have English relatives?'

Polly smiled.

'We'll see,' she said, and sat down. Eloise brought her the coffee, and Polly took her time to enjoy it, while the girl and Jacques attended to their patrons, who gradually began to depart for their homes for early dinner, after which families would take their traditional summer Sunday evening stroll. Before returning to the hotel, Polly received a not unexpected question from Eloise.

'Ma'moiselle, are you able to tell me something about my father?'

'I want to talk to you about him tomorrow, Eloise, when perhaps as it's Monday, your least busy day, your uncle will let me take you out for another picnic. Then we can enjoy a long talk.'

'Oh, I'm sure he will spare me for a few hours,'

said Eloise. 'We're both so pleased to see you again.'

Polly dined at the hotel, and when she was on her way back to the *estaminet*, Albert was bathed in soft warm twilight, and people were sitting at the pavement tables of cafes. Polly, gregarious, did not take long to establish herself at an inside table with some of Jacques' old-established patrons, who welcomed her with some extravagant Gallic flourishes. She was in a quite different frame of mind from her previous visit, she was much more her usual self, extrovert, brittle and amusing.

Later, a lot later, when Eloise had retired to bed, and Madame Duval had intruded her quiet self for a few seconds to say good night to the returned visitor, Polly was given the opportunity to talk to Jacques before he too retired. She had decided it would be the right thing to speak to him first. Jacques listened, absorbed in her story of Eloise's English father. Sometimes he nodded, sometimes he shook his head, sometimes he rubbed his chin, and sometimes he made a brief comment.

'Ah, yes, the war.'

'One accepted such things.'

'Astonishing, astonishing.'

And so on.

At the end he rubbed his chin again, and said, 'Remarkable, ma'moiselle, and all because you decided to come and see me a little while ago. And now, of course, you wish to tell Eloise?'

'You are her uncle, you've given her a home, and you and Madame Duval have looked after her since her mother died, and you have both shown how much you care for her. When I tell her about her father, and that he's coming to see her, it will mean, won't it, that you might have to face losing her.'

'That will be for Eloise to say, that will be her decision,' said Jacques. 'Either she'll wish to go or to stay, and I shall say nothing to move her one way or the other, but allow her to choose for herself. Monsieur Adams, who you say will make an admirable father, is her father, Ma'moiselle Polly, and it's his right to speak to her and to ask if she would like to be with him and his family. And it's her right to make up her own mind. I would only suggest you emphasize the reason why Monsieur Adams did not return to her mother.'

Polly, Boots's ambassador, said, 'I'll do that, Jacques. Eloise mustn't be given the impression that he didn't care enough for her mother. You'll let me take her out tomorrow so that I can talk to her without any interruptions or distractions?'

'But of course,' said Jacques, his demeanour that of an unworried man, which made Polly think he had little fear of losing Eloise.

Albert was sunny but quiet the following day, Monday. Many shops were closed. Mondays in French towns could be very much like an English Sunday. Polly motored into the rolling countryside with Eloise, and with the girl's knowledge of the area they found a very pleasant and secluded spot for their picnic, which Jacques and his wife had insisted on putting together. Not until it was over did Polly begin to cater to the girl's ever-present interest in the English sergeant who had been her mother's lover.

'Yes, yes, Eloise, I'm going to tell you everything about him.'

'Ma'moiselle? Do you know everything about him, then? If so, how do you know? You said you never met him.'

'Not during the war, no. All the same, your father, Eloise, is a very old and dear friend of mine.'

'Is? Is?' Eloise's mouth fell open.

'Listen,' said Polly, and told her story carefully and at length. Eloise had a hand over her mouth, smothering little exhalations of startled and astonished breath, her eyes dilating, her expressions indicative of every kind of emotion. Polly was very careful indeed to explain exactly why Sergeant Robert Adams had not gone back to see Eloise's mother after he had survived the Somme. He could not, he was blind, and unable to offer her anything but the responsibility of looking after him. He had no work, nor could he do any, not even if her mother's parents had been willing to offer him a farm job.

'Ma'moiselle, oh, how terrible, to have been blinded. But could he not have written, or have someone write for him?'

'He thought it best not to, Eloise. If your mother loved him, perhaps she would have replied saying she didn't mind his blindness. Your father, not knowing about you, didn't want her to sacrifice herself, and so he took himself out of her life.'

'There, that showed, didn't it, that he loved her?' said Eloise. 'He gave her up because of his blindness, because he thought he would be a burden to her. Ma'moiselle, I think it was he who made the sacrifice, don't you?'

Oh, ye heavenly gods, thought Polly, am I now to say greater love hath no man for a woman? This dear child is never going to think of Boots in any prosaic way. How on earth did he climb out of the back streets of Walworth and become what he is? He was already a fascination to a girl who had never laid eyes on him, even though he was her father.

'I have to tell you, Eloise, that he married a young woman who lived next door to him and was willing to be his comfort and his eyes.' Those words, of course, almost stuck in Polly's throat.

'Yes, I see,' said Eloise, 'and I understand. But how sad that he did not know about me, and yet how wonderful to know he's alive.'

Polly finished her story by telling the flushed, entranced girl that her father eventually had an operation that gave him back the sight of his right eye. His left eye, however, responded only partially to the operation, and was almost useless. It had a very lazy look that was part of his extraordinary charm.

'Charm, ma'moiselle? Extraordinary?'

I'll give my stupid self away in a moment, thought Polly.

'Oh, perhaps that's the wrong word, Eloise. Gigolos and matinee idols are charming, but don't appeal to all of us. Eloise, your father will be here tomorrow, to—'

'Tomorrow? He's coming to Albert tomorrow? My father?' Eloise put a hand to her mouth again. 'Is this true?'

'Yes, Eloise, he wants to see you and to talk to you.'

'Oh, the blessed saints,' breathed Eloise, 'how am I ever going to sleep tonight? Am I to put my best dress on tomorrow, and have my hair done?'

'I don't think he'll ask you to do that, I think he'll be happy just to see you as you are most days of the week,' said Polly. 'What do you say, Eloise, to meeting him where he met your mother, by the farm? That would be better than in the *estaminet*, don't you think, where there'll be distractions?'

'Ma'moiselle, do you think my knees will hold me up if I meet him there?'

Polly laughed.

'I'm sure they will,' she said.

'Ah, you yourself may be sure, ma'moiselle, but I tell you, even now my knees are shaking.'

'Eloise, I think your father is going to like you,' said Polly. 'And he's going to ask, of course, if you wish to go to England with him.'

Eloise sighed.

'Ma'moiselle, there are my Aunt Marie and my Uncle Jacques.'

'I know,' said Polly, 'and your father knows too. But he doesn't want you to worry. He wants you to do only what you wish to do yourself. But you

314

understand, don't you, that now he knows about you he can't resist meeting you.'

'Oh, I'm glad he wants to see me, very glad,' said Eloise. 'Does he have children at home?'

'A son and a daughter, Eloise.'

'I have a brother and sister?'

'Yes.'

'How am I ever going to sleep tonight?' said Eloise again.

Chapter Eleven

The car slipped out of the traffic in Westminster Bridge Road and turned right into Lower Marsh. It slowed and stopped. Out stepped Sammy. Street kids, still on holiday from school, materialized like magic.

'Cor, is that yer own car, mister?'

'Right first time,' said Sammy. They eyed him speculatively. He eyed them knowingly. He had a soft spot for street kids. He'd been one himself. An urchin, in fact, with Chinese Lady going on at him about disgracing her by looking like a ragamuffin. He always tried to make her understand that a ragamuffin look made nice old ladies feel sorry for him and give him errands to do for a penny a time. The soft spot he felt for street kids related not only to the old days in Walworth, but also to the fact that he was now an established dad. 'Listen,' he said, 'I've got a call to make, so while I'm gone can I trust you not to nick me wheels and me lamps?'

'Mister, we don't 'ardly do any nickin',' said a girl kid.

'We'll look after it for yer, mister,' said a plump boy kid.

'Just for a penny each,' said the girl kid.

'Sounds fair,' said Sammy. 'Let's see, how many of you?'

'Six,' said the plump lad.

'Seven,' said the girl. 'Well, there's me bruvver as well, 'e's just round the corner somewhere. I won't let no-one touch it, mister, I'll bash any of 'em that tries to.'

'Are you in charge?' asked Sammy.

'Not 'alf she ain't,' said a skinny boy, 'she ain't called Basher Bunty for nuffink. She give Georgie Peacock a shiner yesterday for standin' on 'er foot.'

'I'll give you one in a minute, Ernie Spriggs,' said Basher Bunty, a fearsome ten-year-old. 'Mister, shall us mind yer motorcar for yer?'

'You're on,' said Sammy, and fished in his pocket. He brought out five pennies, a sixpence and a threepenny bit. 'See that?' he said, the coins resting in his palm.

'Crikey, it's real money,' said Basher Bunty.

'It's tuppence each,' said Sammy, 'includin' your brother round the corner somewhere, and you'll get it when I come back. Fair?'

The kids decided not to quarrel with that kind of offer.

'Cor, yer a sport, mister, a toff,' said one.

'Right,' said Sammy, 'keep your mince pies on me roadster, then.' He put the money back into his pocket, lifted three parcels out of the car, gave the kids a smile and walked away. He knew about street kids, he knew they liked a deal. It was born in them. Of course, mutual trust had to be established

317

first, and mutual trust was born of the right kind of dialogue.

Mrs Rachel Goodman, answering a ring on the doorbell, went down to answer it. Sammy, laden with the parcels, smiled at her.

'Mrs Rachel Goodman, I presume?' he said.

'Sammy? What a pleasure, ain't it?' said Rachel, whose finishing school education had never prevented her cockney origins from surfacing at appropriate moments.

'Excuse me not raisin' me titfer to you,' said Sammy, 'but I'm lumbered.'

'I can see you're wearing a string of parcels, Sammy, but not your titfer,' said Rachel.

'So I'm not,' said Sammy, 'left it in the car, didn't I? It'll be all right, I've got some kids keepin' an eye on things. Listen, can't stop, so might I dispose of the parcels by placin' them in yer gracious arms?'

'Of course you can stop,' said Rachel, lustrous, velvety, and a high-class picture of health and beauty. 'I should let you disappear when you're on my doorstep? Not likely. What's in the parcels? No, never mind, come up first, lovey.'

'Five minutes, then,' said Sammy, stepping in. Rachel closed the door, and he followed her up the stairs to the spacious and well-appointed flat she and her family shared with her father. Her father, Isaac Moses, was out, her husband Benjamin at his office. Her two daughters, Rebecca, ten, and Leah, seven, were also out, with friends, she said. 'Do I take it you're alone, Mrs Goodman?' said

Sammy, placing the parcels on a settee.

'Not now you're here, Sammy,' said Rachel, 'I get lucky sometimes.'

'Well, Rachel,' said Sammy, 'on the grounds that our wedded respectability will be better off if I push off immediate, I'll do that.'

'My life, have I ever taken advantage of you?' asked Rachel.

'I don't recollect same,' said Sammy.

'And have you ever taken advantage of me?'

'Would I?' said Sammy.

'You could try,' said Rachel. Her affection for him was deep-rooted. Had it not been for her religion, she would have chosen him long ago as her lifelong partner. But whereas Polly was an ever-present danger to Boots and his marriage vows, Rachel never had been and never would be a serious threat to Sammy and Susie. She was a faithful wife and caring mother. However, that did not mean she never had the kind of thoughts about Sammy that she kept to herself. In her younger days and in the vernacular of the time, Sammy had been her one and only. Sammy had always been a character, and was now so sharp that even Old Nick himself would find it hard to put one over on him. But he was also a man in the best sense of the word, as were all Chinese Lady's three sons in Rachel's opinion. She wondered how they would react and how they would fare when another war with Germany landed on the doorsteps of Britain. Her father was convinced it would happen, that Hitler was intent on conquest, and that Britain and France would have to fight him. Rachel asked why. For the sake of humanity and to save the Jews of Europe, said her father. Some are already saving themselves, he said, by coming to Britain or going to America. Hitler, he said, is evil personified. Rachel, dismissing uneasy thoughts, said lightly to Sammy, 'Such sighing nights I had in my teens, lovey, that you never took even the smallest advantage of me.'

'Well, you know, Rachel, me likin' for you was on a par with me respect,' said Sammy. 'There's some girls a bloke always respects, girls that have got warm hearts and nice ways, and I was brought up to be very respectful of same. Tommy and Boots and yours truly have all got highly personal respect and regard for you, Rachel, as an old and valued friend of the fam'ly and a married female woman of tender reputation.'

'Tender, Sammy, tender?'

'Tender it is, Rachel, if I might say so. But I won't mention your remarkable good looks owing to me own reputation as a married man, which prevents me from makin' comments of an intimate kind.'

'How intimate, Sammy?' asked Rachel.

'That's all, I've said me piece, Rachel.'

'And what a piece, Sammy, a lovely speech,' said Rachel, warm voice purring. 'Sit down and I'll make some tea.'

'Due to me limited time—'

'Blow your limited time,' said Rachel. 'Blimey, I should let you push off after all that? On goes the kettle.' Rachel disappeared with a whisper of silk, but was back with a tray and tea things in very quick time. She poured. 'One lump, I think,' she said, and dropped a single cube of sugar into his tea before handing the cup and saucer to him.

'One lump, right,' smiled Sammy. 'Nice that you remember.'

'Sammy, always there are some things women never forget. Wait a moment, you haven't said why you're here. Or did you just drop in to get an eyeful of my remarkable self?'

'I dropped in to deliver the parcels, Rachel, on account of Rebecca's birthday tomorrow.'

Rachel's smile was very warm. There were some things Sammy didn't forget, either, including the birthdays of her girls. It was Rebecca's tomorrow.

'But three parcels, Sammy?' she said.

'Two for Rebecca,' said Sammy. 'A teddy bear and a set of Beatrix Potter books. The other's for Leah, a china doll dressed as Red Hiding Hood.'

'Sammy, you love.' He always did that, he bought presents for both of her daughters on each of their birthdays so that neither should feel left out. It was something he did for her girls alone. Rachel thought it was because he remembered, as she did, what a close and happy friendship she and he had shared when they were young. 'I'll see that they write and thank you. Beccy will love her teddy bear.'

'Well, you've got a sweet first-born, Rachel, and a cuddly second-born,' said Sammy. 'And Boots, by the way, has got an addition.'

'Come again, Sammy?'

'A new daughter,' said Sammy.

'D'you mean Emily's presented him with a baby girl?' asked Rachel. 'I didn't even know she was expecting. My life, such expecting was unexpected after all this time, wasn't it?'

'Have to point out, Rachel me old love, that it wasn't quite like that,' said Sammy, and recounted details of how Boots, just before the first battle of the Somme, fell off a horse or something and landed in the hay with a young French war widow. There wasn't much Boots could do then except play the part of a gentleman. Rachel, agog, said she supposed that didn't mean Boots got up, bowed and walked away. It so happens, said Sammy, that in France, once a bloke's in the hay with a young French widow, the gentlemanly thing to do is roll with her, otherwise she takes umbrage. Rachel said oh, you know that, do you, Sammy? It's what they call common knowing, said Sammy, and peculiar to France. And Boots, of course, was born a gent.

'Boots was born to be obliging,' said Rachel.

'Same thing,' said Sammy.

'So he had an affair, did he?' said Rachel, intrigued. 'Bless the man, a pleasure for her, wasn't it?'

'I can't confirm that,' said Sammy. 'Boots didn't say and I wasn't there meself. But I'll give 'im the benefit of the doubt.'

'So will I,' said Rachel. 'My word, why wasn't I a young French war widow?'

'You happened at the time to be roller-skatin'

with me,' said Sammy. 'Anyway, Boots unfortunately put the lady in the fam'ly way.' He went on to explain the subsequent events and how Polly during a tour of Northern France discovered that Boots was the father of a French daughter. Rachel thought oh, help, Polly of all people, Polly who had spent years wanting Boots and never having him. Boots, said Sammy, was travelling to France tomorrow to see the girl, and taking Rosie with him. Chinese Lady, he said, had called a family conference about it yesterday, and the family had agreed that the girl was an Adams and that Boots should do his best to bring her back with him.

'Well, of course,' said Rachel, 'with her mother dead, she belongs to Boots. My life, Sammy old dear, if I know Boots, he'll want the girl in the family. But what about Emily, how does she feel about it?'

'Well, you know Em'ly,' said Sammy, 'she's her own woman, but she's an Adams herself by holy wedlock, and she'll go along with Boots. Slightly misfortunate the girl bein' born out of wedlock.' Sammy accepted a refill from the pot.

'But it was wartime, Sammy, and for our soldiers it was here today and gone tomorrow,' said Rachel. 'If I'd been a French widow, I'd have gladly made myself a pleasure to Boots.'

'Would you have, Rachel?'

'And more gladly if it had been you, Sammy.'

'I'm touched, Rachel, blessed if I'm not,' said Sammy, 'but what would have 'appened to me respect?'

'Oh, we could have looked for it afterwards, in the hay,' said Rachel. Sammy grinned. 'What did Chinese Lady say about it all?' asked Rachel.

'Well, she handed out several earfuls to Boots, but she made the decision for everybody in the end,' said Sammy. '"The girl's an Adams," she said to Boots, "so bring her home, but while you're there don't get up to any more of your French larks."'

Rachel laughed.

'Your mother, Sammy, is a one and only,' she said.

'And I'll be in my one and only business doghouse if I don't get back to me office,' said Sammy. 'Wait a tick, though, I've got something for you.' He drew a long brown envelope out of the inside pocket of his jacket. 'Here we are, Rachel, all yours.'

'What is it?' asked Rachel, turning the envelope over.

'A certificate namin' you the certified owner of fifty shares in Adams Enterprises Ltd. Boots and me have given you twenty-five each from our holdings. It's in appreciation of your friendship and the loan you once persuaded your dad to make to the firm in its early days. Boots spoke to me about giftin' you self-unanimously, meaning he wanted to do all the honours himself, so I answered him back, and what's in the envelope is the result of a confabulation. Oh, and you're on the board as a director, along with Em'ly, Susie and Lizzy as the female half. Well, you're fam'ly, Rachel, good as.'

'Sammy, oh, you darling,' said Rachel, one more sentimental ambition achieved. It put her closer than ever to Sammy and Chinese Lady's family. Her warm generous heart overflowed.

'Got to push off now,' said Sammy, up on his feet.

'Sammy—' Rachel interrupted herself by kissing him, electing for his mouth, not his cheek. She kissed him warmly, ardently, letting her deep affection escape restraint for once.

'Pardon me,' said Sammy, when it was over, 'but I ain't sure that happened. It's not supposed to, bein' illegal, but since I'm not sure it did, I'll put it down to me imagination.'

'Is it illegal, Sammy, a kiss now and again for old times sake?'

'Well, let's say unmentionable,' said Sammy.

'There's a bright boy, ain't it?' smiled Rachel. 'You won't mention it to Susie, and I won't mention it to Benjamin. Fair?'

'Fair,' said Sammy. 'Except—'

'Except what, lovey?'

'You owe me fourpence,' said Sammy, 'that's me current charge for a kiss.'

Rachel laughed again.

'Same old Sammy,' she said, 'don't ever change.' She regarded him fondly, a Gentile who, along with his family, had given her a friendship she treasured. Her expression changed and she became serious. 'Spare me five more minutes, Sammy love.'

'For you, Rachel, why not?' said Sammy, noting her change of mood.

'Did you know that dreadful man Hitler is set on forcing all Jews out of Germany?' she asked.

'I've heard he's not too fond of them,' said Sammy, 'but I think Boots knows more than I do, and so does me stepdad. He and Boots are keepin' track of what Adolf Hitler's up to. They get together with Polly's dad sometimes and talk about it, so I hear. You worried, Rachel?'

'Not for myself, I'm lucky,' said Rachel. 'I was born here as a subject of our sovereign monarch. I'm English, Sammy, of Jewish faith. So are my daughters, so are my husband and father. The unlucky Jews are those who live in Germany, and some are being wise enough to leave. My father has spoken to several of them. Did you know the Germans have built what they call a concentration camp at a place called Dachau, into which they herd Jews and political prisoners?'

'That's news to me,' admitted Sammy.

'Well, do you know about the Gestapo?' asked Rachel.

'Not much,' said Sammy, 'but I think my stepdad does. He's got a job with the Government.'

'My father says the Gestapo is the evil arm of an evil man, and the German Jews he's spoken to say awful things are happening that the outside world doesn't know about. Sammy, there's going to be a war, and Britain and France will have to fight Hitler.'

'I can't believe that,' said Sammy, 'not after what the last one was like. No, it couldn't happen. And if you're thinkin' Hitler's goin' to come goosesteppin' down Piccadilly, that won't happen, either. Nothing's goin' to hurt you or your fam'ly, not while all the Adams fam'lies are on your side.'

'Sammy, what would I do without your friendship, if I'd never met you?' asked Rachel.

'Well, you could come to the offices and ask for an interview, and I daresay that once we'd been introduced we could get to like each other,' said Sammy. 'Always remembering, of course, that we're both respectably married.'

'Sammy, I had a wish during those days when I went roller-skating with you,' said Rachel, 'a wish that we'd be friends for life. And we shall be, won't we? I treasure that. Bless you, lovey, it's heartwarming, ain't it?'

'It's a good old Union Jack,' said Sammy.

'Here in this home we treasure that too,' said Rachel.

'Well, if I had more time I'd get you on your joanna and we could sing "Rule Britannia" together,' said Sammy, 'but I'm pushed now and must buzz off. So long now.'

'Yes, Sammy, thanks,' said Rachel, 'and give Boots my best wishes.'

Sammy smiled and left. He found the group of street kids standing guard around his car.

'Oh, 'ello, mister.'

'We looked after it, mister.'

'It's all 'ere, mister, its lamps as well,' said Basher Bunty.

Sammy eyed her. There was a bruise on her forehead.

327

'Hello, who did that?' he asked.

'Oh, some kids come round from Murphy Street,' she said, 'and wanted to sit in yer car. So we 'ad to bash 'em. We didn't let not one get in it, honest. Me 'ead knocked itself against one kid's knee, but it didn't 'urt.'

'How'd his knee get in the way of your head?' asked Sammy.

'Well, 'e was on the ground,' volunteered the plump boy.

'An' Bunty was tryin' to bite 'is leg orf,' said another boy.

'Yes, it was a sort of accident,' said Basher Bunty. 'Mister, can we collect now, tuppence each for ev'ryone?'

'Well, seein' you collected a knee in your loaf, and your gang saw off the interlopers,' said Sammy, 'share this out among you.' And he placed half a crown in her eager hand. She gawped and so did the rest of the kids. 'Now go home and run some errands for yer mums. So long.'

The happy kids waved him goodbye when he drove off. Not until he reached Camberwell and had parked his car did he discover his hat was missing. He'd left it on the back seat, and it was relatively new. He reckoned that by now Basher Bunty had sold it for fourpence to a second-hand clothes stall. He took the loss philosophically. Street kids had to keep wolves from their doors.

Chapter Twelve

'I think I'll phone Boots,' said Vi after supper that evening.

'What for?' asked Tommy, watching his kids through the window above the kitchen sink. They were playing in the garden. So far, no damage had been done. 'What's on your mind, Vi?'

'Oh, you know,' said Vi.

'His French daughter?' said Tommy. 'It's all settled. Chinese Lady settled it.'

'Yes, I know,' said Vi. 'I'm fond of your mum, Tommy, I always 'ave been, but I've been thinkin' today it was a bit hard on Boots gettin' everyone there yesterday to talk about what was really nothing to do with any of us except 'imself and Em'ly.'

'Good point, Vi,' said Tommy, drying dishes, 'but as far as Chinese Lady was concerned, y'know, it was fam'ly. She'd made 'er mind up about that, that it was something the fam'ly 'ad got to talk about, and she'd made up 'er mind as well that everyone had got to come out in favour of Boots, or else. And Boots didn't object to the fam'ly conference. He can take that sort of thing, he's got a bit of iron in 'is backbone, Vi. Sammy and me wouldn't let 'im lord it if he didn't have.'

'He might 'ave looked as if he didn't object,' said
Vi, 'he's good at keepin' the peace, but I'm not sure
he really liked it, the whole fam'ly goin' round to
talk about what was his own concern mostly. I
mean, if Em'ly had accepted the girl, which she
had, it wasn't right for the rest of us to 'old an
inquest.'

'It was only you girls that talked about it, the rest
of us played cricket,' said Tommy. 'So did Boots
'imself.'

'Yes, but what was he thinkin', I wonder?' said
Vi. 'That we'd all got a blessed cheek?'

'It was fam'ly, Vi, it was what Chinese Lady
wanted, to settle things once and for all,' said
Tommy.

Vi said that over tea, later on, she was sitting
opposite Boots. She looked at him once, she said,
and he was looking at her. At least, she thought he
was, then she sort of felt that he wasn't seeing her.
He wasn't seeing anything of anyone there. You
know how Boots is, she said, he always looks as if
he's about to tell a funny story, or is about to listen
to someone else telling one. Well, he didn't look
like that then, she said, he was far away, and she
thought that because of everything, he was remembering the war and all the comrades he'd lost, and
perhaps the days before the battle of the Somme
and the young Frenchwoman.

'I thought then,' said Vi, 'what are all of us doing
here, poking our noses in? I glanced at Lizzy, and
Lizzy was looking at Boots. She caught my glance
and made a little face at me. Boots never talks

about the war, he's always kept it to 'imself, but for once I think he was rememberin' it, Tommy, with all the fam'ly around him. Then Annabelle said, "Penny for your thoughts, Uncle Boots." He gave her a smile and said that over in France there might be one more like her, in which case who was going to complain? I think I will phone him, Tommy.'

'All right, Vi, if it's goin' to make you feel better.'

Vi phoned. Rosie answered.

'Is your dad there, Rosie?'

'Oh, yes, Aunt Vi,' said Rosie, 'he's supposed to be doing his packing, but I'm doing most of it for him. What a shirker. Hold on and I'll get him.'

Boots came on the line after several seconds.

'What can I do for you, Vi?' he asked.

'Oh, I just wanted to say you stood up to all of us so well yesterday,' said Vi. 'Tommy and me want you to know – seriously, like – that – oh, you know, Boots.'

'That I'm not in the doghouse?' said Boots.

'Never,' said Vi, 'not with any of us. Boots, did you – did you mind that we all descended on you yesterday?'

'Mind? Of course not, Vi. What's better than a Sunday tea with everyone present?'

'It was a bit more than that,' said Vi, 'but you really didn't mind?'

'Not a bit,' said Boots.

'Oh, that's good,' said Vi.

'Don't give it another thought,' said Boots. If Tommy was the most soft-hearted of the brothers,

331

Vi was the gentlest of the wives, and Boots knew it.

'Tommy and me wish you ever so much luck when you get to France,' said Vi.

'I'll need a little at least,' said Boots.

'Oh, she'll come home with you, Boots, I'm sure she will, now or a bit later.'

'We'll see,' said Boots.

'Bless you,' said Vi.

Boots smiled to himself. Vi had a nice way of blessing everyone.

'Bless you too, Vi,' he said, and she rang off.

In another Adams' household, it was not until well after supper and the children had been bathed and put to bed by Susie and Sammy that he spoke to her about Rachel.

He began by saying, 'Concernin' our friend Rachel, Susie.'

And Susie began her part in the dialogue by saying, 'Are you referrin', Sammy Adams, to your old girlfriend, Mrs Rachel Goodman?'

'Well, I did tell you, Susie, I was goin' to drop in on her to give her that share certificate and the birthday presents for her girls.'

'Oh, yes, so you did, Sammy, and I told you, you weren't to cross her doorstep into her parlour.'

'So you did, Susie. Well, after I'd bestowed the certificate on her—'

'Just a moment, Sammy, you're not lookin' me in the eye,' said Susie.

'You've got blue eyes, Susie, did you know that?' said Sammy. 'I can't remember the number of times you've used them to me pathetic disadvantage. Anyway, as I was sayin''—'

'Look at me, Sammy, when you're talkin' about this person that's someone else's married wife.'

'Believe me, Susie, Mrs Rachel Goodman's not the kind of headache to you that Polly is to our Em'ly.'

'If she ever was, Sammy Adams, I'd fit my heavy jam saucepan over your topknot and someone would have to cut your head off to get rid of it,' said Susie.

'Susie, is that Christian, is it charitable?' said Sammy.

'Just a little warnin', Sammy.'

'Now, Susie—'

'Now, Sammy.'

'As I was saying,' said Sammy, and went on to let Susie know all that Rachel had told him about what was happening in Germany, that Jews were being hounded and Hitler was going to make war.

'Well, that's happy news, I don't think,' said Susie. 'Except you know what your stepfather thinks about Hitler and his kind of Germans, and he's probably got good reasons for his opinions seeing he works for our government. Well, he'd know things we don't, wouldn't he? It's a shame there's the rotten kind of Germans. I bet most are like everyone else, good at heart, and I just don't know how that man Hitler got where he is.'

'There's a lot of people in this country that support him,' said Sammy, 'they reckon he's doin' wonders for Germany. But Boots doesn't think much of him, or trust him, either, and Polly said once that her dad would like to shoot him.'

'If Boots doesn't trust him, then I don't, either,' said Susie.

'Might I point out that I ain't in favour of you and Boots gettin' to be bosom chums?' said Sammy.

'What a sauce,' said Susie. 'You and Mrs Rachel Goodman have been bosom chums for I don't know how long.'

'Susie love, no worries, believe me,' said Sammy.

Susie smiled.

'I know, Sammy. Only teasin'. But I just can't believe there'll be another war when the last one was so awful.'

'My sentiments exactly,' said Sammy.

'Yes, let's be optimistic,' said Susie, and smiled again. 'Give us a kiss, then.'

Sammy gave her one. Halfway through, Susie uttered a muffled little yelp. Sammy was interfering with her bosom, on the principle, as he always said, that what was hers was his as well. And she did have a nice bosom. And there was a certain satisfaction in knowing Sammy still appreciated it. On those grounds, Susie suffered interference without complaint, apart from that one little yelp.

'Ned,' said Lizzy Somers to her husband, 'what d'you think really about Annabelle wanting to get engaged to Nick on her birthday?'

'I thought we agreed last night that if it was what she wanted, we should accept it,' said Ned.

'Yes, but I'm still havin' thoughts about it myself,' said Lizzy.

'That's because you'd still prefer her to marry someone like a dentist,' said Ned.

'Not a dentist, you daft thing,' said Lizzy, 'he'd always be bringing home someone's teeth he'd just pulled out. Like a sort of prize for the day. I meant a doctor. A doctor would be right for Annabelle.'

'At the moment, Annabelle thinks the only right bloke is Nick,' said Ned.

'Well, I like him, of course,' said Lizzy, 'I can't say I don't. Then there's Boots findin' out that that Frenchwoman had a daughter by him.'

'You've been thinking about that as well?' said Ned. 'Don't alarm yourself, Eliza, Boots'll work things out to everyone's satisfaction.'

'He hopes he will,' said Lizzy, 'but I don't think he's sure.'

'Well, I am,' said Ned.

'Ned, does the war sometimes make you feel sad?'

'It sometimes makes me wonder what the hell it was all about when it cost so many lives and old soldiers couldn't find jobs when it was over,' said Ned.

'Only I thought Boots looked a bit sad once or twice yesterday,' said Lizzy.

'Boots? Sad?' said Ned.

'Well, I did think so,' said Lizzy.

'Ghosts creep up on some of us sometimes,' said Ned, 'even on Boots.'

'But he's pleased about this girl Eloise, I know he is,' said Lizzy.

'Yes, but it made him remember, Eliza.'

'Remember what?'

'The sound of the guns,' said Ned.

Boots received another phone call, this time from Sammy, who told him what he had heard from Rachel about the Jews of Germany, some kind of concentration camp at Dachau, and the Jewish conviction that Hitler was going to launch another war. For all his natural acumen, Sammy had a lot of respect for his eldest brother's thought processes.

'Sounds serious, Sammy,' said Boots.

'Well, if it's true, it ain't funny,' said Sammy.

'I think our stepdad would like to talk to these people from Germany,' said Boots. 'I'll get him to phone Rachel so that he can arrange to meet them.'

'Good idea,' said Sammy. 'What's he been sayin' lately about Germany?'

'That Hitler and his fascists are the next worst thing to a dustbin of leavings.'

'I've got a feelin' he might be right,' said Sammy.

'Thanks for calling,' said Boots.

'Well,' said Sammy, 'you're not just a bag of peanuts. You've got an educated head on you, Boots.'

'Kind of you, Sammy.'

'Don't mention it,' said Sammy. 'I – Susie, leave off.' But he lost the phone to Susie.

'Boots lovey?' she said.

'I'm here,' said Boots.

336

'Sammy should get serious about Hitler, shouldn't he?' said Susie.

'I'd say so, Susie.'

'I knew you would. And, Boots?'

'I'm still here,' said Boots.

'Everyone's happy about your new daughter,' said Susie. 'And I'm sure that when she meets you, she'll be happy too.'

'We'll see,' said Boots.

Chapter Thirteen

The afternoon sun was a shining brightness, but the ubiquitous French plane trees, lining a straight stretch of the road between Doullens and Albert, diffused its rays, and light and shadow fell over an open car.

'Damn, I forgot,' said Boots at the wheel.

'Forgot what?' asked Rosie. They had both taken their hats off, and the wind and the slipstream tugged at her hair and frisked around her father's.

'I forgot to phone Polly to tell her you were coming with me. I should have done so on Saturday evening after the domestic earthquake had stopped rumbling.'

'Never mind,' said Rosie, 'I'll just walk about all night and find out what a sleeping French town feels like. The experience might come in useful for an essay. I could call it, "When Albert Slept", except that my tutor might think he was going to read about Queen Victoria's Albert having forty winks when he was supposed to be pruning the roses.'

'You'd do that, walk about all night, would you?' smiled Boots, the long straight stretch pulling him on to Albert and his new-found daughter.

'I'm giddy enough to do the barmiest things,' said Rosie. 'I'm in France, the sun's shining, and we're going to meet your daughter. Are you very emotional about it, meeting your very own daughter?'

'Well, it's not quite like meeting the postman,' said Boots, 'nor quite like a one and only. I already have a very own daughter.'

'No, it's different,' said Rosie, 'Eloise was born to you.'

'So were you, poppet, in your own way, when you first sat on our Walworth doorstep with me.'

'Bless you, Daddy old thing, I still like you saying things like that,' said Rosie, as the plane trees ran by and the filtered sunrays flashed at them. She had never attempted to monopolize her adoptive father's affections, she had always made room for Annabelle and other nieces, and for girls like Cassie Ford who had special feelings for him. And she had always encouraged Tim to become close to his father, to become his young pal. Because of her nature, Rosie was far more intrigued by the advent of Eloise than worried about whether or not it would displace her. She had never felt less than absolutely secure in the love of her adoptive parents, and in her instinctive certainty that she was very special to Boots. That was enough for her, and she suffered no jealousies. There was only the feeling that if Eloise joined the family, there would be fewer times when she could have Boots to herself. But then for much of each year she would be away at university, anyway. 'I simply can't wait to see exactly what Eloise is like,' she said.

'Well, we'll find out,' said Boots, 'but first we'll make sure you don't have to walk around the town all night.'

Polly had arranged to reserve a room for him at the town hotel, and to meet him there sometime during the afternoon. As soon as a room had been reserved for Rosie too and they'd unpacked, the meeting with Eloise could take place.

'There's the town,' said Rosie, as the plane trees fell away, the vista opened out and the rooftops of Albert appeared in the distance. 'Heavens, how excited I am, and glad to be here safe and sound.'

They hadn't encountered a great deal of traffic, but what they had engaged with had convinced Rosie that French drivers were madmen. It's their French dash and devilry, Boots had said. Well, their dash and devilry won't last some of them a lifetime, said Rosie, it'll take them to a cemetery while they're still trying to grow their first moustache.

It was a little after four when they reached the hotel. Polly was waiting for them in the lobby, reading a glossy French magazine to while away the time. She came to her feet as she saw Boots entering, then raised an eyebrow as she immediately noted Rosie was with him, her dress bright and colourful, her hat in her hand, her face alight with excitement and anticipation. Well, I like Rosie, I almost adore her, thought Polly, but if she'd stayed at home I could have had Boots to myself some of the time.

'Here we are, Polly,' said Boots.

'Yes, here you both are,' said Polly wryly.

'Aunt Polly, a glad hello to you,' said Rosie.

'Dear girl, how enchanting you look,' said Polly, 'but is it fair to outdo me, and in France of all places?'

'Flattery will get you a special place in my diary, Aunt Polly,' said Rosie.

'Sorry I forgot to let you know Rosie was coming,' said Boots, 'I'll just get her booked in.' He made the reservation with the clerk, and was given two keys, together with the assistance of the porter to deal with the suitcases. Polly went up with them, noting with a look of rueful resignation that they'd been given adjoining rooms. Her thoughts of exciting moments took a downward turn. Nothing ever worked in her favour where her relationship with Boots was concerned. God, she thought, I hope it won't eventually sour my sweet nature.

'Did you have a good journey?' she asked with mock interest

'Hair-raising out of Calais,' said Rosie, 'but Dad fought the good fight with all kinds of fiery French roadsters, and we emerged flying the flag of victory. Now, Aunt Polly, tell us more about Eloise. What's happening, when do we meet her and where? What is she like exactly, and how does she feel now she knows her English father's alive?'

'Eloise is a sweet girl, Rosie,' said Polly, 'and I've arranged everything. Now that you've arrived, you'll probably want to freshen up and perhaps have some tea, while I go and talk to Eloise before

341

taking her to the meeting-place. We agreed that her uncle's *estaminet* isn't too suitable. Then I'll come back and pick you both up and drive you to the rendezvous. But you and I should stay in the car, Rosie, and let the first meeting be between just Eloise and Boots.'

'What has she said?' asked Boots.

'That she's very glad you're alive and want to meet her,' said Polly, 'and that she has her Aunt Marie and Uncle Jacques to think about.'

'Which means, I suppose, that she favours them,' said Boots.

'Are you surprised, old sport?' asked Polly.

'Not in the least,' said Boots.

'Keep hoping,' said Polly.

'I'll settle for optimism,' said Rosie, and Polly studied her. She knew how close Rosie was to her adoptive father, and she wondered how she felt about Eloise. Was she thinking Boots might give pride of place to his natural daughter? Polly didn't think he would, she didn't think he was that kind of man, but Rosie might have her doubts.

'Well, I'll leave you and Rosie to yourselves for a while, Boots, but it won't be too long before I'll be back to pick you up. Oh, and after you've met Eloise and spoken to her, you'll have to meet Jacques and speak to him too. He wants to take stock of you and find out if you look like a decent old bloke or a bank robber.' Polly's brittle smile showed. 'See you, old things,' she said, and off she went.

She returned in forty minutes, by which time

Rosie and Boots had freshened up and enjoyed a pot of tea that was served with the option of lemon slices or milk.

'It's now, Aunt Polly?' asked Rosie, who had changed her dress and was looking a slender bloom of summer in golden yellow. Boots had changed too, into a light grey flannel suit that was cool enough to make the hot afternoon bearable.

'Yes, it's now,' said Polly, 'so come along and bring your optimism with you.'

When they were out of the town and on a road leading south, Boots said, 'I've a feeling I know where I am.'

'Well, all around here are the places you knew, didn't you, all those years ago?' said Rosie.

'There's a farm not far from here,' said Boots.

'Heavens, not the very farm itself, is it?' asked Rosie.

'It will be when we get there,' said Polly, and in a little while she turned into a country lane and pulled up outside a gate that led to a farm lane. 'She's here, Boots, you'll find her just a little way down the lane. You can meet her not far from where you met her mother.'

'Did it have to be like this?' said Boots, getting out of the car.

'Oh, well, roses are red, and violets are blue, you know,' said Polly, 'and Eloise is a romantic. I know you won't rush her, so I'll say no more.'

'Polly, you're a treasure,' said Boots, 'and whatever happens, you're due for a medal and a certificate.'

'Oh, just a bunch of red roses will do,' said Polly, her smile hiding all she felt about events that had never favoured her.

'With a mention in despatches,' said Boots.

'Good luck, Daddy,' said Rosie, and watched as he walked to the gate, opened it, went through to the lane, turned left and disappeared between hedges. 'Aunt Polly, it's a bit much, isn't it, arranging for them to meet here, in this very particular spot?'

'Well, Rosie dear girl,' said Polly, 'I'm on your father's side.'

'That makes a whole lot of us,' said Rosie, 'including Emily.' Her adoptive mother's name slipped out in easy fashion. 'I don't know how he does it, do you?'

'It's difficult for anyone to dislike your father, Rosie,' said Polly lightly.

Boots, walking down the lane that led to the dairy and the farmhouse, the large barn at his back, saw the girl. She was standing quite still, but turned as she heard him. They saw each other then, at a distance of twenty yards. She wore a waisted dress of apple green, and her light brown hair, stirred by a faint breeze, was caught by the sun. The skirt of her dress fluttered. Her right hand went up to her mouth as Boots walked slowly up to her, and she saw him clearly then, a man distinctively personable. He was hatless, his hair thick and dark brown, his eyes a deep grey, and his smile whimsical, as if he was thinking what she was thinking, how strange it was that they were father

344

and daughter meeting for the very first time.

'Mademoiselle Eloise Lacoste, I presume?' he said in excellent French. The gentle humour of that was lost on Eloise. The meeting of the explorer Stanley and Dr Livingstone had never been mentioned in her French history lessons.

'Oh, m'sieur,' she said faintly, letting her hand drop, 'yes, I'm Eloise.'

'During the war I was Sergeant Robert Adams,' said Boots, 'and I think I'm a little late.'

'Oh, no, m'sieur, not at all.'

'Are seventeen years not at all late?' smiled Boots, noting her prettiness, her nervousness and her shyness.

'Oh, I see.' Eloise was overwhelmed. Such a tall and fine man, and not a single sign of blindness about him, except, yes, perhaps his left eye did look a little lazy. 'M'sieur, yes, I see. Seventeen years. Oh, my knees are having a terrible time trying to hold me up. Isn't that silly of me?'

'I've had trouble with mine on past occasions,' said Boots, who was not going to rush the girl in any way.

'In the war, do you mean? Oh, how could you help that? Everyone says it was a terrible war. M'sieur, are you really my father?'

'Yes, Eloise, and I'm sorry we haven't seen each other until now, and I'm sorry too that you've lost your mother. I met her, as I think you know, at the end of this lane, by the dairy. Is it still there?'

'Yes, m'sieur, but it's best to stay here,' said Eloise, troubled by her erratic breathing. 'My

345

mother's brother has the farm now, and he likes chickens and cows more than people, yes. M'sieur, I – I am very happy to meet you.'

'Well, that's a good beginning,' smiled Boots, 'for I'm delighted to meet you. Tell me about yourself.'

'Oh, there's little to tell, m'sieur, except that I was brought up by my mother and my grand-parents, and they're all dead now. So I live with my Aunt Marie and Uncle Jacques, who are very kind to me. M'sieur, you look very kind yourself, and very handsome.'

'Handsome?' Boots laughed. 'No, it's my brother Tommy who's renowned for being handsome. But at least I seem to be the father of a very pretty girl.'

Eloise regarded him with less shyness now, the deep grey of her eyes matching his. The sunlight tinted hers with blue. She smiled.

'See, my mother and I tried to find your grave,' she said, 'and all the time you were alive. Oh, I'm so sad that you couldn't come back to her because the war blinded you, but you have come to see me now that you know I exist, which makes me happy for both of us. You have a family in England?'

'I've a wife, a son and a daughter,' said Boots, and spoke of them and of his mother and stepfather who lived with them. He did not, however, say that Rosie was adopted. Eloise listened, all eyes and ears. She looked at him, and kept looking, at his sound eye and his lazy one, at his firm mouth and the little smile that seemed close to the surface all the time. She felt she knew then why her mother had fallen in love with him.

'*Mon pere*, I think perhaps you have a lovely family.'

'It's a very talkative one,' said Boots. 'Eloise, my daughter Rosie is with me, wanting to meet you, and we'll spend several days here. Shall we get together with you, so that we can all come to know each other?'

'You would like that?' said Eloise.

'Yes, very much,' said Boots. 'There'll be the question of what you'd like to do, whether you'd like to come and live with us or stay with your aunt and uncle. It's not something I'd ask you to decide while we're here. You can take as much time to think about it as you want. If you should decide in our favour, then I'll come and fetch you. Are you happy with that?'

'My aunt and uncle, I must think about them and all they have done for me,' said Eloise, 'but yes, I am quite happy with your suggestion.'

'Then come and meet Rosie, your sister,' said Boots, and she put her hand in his and walked back with him to the gate. Polly and Rosie were out of the car and standing at the gate. 'Rosie,' said Boots, 'here's your new sister, Eloise.'

'Eureka and shining stars,' said Rosie. She opened the gate and came through, to look at Eloise and to smile at her. 'Oh, yes, you're my father's, aren't you? I'm so pleased to meet you.'

'Excuse me?' said Eloise, thinking Rosie quite beautiful.

'Try French, Rosie,' said Boots.

Rosie, fluent, said in French, 'Eloise, I'm Rosie, and I'm so pleased to meet you. We're sisters. Isn't that simply wonderful? And isn't our father lucky in having two daughters like us? We're both treasures. There, may I kiss you?' And Rosie kissed Eloise on her cheeks.

From the gate Polly looked on, seeing the three of them together, Boots and his two daughters. None of them belonged to her. She stood on the outside, although for many years she had longed to be on the inside, and still did. The old bitterness might have surfaced then, but didn't. She might have said something sweetly acid, but didn't. A girl, Anglo-French, had found a family, and Polly could not bring herself to spoil the moment.

Boots turned.

'Polly, stop cuddling that gate. Come and join us,' he said, 'you're the best part of this event.' He moved and pulled the gate open. His hand touched hers, took hold of it and for a brief moment pressed it warmly. Then, lightly touching her arm, he brought her forward, and Polly could hardly believe that she of all people had to fight the emotional sensation of eyes turning moist. 'We owe you, Polly. I owe you.' Then he said in French, 'Eloise, by the way, is going to think about whether she'll come and live with us in England or stay here with her aunt and uncle. We'll let her take all the time she wants to make up her mind.'

'Eloise, you will think about living with us, won't you?' said Rosie.

Eloise, emotional, said, 'But yes, how could I not? I belong to my father. It is just that I could not leave my aunt and uncle too quickly. See, I will come and spend Christmas with you, and then if I come again, it will be to stay, it will be to say my aunt and uncle are happy for me to do so. But I speak only a little English.'

'But you do speak a little?' said Rosie, smiling.

In English, Eloise said, 'Oh, 'ello and 'ow are you, please, and also 'ow much.'

'That would make a very good start,' said Boots.

'Lovely,' said Polly. 'Anything else, Eloise?'

'Yes, what the Tommies used to say.'

'And what's that?' asked Boots.

'Oh, it's what Uncle Jacques told me,' said Eloise. 'Shall I say it?'

'We'd all like to hear it,' said Polly.

Eloise said in English, 'It's cheeri-oh and gawd blimey.'

In the farm lane, close to the barn that had seen the West Kents resting out of the line in the summer of 1916, Boots laughed his head off.

Which, for Polly, brought back the laughter of the men of the trenches.

THE END

MISSING PERSON
by Mary Jane Staples

The house in Caulfield Place, off Browning Street in Walworth, was haunted, or at least that's what the street kids said. So when two men, a woman, and a parrot moved in, everyone was very interested, especially fourteen-year-old Cassie Ford, who was particularly fascinated by the parrot.

And it was just about this time that Mr Finch, Chinese Lady's husband, and Boots's stepfather, began to get mysterious telephone calls. Mr Finch had never told the rest of the Adams family – except for Boots – the secrets of his past, or what kind of work he did for the government, and he decided not to tell them about the slightly sinister telephone calls either.

It was when he took Chinese Lady on a summer's day jaunt in his Morris motorcar that things began to happen. For, in the Hog's Back Hotel, Chinese Lady went to the cloakroom, and when she came back Mr Finch had vanished. It took all of Boots's ingenuity to finally discover what had happened, and Cassie's knowledge of the Caulfield Place parrot was to prove a vital clue in unravelling the mystery.

Here again is the Adams family from *Down Lambeth Way, Our Emily, King of Camberwell, On Mother Brown's Doorstep* and *A Family Affair*.

0 552 14230 1

PRIDE OF WALWORTH
by Mary Jane Staples

There was a new family in Browning Street, Walworth – the Harrisons. Respectable and well-behaved, the only thing unusual about them was that Mr Harrison was never there. He was a sailor, said Ma Harrison, away fighting pirates in the China Seas. Actually, 'Knocker' Harrison was in Marsham Gaol – he had unfortunately burgled a lady's suite when she happened to be there. Pa wasn't really a very good burglar.

When young Nick Harrison, eldest son and heir of Ma and Knocker, met Annabelle Somers he found himself in a very difficult situation. For seventeen-year-old Annabelle was a peach of a girl, was related to the highly respectable Adams family, and was really quite keen on Nick, very interested in him and in his family. What with keeping Annabelle at arm's length in case she found out about Pa, *and* with the problems of running the Browning Street Rovers football team (the ball was owned by Chrissie Evans who laid down her own rules about the team) Nick sometimes wondered if his life would ever be sorted out.

Here again is the Adams family from *Down Lambeth Way*, *Our Emily*, *King of Camberwell*, *On Mother Brown's Doorstep*, *A Family Affair* and *Missing Person*.

0 552 14291 3

A SELECTED LIST OF FINE NOVELS
AVAILABLE FROM CORGI BOOKS

THE PRICES SHOWN BELOW WERE CORRECT AT THE TIME OF GOING TO PRESS
HOWEVER TRANSWORLD PUBLISHERS RESERVE THE RIGHT TO SHOW NEW
RETAIL PRICES ON COVERS WHICH MAY DIFFER FROM THOSE PREVIOUSLY
ADVERTISED IN THE TEXT OR ELSEWHERE.